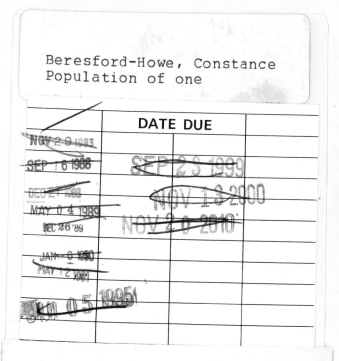

Beresford-Howe, Constance
Population of one

	DATE DUE		
NOV 2 3 1983			
SEP 1 6 1986	SEP 2 3 1999		
DEC 27 1988	NOV 1 3 2000		
MAY 0 4 1989	NOV 2 0 2010		
DEC 26 '89			
JAN 8 1990			
MAY 1 2 1991			
JUN 0 5 1995			

DEMCO

A POPULATION OF ONE

A Population Of One

A NOVEL BY

CONSTANCE BERESFORD-HOWE

ST. MARTIN'S PRESS   NEW YORK

Fic

First published in America in 1978 by St. Martin's Press by
arrangement with The Macmillan Company of Canada
Copyright © 1977 by Constance Beresford-Howe
All rights reserved. For information, write:
St. Martin's Press, Inc., 175 Fifth Ave., New York, N.Y. 10010
Manufactured in the United States of America

Library of Congress Cataloging in Publication Data

Beresford-Howe, Constance.
     A population of one.

     I. Title.
PZ3.B45166Po 1978 [PR9199.3.B4] 813'.5'4 77-92976
ISBN 0-312-63150-2

I am grateful to the Canada Council for their award of a Senior Arts Grant to assist in the writing of this book.

Lavenham, Suffolk
April, 1976

Contents

FOR RACHE LOVAT DICKSON
With much affection and respect

A POPULATION OF ONE

The Project

ON THE GREEN APRIL MORNING when I leave for Montreal to
be interviewed for a teaching job, I have in fact two objec-
tives. One, of course, is to get the job: I've always wanted to teach.
The other is to marry somebody as promptly as possible—or at
the very least to have an affair. This latter plan is new. I have
labelled it The Project, a phrase light enough to keep Fate and me
both safely defused, or so I hope. On balance, though, I feel
cheerful and confident about the whole thing. It can't be really
hard, can it, to find a nice man?—though my mother would call
that a contradiction in terms. Of course either or both categories
of my project might turn out to be a little more complex than I
anticipate. At this thought, several large, restive birds I seem to
have swallowed recently flap inside me, disturbing my breakfast
and my composure.

I am the first one aboard the Turbo. This makes it hard to play
the sophisticated traveller with chic little case and copy of the *New
Yorker*. The one sleepy club-car attendant to notice my existence
remarks disapprovingly, "We're late today—won't leave till two,
Madame," and looks at me as if I were a social error.

After trying one or two different locations, I choose a window
seat. (Which end is the Ladies? There doesn't seem to be one at
either end; how odd.) My first impression of which way the train
is pointed also has to be corrected. I want to be on the lake side, in
order to see as much as possible. These various exertions cause a

long run to pop down the back of my pantyhose. I feel hot in my New Season tweed suit, and the birds are restless. But nothing can spoil the joy of waiting for the train to move, the journey to begin. How right I was to dodge my sister Lou's offer to see me off. She'd be nagging away: Have you got your ticket? Is your money in a safe place? . . . you'd think I was three, not thirty, the way she goes on. (Where the hell *is* my ticket, anyway?—oh yes; all right.) But without her, waiting to leave is half the fun. *Partir c'est vivre un peu.* You'd think anyone would know that, but French philosophers are always so depressive.

Nobody aboard yet but those two nuns; isn't it queer? Can this be the wrong train? Deep down, both Lou and I know I am just the kind of person to be whirled nonstop to North Bay or Yellowknife. But no, the Information man said Track One, and so did that squinty-eyed porter. . . . My skirt is twisted. I stand up and, with a furtive glance at the nuns, hitch it straight. Sitting down again, I try to smooth the heather-coloured wool over my knees. "It's gauche to cover your knees this season," the Boutique girl told me. How marvellous to be so sure what's gauche. The birds give a leap as I notice a smudge of something—oil?—on the new-smelling edge of my jacket. Damn. Must have got it clambering up those ridiculous high steps into here, cumbered by case, umbrella, handbag, and magazine, not to mention those plans. Is it the forces of chaos in the year 1969 that keep me so dishevelled, I wonder, or some discord inside me, conflicting with the year? Whatever it is, it tends to keep me looking as if I'd just been shot out of a cannon.

Wait—here's somebody else. A man. Pushing sideways down the aisle, butting a briefcase ahead of him with his knee. Quite a good-looking man. Youngish, nice grey pinstripe. He plops into the window seat across the aisle and pulls down the shade. A barbershop smell comes from him as he rubs both hands over his face and head.

Now more people. Two pink-haired old ladies looking gift-wrapped in plastic raincoats. A long string of men with folded *Globe* and attaché case, like joined paper dolls. Mother with three children and bag of oranges. Two more nuns, their skirts to mid-calf. Gauche. A portly middle-aged couple in trousers; the man is presumably the one with the cigar. Now the sleepy attendant is all over the place with reaching arm, big smile, and Take your coat, sir. He seems to know many of them. It's almost like a club, to which I don't belong. The seats are filling up. The birds flutter. Soon we'll move off.

A bearded young man pauses at the empty seat beside me, then moves past, even as I look up at him and smile. Well, perhaps he wants a window seat himself. A very old couple stand at my elbow, clogging the aisle helplessly. They lean over me murmuring "Would you mind very much?—so we can be together?—it would be so kind—" And (down, birds) I realize they are asking for my seat, damn them. How to refuse? They look about ninety. So I struggle up, dragging my case after me, and cross the aisle to sit beside the barber-smelling man, who is now asleep, or pretending to be.

It's twenty after two, but the train hasn't yet given a twitch. The frail old couple in my seat are ordering Scotch-and-water. All the places are filled. The warm air smells of oranges and people. I try to read my magazine, but the print seems to jiggle. I feel terribly thirsty. Then, suddenly, from the corner of my eye, I catch a station pillar gliding backwards. My birds give a great heave. We're on our way.

An electronic voice then makes it official, announcing the next stop and advising us all, bilingually, to remain in our seats. Unfortunate for anyone who (like me) feels a sudden, urgent call of nature. As we slide out of the station, rain traces horizontal streaks on the window, a tangle of track and overhead wire flashes by, and soon the train begins to make generous, swooping lurches. The man beside me opens his eyes and gives a mini-groan, and I wonder if he shares my qualmish memory of being five and carsick.

"A bit rough, isn't it?" I say brightly.

"Mah."

"They travel fast, these trains, don't they? Is it ninety miles an hour?"

"Yoh."

"Do you often make this trip?"

"Uck, uck, uck." He clears his throat of an apparently massive obstruction.

"This is my first. Time on the Turbo, I mean. I hope they've ironed out all the bugs by now."

"Good service. I come up to Toronto every month," he says

huskily. "Christ, it's hot in here. Where's that damned waiter? Eh, Pascal — a Canadian Club here, lots of ice ... Uh, maybe you'd like a drink?"

"Oh. Well ... perhaps — yes, I'll have a little sherry, then. Thank you very much." Nice of him. My stomach gives a loud growl; I wish I had something to eat.

"I suppose you come to and fro on business."

"That's right." His slightly watery blue eyes are unfocussed, without interest; but after the drinks have come and he has gulped half his, he seems to feel much brighter. His cheeks pinken, he leans forward to offer a cigarette, and gives me a quite charming smile.

"God, that's better. Fact is, I had a pretty late night."

"Did you really? Business deal, I suppose."

His lips twitch. "Yeah. Right. Big deal. Toronto's quite a town these days. You just visiting Montreal?"

"Well, not exactly. I've got a job interview. Actually I've never been there before, so I'm quite — "

"Never been to Montreal? Lady, where you been? — in jail?"

"Well, not exactly," I repeat, feeling silly. "I've always lived in Toronto. With my mother. Only now she's gone — "

"Pascal — excuse me — a refill here; and you'll have another? Sure? Just the rye, then ... You'll like Montreal. Still has something, I don't know, zing, personality. Take Westmount, it's mostly Wasp there, you know; but it's still no way like Toronto. Only thing is these damn peasoups, all this crap (excuse my French) about a separate Quebec; and some of them are crazy enough to try and shoot the place up, you'd better believe it."

"Really?"

"Bet your life. I'm in real estate, been with the same company for nineteen years, and you'd never believe what's happening to property values in Quebec now. Incredible."

"Well, all kinds of values are getting a shake-up now, aren't they? I mean moral values and all that. You hear a lot about young people — "

He flashes me a dramatic look.

"Christ, don't talk to me about young people. I got two teen-agers, and I tell you — I mean they simply haven't got a clue what life's all about. My dad walked out on us when I was sixteen; you can guess where that left me, oldest kid of three. No college. No travel. No nothing. Get a job and work my ass off. Absolutely no choices. Then comes my son, everything on a platter, and he flunks out of Cartier his first year."

"Oh, Cartier College? That's where I'm — "

"Excuse me — hey Pascal — you'll have another one, eh? No? Just one for me, then."

"Cartier has a good reputation, hasn't it? I mean it's not McGill, but — "

"Aw, I don't know. All these places're full of separatists, pot-smokers, left-wingers ... I went to see my son's Math professor, turns out to be a guy in a headband with a *swastika* round his neck, for God's sake. Anyhow, I said to Jamie, look, boy, it's work or out. You cut classes, you fail; okay, OUT. So he's living right now in some kind of crazy commune in a tenement full of bugs on Jeanne Mance. And there you are. You a teacher, then?"

"Well, I have a PHD ... the nineteenth century's my field. But this will be my first real teaching job. If I get it, that is. Wish me luck, will you? Teaching is — well, specially the humanities — something of value — you're giving civilization a sort of friendly leg-up, in a way ... "

"Lady," he says with a bloodshot glance, "you may be in for a shock. These kids today don't give a sh — I mean a damn — for anything, never mind civilization. My daughter's on welfare, how about that? I put her out of the house. Caught her and the boyfriend in bed, drunk as frogs. I mean, they just deliberately cock a snook at everything. They seem to hate us."

He looks out of the window briefly, his eyes so sad I almost reach over to give him a comforting pat. Permutations and combinations of wet field, red barn, and clumped trees, whirl past in endless succession. He clutches his empty glass on his knee like a weapon.

"I suppose your wife — "

"Yeah, well, we're sort of — like separated. Pascal! No, look, take away that damn plastic food; keep it; just give me another rye here, lots of ice. You really going to eat that? — all right, I'll buy you a brandy later on, you'll need it. No, I wouldn't want to be a teacher, I tell you that. Uh — where you staying in Montreal? Got friends there?"

"No." I almost add the name of my hotel; but that might be unwise. Mother's training. Of course she was terribly old-fashioned, God love her. "Never take out your house keys in a public place," she used to tell us. "It looks like an invitation. You know what men are."

"My name's George. George MacKay." He is running his eyes over me now with so much interest (could Mum be right?) that I'm too shy to go on munching my crusty roll, and feel myself starting to blush.

"Well, I'm called Willy — short for Wilhelmina — my grandmother used to admire that old Dutch queen."

"No kidding. You not married?"

"No." I add nothing, of course, about those intentions of mine. But they are firm. Partner unknown as yet. Details likewise. But I am fed up with being a virgin. A pity there is no refined way I can convey this sentiment to George MacKay.

"Yuh, smart girls stay single," he mutters. "Smart guys, too." (You may be right. But *partir c'est vivre* —)

"I'll be forty-five next month. By God, it sometimes feels like a hundred."

I say nothing. Thirty is surely not too old for *everything*. The Project should be perfectly simple to accomplish, if I just organize properly.

"Like to show you round Montreal some time. Nice town, specially this time of year. All right, Pascal, take this junk away, right, and bring the lady a brandy. No? Aw, come on. Sure? Well, the same again for me."

I haven't kept count, but he says quickly, "Don't worry. I got no problem whatsoever with drink. None whatsoever. The thing is know your capacity, that's all. Greatest tranquillizer there is, you ask me. All this crap about brain damage, liver damage, it's all a load of horse manure. Doctors always got to croak about something. Wife's a nurse; same thing, on and on. Where'd you say you were staying?"

"Tell me — in your business you'd know all about it — where could I find a nice modern apartment . . . maybe in Westmount?"

"Thousands of 'em," he says vaguely. His head slips forward a little and he swallows a belch. But when the waiter brings along his new drink, he sits up like a man prepared to do a man's work.

"Cheers. Yes, I'd sure like to show you around. You're an attractive gal, right? You know what that curly hair means, and those little gaps between your teeth . . . if not, I'll explain some time. We'll get together. Montreal can be a very lonely place."

"So you know that," I think. The train rocks us gently together. I smooth my skirt over those gauche knees. "Yes, cities are lonely. Do you ever feel as if you might as well be on a desert island, because there's absolutely nobody you can really talk to? I mean you can have family, friends — I've got my kid sister Lou — well, she's twenty-five, married to a nice swinging lawyer — and yet we can't *talk* to each other. We love each other, I suppose; but that's not enough. That's why I sometimes think marriage, if you just *liked* your mate, would be the answer. To loneliness, I mean."

I feel the blush again, hot on the forehead. My mother would have had a fit to hear me talking like this to a strange man. But as it happens, there's no need to worry, because he has at some point or other dropped into a deep sleep. His head is tilted against the corner of the seat, and his mouth is a little open, letting out a faint snore.

All through the carriage now there's a drowsy, post-lunch lull. The silence oppresses and depresses me vaguely. Yet I should be used to silence. God knows. Didn't I live in a silent house for more than twenty years? A time and space where my parents never spoke to each other except through me.

"Be good enough to tell your mother, Willy, that this month's laundry bill is preposterous, and I have no intention of paying it." "Kindly remind your father that the property taxes have been owing for two months now." "It's her house, as your lady mother is never tired of reminding me. Let *her* pay the taxes."

On Lou's wedding day he did say stiffly to her, "I understand, Mary, that we're expected to sit together in the church." She nodded. And sit together they did, formally dressed, side by side in the front pew, never once glancing at each other or exchanging another word. The extraordinary thing was that no one but me seemed to hear their silence. The years and years of it, when I lived with them in that Rosedale house, filled with the silence of glass under tension. The creak of her rocking-chair all day behind the locked door of her room. The fumble of his key in the lock late at night. His muttering progress up the stairs; his stumble in the upstairs hall. As he passed her door, he sometimes gave it a violent bang with the flat of his hand.

And that is why *vivre un peu* is so important to me; why The Project is more than just a joke, and why George MacKay, even with his head joggling and mouth open, has a certain allure, though not of the romantic kind.

Just the same, if this were a novel, I think, and right now Chapter One, it would surely be a love story. You could always trust them in the nineteenth century, for instance. After all, even Lucy Snowe met four men on her first night in Villette. Yes, strangers meeting. Two lonely people. Enough problems and obstacles to make a satisfactory plot. Then the happy ending... lovers united. No more loneliness. Trollope, Brontë, Dickens; they all agreed. So it must be possible. As a matter of fact, I feel quite drawn to George MacKay, in spite of his personal prose style. Those rather bewildered blue eyes appeal. You can see in there sometimes, just for the flick of a second, the child he was. Often can't see that at all in people. One reason I'm so different. The child in me is still there whole for anyone to see, swinging upside-down in the tree-house of adult Willy Doyle, grinning hopefully at the world with gaps in her milk teeth.

After a long and inexplicable stop in the middle of a flat, wet limbo, we shoot on through a blue dusk blotted with fog. George MacKay's head rolls a little. Too much to drink, of course. But in the novel, that would be all right. She would cure his loneliness. Not that in life She cured any such ills in her drunken old ripsnorter of a father, did She? What was that he told me—that when he was a kid his dad ran out on them? — now there's a common bond for you. Makes us soul-mates. Or is it just that basically everybody's father is a bastard? One of those archetypal situations.

The train swings. We are crossing a bridge onto the island of Montreal. Suddenly a geometry of city light appears; neon signs flash, highway lamps of iceberg green form loops of light. The birds wake up smartly. I powder my nose and in the little square mirror pull at bits of my hair that look strangely distraught. Maybe Lou was right about my new Afro-style permanent. "You don't look like yourself," she complained, and was cross when I said "Good."

"Do—o—o—rval," calls the conductor, swinging through the car.

"Come on, Mr. MacKay," says Pascal, giving him a not particularly gentle shove. "Your stop. Come on, wake up. Your wife will be at the station for you. Come on, Mr. MacKay, pull yourself together. And here's your check. Lady, can you hold onto this for him? — I got to get the luggage up front. Thanks."

I shake him. Harder. His head finally snaps up. He gives me an offended look.

"It's your stop," I say in self-defence.

"Oh. Yuh. You going on to Central Station? 'Scuse me, get past. Nice talking to you. Lots of luck. Night."

Yawning horribly, he drags his briefcase clumsily past my knees and then hurries to push into the queue lining up as the Turbo hisses and slows. When the doors are unsealed, a cold gush of rain-wet air bursts into the stuffy carriage.

"Wait—" I say. "You forgot—" But it's too embarrassing to call after him. The line of people is shrinking fast; it disappears and he's gone. He's forgotten the bill for the drinks, and Pascal has reappeared to stand expectantly by. What can I do? I pay it. Novels, indeed. Goodbye, my hero.

At my time of life, it's odd to be facing a job interview for the first time. (Lady, where you been — in jail?) Uncomfortable business, to be offering yourself with a good prospect of being refused. Greg says academic appointments are getting scarce, and I have no experience. But I want this job so badly! Somehow, though, I have got to seem both keen and cool, a discouraging combination of challenges at the best of times. If only my love and respect for the humanist ideals would make me desirable at a glance to any faculty committee, instead of, as they do at the moment, painting an intense pallor under my freckles and clenching my stomach into a fist.

In these circumstances, the only tactics I can muster are to look respectable and get there on time. To this end I've had the heather-coloured suit cleaned and pressed at the hotel, and a taxi has delivered me at Cartier College twenty minutes early, over-doing things a little.

The rain has stopped, leaving a soft coolness in the air. Trees at home are getting green; here they're still in bud. The sky is bright in pools that patch the broken pavement of the steeply rising road. I walk uphill past the college—a penitentiary-style affair of eight or nine storeys in pleated concrete, built, from the look of it, just last week, in the new mode without windows. What are they afraid might get in — or out — I wonder?

But how attractive the old houses are on this street, with their tall, narrow windows, slatted, some of them, with folding indoor shutters. The dove-coloured mansard roofs shine in the sun. Turning the corner I find a charming crescent of terraced Edwardian houses wearing crowns of wrought-iron lace, their doors painted bright red, blue, orange, and green. Up the next street looms Mount Royal, a purple thicket of leafless trees; it forms a massive and mysterious backdrop to white blocks of high-rise apartments. I climb toward it, fascinated as the big Jacques Cartier cross comes into view. Last night at the hotel, when I couldn't sleep, I kept getting up to look out at the ocean of city lights lapping frivolously against that dark island of silence. Even by day it looks aloof, alone. That mountain might almost have been put there by someone with a taste for Canadian symbolism.

Time to turn back. I stroll down a block, turn along a curved street full of shabby rooming-houses; descend again — then discover I'm on a street completely new to me — I've made a wrong turn somewhere. And it's already ten-thirty: I'll be late. Serves me right, fiddling about with symbolism in broad daylight. Panic breaks out all over me like a series of little rockets bursting through my skin. I hurry back to take the opposite turn; then after another block I realize I'm climbing again toward the mountain. Oh, for Toronto with its no-nonsense grid-pattern, instead of these twisting, illogical streets! There's no one around, either, to ask for directions. I hurry frantically to the next corner. There's a taxi — I flag it in desperation. "Macnaughton Street — Cartier College," I say, clutching the door-handle like a prayer.

"Mais vous y êtes, madame," says the driver. "Là-bas, là, vous voyez?" I don't understand a word of this at first—it doesn't even sound like French to me — but his poking gesture to the right reveals the grim grey profile of the college, sure enough, only fifty yards further down the street.

By the time I reach the door of the penitentiary, I am twelve minutes late, perspiring heavily, and hot all over with guilt. "Excuse me," I say to a passing girl, dressed like someone from another planet in black leather clothes. "Can you tell me where to find Dr. Benson-Clarke? Head of the English Department?"

The girl looks at me blankly before shifting her gum to the other cheek. "No idea. I'm Science," she says, and turns away. After I've approached two more students I finally learn that all the administrative offices are in a house farther down the street. By now I'm fifteen minutes late. It's more that twenty before I whizz at last into a dignified stone mansion with broad bay windows and panelled walls. Breathless, I climb the scuffed grandeur of a carved walnut staircase to the floor where a lad in granny-glasses has promised I'll find the Department of English offices.

Through an open doorway I meet the truculent eyes of a fat old man, sunk amid crumpled tweeds, a pair of half-glasses on the extreme tip of a beaky nose. He is smoking a cigar that curdles the surrounding air. A fierce-looking bush of grey hair makes his big head look even bigger. His cheeks are bright pink and his aggressive stare very blue. He looks like an Englishman.

"My name is Doyle, I'm looking for Dr. Benson-Clarke," I say with what's left of my breath.

"A bizarre quest, young woman."

"Well I have—or maybe had—an appointment with him. I'm afraid I'm awfully late for it."

"Eh? What's that ye say? Speak up!"

I obey, feeling ridiculous. Yes, he's English all right. Knows how to keep the natives down.

"I'm terribly sorry ... I had some trouble finding this place. Are you — "

His only reply is a grunt, but he makes an ungracious gesture toward a wooden armchair, so I move discreetly into the smog and sit down, trying not to cough. Then for the first time I notice someone sitting behind a desk at the back of the room — a not-quite-young man in a corduroy jacket of the same colour as his brown eyes. He is actually standing up politely and offering his hand.

"Oh," I say, relieved. "Dr. Clarke, I do apologize for being so late — "

"I'm Bill Trueblood ... is it Mrs. Doyle? Miss. How are you? This wicked old gentleman is Dr. Clarke."

The old man gives a snort. Either the cigar has got to him at last, or he is laughing. "Go and ask Molly to come back, will you, Bill? She's gone to her office, I think."

While we're left alone I try to get my wits together and appear serene. Neither attempt is very successful. My eyes water in the reek of smoke. The chair is hard. The old man closes his eyes and lets his head sink forward with the weight of its great Roman beak of nose. He is apparently lost in the contemplation of some Great Thought. Or, like my hero on the train, he may simply be in the toils of a formidable hangover. Eventually he rumbles, "For Age, with stealing steps / Hath clawed me with his clutch." This effectively aborts a hopeful remark I'm about to make about the weather.

A very long time seems to elapse before Trueblood (can that really be his name?) comes back, escorting a pretty, petite young woman with dark hair smoothed into a modish French knot. She is wearing a pleated skirt and cashmere sweater whose rose colour sets off a clear, pale complexion. The sight of it makes my own red face feel redder. She is carrying two cardboard containers of coffee, and offers me one with a pleasant smile.

"Hello; I'm Molly Pratt. I teach Can. Lit."

Can. Lit. What a pity it sounds like a corporation.

"Now, Miss Doyle," says Clarke, sitting up in a great hurry like one of the more eccentric creatures in *Alice in Wonderland*, "there was no opening here for you at all, as I told you in my letter last February. But since then we've unexpectedly lost our man who teaches the nineteenth-century novel. That, I believe, is your field."

The coffee is so hot it scalds my tongue and I am glad when Molly Pratt remarks, "Yes, Sandy ran out on us, the fink. Went to Trinidad for the spring break and sent us a happy telegram to say he wouldn't be back."

"Never mind all that," growls the old man. "Miss Doyle, you got your doctorate five years ago—it would have been natural for you to go straight into the academic life. Why have you done no teaching?"

"Well, you see my father died the spring I graduated" (. . . Yes, Gerald Wellesley Doyle fell down the Bloor Street subway stairs and broke his neck when drunk, if you want the truth) "and then my mother was very ill and there was no one to look after her." (There was enough money. I filled up the spare time with Red Cross work. Of course the darling often said 'It's not right, Willy . . . ' but that long, long story trails after me even now like a paper shadow pinned to my heels. And *you* are the last person in the world I'd ever tell about it.)

Clarke gives me a dissatisfied stare over his glasses, as if he somehow gets an echo of these defiant thoughts.

"But you finished graduate school with great distinction, didn't you," says the brown-eyed man kindly. "And I think your letter said your thesis on Mrs. Gaskell was published?"

"Yes. I was amazed to think anyone would print it, but they did."

What attractive eyes the man has. There are a few threads of silver in his curly brown hair. Comely hands, too, with nice long fingers and polished nails. His smile is easy and pleasant; you can see he is full of kindness. He wears no wedding ring; but of course that doesn't mean —

"With no teaching experience at all, do you think you could cope with a full-time appointment?" The old man looks gloomily at his cigar rather than at me. "The preparation alone would be a big job, at this late date. And the workload here is heavy. All of us teach the first-year survey course, Chaucer to Hardy. Then it was decided last year by a dread of deans that wasn't enough, so we now all see a list of first-year students for regular counselling. That's on top of the usual conference work with one's own students preparing term papers and so on. Do you think you could manage all that?"

"Oh yes, I'm sure I could." I'm not, of course; but damned if I'd ever let *him* know it.

"Ha-kapff," says Clarke, obviously far from convinced. What an old rhino. It's so obvious he hasn't the least intention of hiring me that the others are embarrassed. Oh well, there must be other teaching jobs in Montreal. Private schools or whatever. I'll look in the yellow pages when I get back to the hotel. For one thing, I like this island city. I want to stay here.

"Unfortunately our salaries here are well below the C.A.U.T. average level," says the young man, as if to console me. "That's because, as you probably know, our grants from the province aren't statutory—we never know from year to year what we'll get. Or even if. However, there are lots of compensations. Montreal is one fringe benefit; it's fun living here."

"Yes, I'm sure it is."

He gives me something that is almost a wink; it makes his face more agreeable than ever. Molly looks thoughtfully at her fingernails. The old man seems about to lapse into sleep again; but suddenly shifts himself with a pettish sort of flounce and points his cigar at me with such abruptness I give an involuntary jerk.

"No need to keep you, Miss-er-Boyle. We'll be writing to you after we've completed all our interviews. Thank you for coming along. Good day t'ye." And without another word he shuffles his tweedy bulk and his cigar out of the room.

"Good day," I repeat obediently. I get up and find a place on the desk for my coffee container. It is still hot. So am I. The old bison. Why ask me to come here at all, when it's so obvious he has no —

I shake hands with the girl and with Bill Trueblood, who leaves my hand with a friendly little squeeze in it. Just the same, when I leave the building I have to grip my jaws tight and stare fiercely at the bright day in order not to cry.

One of the things I've learned never to do is dream ahead about how things will be; they have such a nasty habit of letting you down. But there's no harm in improving them afterward, now is there? So all the way home on the train I construct a big improvement on The Interview, and it comforts me quite a lot.

"Can you be Dr. Doyle?" the big tweedy man asks, hurrying up to me in the lobby. "Please forgive me; I'm twenty seconds late — but you see we were watching for someone much older. It was tremendously good of you to come all this way to see us. Do come into my office, will you?" Before ushering me in, he squirts the room lavishly with air freshener. Then he pulls forward a chair, tucks a cushion at my back, and carefully places a footstool under my feet.

I sit down gracefully and light a cigar. He shuffles papers on his desk with tremulous hands. He is very nervous, or perhaps just shy. Obviously this interview is very important to him.

"Ah, Bill," he says to the young man hovering in the background. "I would introduce you to this charming woman, but I'm not feeling that generous. Go away for half an hour, will you; then you and Molly may come in just to shake hands. What I'm planning to do is adjourn this meeting almost immediately and take the lady to lunch at the Faculty Club."

I puff the cigar nonchalantly and nod farewell to Trueblood.

When we're alone, Clarke tries to rub out an anxiety-frown. "Have to keep the youngsters in line, you know. Never trust anybody under thirty. Now I don't know whether you'd be willing to accept the post we have to offer, Dr. Doyle ... we're just a small college, and you're probably snowed under with better offers. But the appointment is yours if you'd do us the honour ... "

I wave the cigar to check any thought he might have of getting down on his knees.

"Yes, actually I think I'll take it. You can write me the details later. Unfortunately I must go now; I have a luncheon engagement. At the Mount Stephen Club, with Sir George MacKay. Good day to you."

Well, of course it's childish; but say what you like, it helps. After a few days, this much-improved version of life's first draft can even give me a laugh.

In any case, I've almost forgotten the whole thing when two months later I receive a Special Delivery letter signed A. C. Benson-Clarke, D. Litt., offering me the post of Lecturer at Cartier College, on two-year probation, at a salary of $12,000 a year. I am so astonished and wildly excited that I immediately phone to tell my sister Lou.

"You're kidding, Will!"

"Not very complimentary, are you?"

"No, what I mean is of course it's great—only they didn't seem very interested when you went down there; or so you said."

"Well, somebody else probably let them down. After all, June's half over. They must be a bit desperate."

"Oh, don't keep running yourself down all the time. You won't be coming to us for long, then. And you won't want that Dale Avenue apartment you thought about. Oh, I hope you'll like Montreal, but I don't know ... all this separatist bother ... they say there are real terrorists in the ranks, trained in Cuba and all that. I've even heard the *Mayor* is a sympathizer. Some people think there'll be shooting in the streets ... I do wish you could have found a job here instead."

"You trying to cheer me up or what? I can't wait to get there. I'm going to call Greg right away and ask him to wind up this house sale as fast as he can."

"That shouldn't take long. He said something last night about it —the deeds and things are being typed in the office now."

"Good. I'll drive up to Montreal in a day or two and find myself an apartment. Buy furniture and all that."

"Lucky for you the house fetched such a good price. I suppose you're still determined to store all Mum's furniture."

"Oh, yes, I couldn't ... somehow — sell it."

"Well, no point arguing about it again, I suppose. And what will you do with all those books?"

"Take them with me, of course."

"But Willy, there must be *thousands* of them. You'd better send them by freight."

"Yes, I suppose so. About the furniture, Lou, of course I want you to take Mother's piano for Dougie. She'd have wanted him to have it."

"He won't be three till November, you know. However — "

"Or anything else, come to that, you feel like having as a memento ... "

"There's nothing, thanks." And I can almost feel Lou's shiver at the other end of the wire. She spent so much time away at school she has none of the feeling for the house — or come to that, the family — that I have. We are totally different people. However, she now makes a sisterly effort to steer us away from the probability of a quarrel.

"Well, it's going to be a busy summer for you, that's sure. Look, why don't we go up to Montreal together next week — I could stay a couple of days and help you apartment-hunt. Mrs. Chan could look after Dougie."

And have you try to decide everything for me? No thanks.

"No, thanks, Lou; I'll be able to manage fine. Come up for a few days when I'm settled. You know I spent quite a bit of time exploring Montreal when I was up there in the spring. I know just where in town I'd like to be, and what kind of place. A nice modern high-rise with a view of the city, and underground parking for my nice new Porsche."

"Look out, Willy; rapists love that kind of setup. And if you're planning to drive, for God's sake watch out on the 401, it's like a raceway. Also Quebec drivers are a special breed, you know."

I pause to control myself. "I'll watch it."

Well, I couldn't wait to call her; now I can't wait to hang up. Why is it that I love the bitch and yet she annoys me so? In ten minutes' chat she's managed to squeeze most of the joy out of my wonderful news. I'm full of qualms and doubts now. I even wonder (though of course I'll write and accept the job before dark) whether I'll really be happy at Cartier College, working with Acid Coughdrop Benson-Clarke, who made it so clear he disliked me.

Highway 401 to Montreal is as broad as the road to destruction, but much more monotonous. Its four lanes cut straight as a paper knife through flat, empty, forgettable countryside so featureless you have to stop occasionally just to break the numb grip of boredom. But nothing in the fake-colonial triteness of the restaurants along the way tempts you to linger there, either. The coffee is bad and hot, the Muzak is bad and loud—it's a relief to climb back into the car and put your foot down. Then the excited feeling of adventure comes back, and I'm happy.

The new white Porsche zips along smoothly and I enjoy the envious and admiring glances it gets. When various salesmen asked what kind of sports car I had in mind, I told them whatever was in. I have been out—out of everything—for so long. Now I want to be *in*. Of course Lou disapproves. "What was wrong with your nice little Volks? It's barely a year old." But there's no use trying to explain. Greg comes closer to understanding, maybe. His face spread into a broad grin when he saw it, and he asked at once, like a kid borrowing a new toy, if he could run it around the block. On the other hand, maybe Lou *does* understand. "You can't even get out of the thing without showing your pants," she said to me severely. It might almost be Mother's voice. Oh, how good it is to be streaking at seventy-five miles an hour away from Toronto, away from everybody I know at the Red Cross and the Alumnae Society, away from those dead years. How wonderful to be running toward something new, a future with possibilities.

Just as I cross the bridge onto Montreal Island a heavy rain begins to stream down; but it is still so hot I leave my windows open, and the asphalt streams like a jungle trail. The traffic thickens, and I creep by inches into the centre of town, competing for space with other drivers of impressive ferocity and lawlessness. But I am enjoying myself. The garish jigsaw of neon signs reflected in wet black pavement pleases me. So does the gassy, polluted, saturated air that tangles my hair, and the nervous, hustling crowds on the streets, who push across intersections without the slightest reference to the current colour of the traffic lights. Every word of Lou's about the trip has proven true; and I don't care.

I arrive at the Queen Elizabeth hungry as a wolf and overtip the parking boy for remarking "Voilà un neat char, là." I'm still happy, even when I discover the only hotel room I can have is a cubicle overlooking noisy Dorchester Boulevard, and the elevator whining outside my door guarantees a sleepless night. But I sing in the shower. Nothing can depress me.

The first thing I do in the morning (without having consciously planned anything of the kind) is to open the Yellow Pages to Real Estate and begin calling the bigger companies in alphabetic order. Each time, I ask to speak to Mr. George MacKay. Well, why not? There wasn't a speck of harm in the poor soul. He could find me the ideal apartment in half the time it would take me alone. Perfectly sensible to contact him. Besides, I liked him. And he liked me. Well, I think he did ... if he remembers me at all. The thing is, having met him, I can't waste him, can I? Lucy Snowe didn't waste a single soul among the men she met that first night in Villette ...

On the fifth call, I'm lucky. That is, up to a point. Mr. MacKay, it appears, is on holiday. They don't expect him back for ten days. But at least now I know where to find him. If I want to, I can give him a call some time, just to say hello. Friendly, he was. Lonely. And I think he liked me.

I spend some time over coffee studying a city map and the classified ads in the *Gazette*. There are several apartments for rent on the mountain slope near Cartier College. Cheerfully I set out in a taxi to inspect them. As we draw up to the first building, I note that right next door to it is a huge service station, full of metallic clanging and drilling. Feeling clever, I tell the driver to move on. The next place on my list sits behind a strip of lawn and a bank of bright flowers. It is white as a many-tiered wedding cake, with a long, festive canopy sheltering carpeted steps. Wide doors of thick glass lead to a lobby carpeted wall to wall in purple broadloom.

I buzz *Sup't*. After a considerable pause, he appears, a thin, rather stooped French Canadian who needs a shave and, from the sexy look in his hooded, impudent eyes, a whole series of cold showers. His shirt is open halfway down, and two religious medals are tangled in the hair on his chest. Without troubling to remove a hard-worked toothpick from his mouth, he assures me this is a very chic apartment house. The night-club singer Danielle lives here, and several newspapermen from *Le Devoir*; lots of lawyers, musicians, very swinging people.

He takes me up in an elevator, whistling faintly while he analyses my figure in close detail. When he unlocks the door of 1204 I edge past him rather apprehensively. It distracts me as I walk through the two big, empty rooms, to know he is still inspecting my legs and bottom with the eye of a man whose hobby never palls. A huge window occupies one whole wall of the sitting-room, and outside it runs a balcony with a white, curly-iron perimeter. Inside, the walls and woodwork are a dreary, dog-biscuit beige, but the bathroom is tiled in black and white, and the tub and basin are black porcelain. This I like very much.

"We gon' decorate all new," the janitor remarks, shifting the toothpick expertly to the other side of his mouth. "No need for air-condition, neither, because you get a cross-draft from dese bedroom window, very cool."

I wander across the hollow sitting-room floor again. The big window frames a large vista of the city spread below. The kitchen is just a narrow galley separated from the main room by a waist-high bar. Good. I don't intend to do a lot of cooking. My decision is as good as made.

"Well, it's quite nice ... what did you say the rent was?"

When he tells me, I'm surprised, but not shocked. He eyes me with a half-smile. "You like?"

"I like."

Five minutes later, M. Louis-Philippe Mackenzie and I are sitting across from each other in his tropically hot little business room downstairs, where he produces a six-month lease for me to sign and asks for a month's rent in advance. I can occupy the place in two weeks, after the decorators have finished. He is very businesslike now and seems to have lost all interest in my anatomy. He explains that I will have to pay a water-tax in addition to rent, as well as a monthly charge for window-cleaning and another for cable TV. The management (an Italian company, it turns out to be) also requires a deposit against possible damage. (With all those chic tenants?) "But if anyt'ing go wrong wit anyt'ing, mademoiselle, you just call hup, night or day. Always 'appy to do my possible for all nice people here, specially ladies like you."

"I'll bet you are," I think; and then blush up to the top of my scalp because I can see he's caught my thought and is grinning broadly in his leering way. Damn. Why can't I keep a more inscrutable face; everything shows on it. I hasten to collect my oversize straw bag, say good-bye, and depart, trying to freeze him with an air of calm hauteur. I'm not terribly successful.

After sending the taxi away I walk downtown for a tour of the big shops. This gives me time to reflect how ashamed I ought to be to admit that Mackenzie's kind of insolent male appraisal is obscurely exciting, even while it repels. It can't be dismissed as it ought to be, ignored as silly, or put aside as insignificant. Not by me, at any rate.

These rueful thoughts soon melt away, though, in the fun of looking for new furniture. Soon I'm deep in negotiation with a diffident young man in a Scandinavian shop, who soothes me with his large Adam's apple and nervous stutter. He couldn't make me blush if he tried. (Indeed, I make him laugh once and colour up a bright pink.) I am happy choosing a free-form coffee table topped with black glass; so happy I could laugh out loud. In a department store I buy a shaggy white rug like yak fur, and roughly half a mile of zebra-striped fabric to curtain the sitting-room. These will look grand with my new Swedish furniture. I also buy a queen-sized bed and some psychedelic sheets, all huge red and pink flowers. If all this isn't in, nothing is. A tremendously satisfactory day. The only remaining problem is how to wait for two long weeks until I move into my new apartment and begin serious work on my job. And on The Project.

TWO

Colleagues

F LIFE WERE ONLY MORE LIKE LITERATURE, there'd be a whole lot more satisfaction in living. No self-respecting Victorian novel, for instance, would at this interesting point come up with an anticlimax. But the fact is that once I am settled into my bright, paint-smelling apartment (where the zebra curtains, the yak rug, and the queenly bed look marvellous), time seems to stick. The slow evenings creep past; the long days are flat and empty. Nothing *happens*. It's bad art. It's also very depressing.

Of course I spend hours every day at the library preparing my courses, and I do a lot of conscientious re-reading of the nineteenth-century authors I already know almost too well. But mealtimes gape, open and vacant as three yawns, and in the late evenings, with the electric glitter of the city spread out below my window, I feel enclosed in glass and silence, suspended outside both world and time. Not an agreeable sensation. Partly because it's not what I expected; though exactly what I did expect isn't really clear to me either.

For one thing, when I presented myself early in July at Cartier College, in all the dignity of my new Faculty status, I found the Department of English deserted, brooding stuffily in its own dust and hooded with yellow blinds drawn against the heat. All the office doors were inhospitably closed. The silence was so thick even the air seemed asleep. I followed a dim little corridor in pursuit of one faint noise — "Ya. Ya. Ya." repeated on the same flat note—and found a young woman in a tight pink pantsuit with the phone cradled under one ear to free her hands for a manicure. Without hurrying, she wound up the conversation and, when I identified myself, stuffed my hands full of mimeographed papers and forms. She added a few sketchy directions about the location of the library, bookstore, washrooms, and other useful institutions. As an afterthought she produced a key and unlocked the office I'd been assigned — though it is so tiny it must surely have begun life as a broom closet. Pinky then wiggled off, and a moment later I heard her again. "Ya. No kidding. Ya. Ya." In short, at the moment, there isn't much at Cartier to encourage loitering.

The smouldering heat of Montreal makes exploration on foot very wearing; but I blister my feet anyway on long walks. My reward is to discover a number of charming little squares with trees in heavy leaf, where green statues of generals and other heroes lift chins and swords bravely into the hot, traffic-throbbing air. I climb narrow, cobbled streets; I gaze at pagoda-shaped telephone booths in Chinatown and am diverted to find notices for Mass on a church wall in Chinese. In a downtown square in Old Montreal I discover a large statue of Nelson and wonder how it got there. Across the street is Rasco's Hotel, where Dickens once stayed. (He hated it.) I visit St. Joseph's Shrine on the mountainside, picking my way tactfully among the faithful, who clot the long stairway as they climb to the top on their knees. I am suitably impressed when I discover part of the establishment is a museum with relics of the saintly life of Brother André. In one glass case his truss has been reverently preserved.

When the blazing sun becomes too much, I take refuge in the marble dignity of the Fine Arts Museum, where there is a magnificent El Greco, or cross the street to have tea in the recessed garden of the Ritz-Carlton, where a fountain and glass-topped tables give an illusion of coolness. Another refuge is the wildflower-and-bird sanctuary on the flank of the mountain, where a bold young pheasant pecks some of my picnic crumbs. And yet, for all this, it's hard to fill the time. As for The Project, it recedes rather than advances.

Unfortunately, there are many things I cannot do. I can hardly bring myself to read newspapers, for instance, because all those chronicles of cruelty, stupidity, and wasted time fill me with horror. I persist only in the hope of understanding the world better—and the dimmer hope of finding a place for myself in it. Nor can I often watch TV, because the regular alternation of gunfire and advertisements for deodorant makes me twitch. The wide-screen movies showing locally are even worse; you have to choose Disneyland or the kingdom of sado-masochism—though I suppose anything in between would be even worse. The concert season doesn't begin till autumn, and there is little or no live theatre even then, except in French.

Churchgoing might be one answer; but not for me. I believe absolutely in God, without understanding a single thing about Him. And I love the stately Tudor music of the Book of Common Prayer. But go to a new church and you are likely to find that a thankless Anglican establishment has flattened that noble prose into Basic Modern English—an outrage, like reducing Goya to paint-by-numbers. Another serious drawback to church is my lifelong affliction of irrational, violent seizures of giggling. The last time I went, the visit was sabotaged by a dim small boy in the pew ahead, beguiling away the sermon by putting on his mitten. He got it on the wrong hand, and puzzled long over the enigma of the thumb sticking out of the wrong side. After deep thought he took the mitten off, inspected it, put it back on. The thumb still protruded on the wrong side . . . I had to sneak out rapidly, under cover of the blessing.

That leaves people as the only remaining pastime. The trouble is that in this city I literally don't know anybody. I live as solitary as Crusoe, though my island contains a million souls. Louis-Philippe Mackenzie is, for obvious reasons, not somebody I'm keen to cultivate. When I ring Bill Trueblood (he's not hard to locate, with that name) there is no answer. And for some reason or other, I now can't bring myself to call George MacKay, though several times I lift my bright new red phone and look at the lighted dial before putting the receiver back on its hook.

Such neighbours as this building affords seem to consist mostly of brisk, well-groomed young men in the bright shirts and wide ties of the moment. They all carry briefcases and a look of profound preoccupation. The smart little women who whisk in and out are mini-skirted, their eyes outlined in green, blue, or purple, their lips coated with whitish-pink gloss. They look unreal to me, like Barbie dolls, with stiffened eyelashes and tiny clothes made to take off at a moment's notice. If you say "Good morning" in the elevator to any of these people, he or she is likely to give you an incredulous, almost angry glance, and few of them make any distinguishable answer.

Lou and Greg did come down one weekend in August to inspect the apartment and take me out to dinner, and that crammed one day wonderfully full. It was grand to see Dougie stumping around my rooms on those fat legs that kiss at the inside of the knees. He pulled open all the drawers, rolled on the yak rug, jumped on the bed, his fair hair flying. He filled the whole place up with life, God love him. When he saw a bird on the balcony railing, he pointed a stubby finger at it and shouted "BUIDIE", his funny, hoarse voice loud with joy. Before he left, we two had a good round of a chase-and-tickle game my father long ago invented for me, called Let's Be Two Horses Laughing.

It was so good to see them all that I didn't get irritated once, not even when Lou said Good God to my wonderful curtains, or when Greg advised installing a special bolt on the door. When they left, I gave Dougie three hard kisses on the head. I could hardly say good-bye for the fat lump in my throat. It was so nice of them to come. But that night I couldn't sleep because I buzzed all over with a restless, meaningless overcharge of excitement. Probably Crusoe felt the same after his first visitors.

Insomnia is an old friend, of course; for years I've sat up reading most of the night. Even when I do sleep, by six in the morning I'm always awake and ready for the day. It's been this way for so long that the night feels like my private environment now. It's good to be alone while everybody else sleeps. The dark is tranquil and undemanding, restful in its silence. Even in the Rosedale house there was a truce in the small hours, most nights.

There are times, though, when the friendly dark turns traitor and twists dreams around my neck; dreams made of long chains of remembered words, pictures, faces, silences, from those closed years. My father drunkenly singing the most sentimental of Moore's songs — or noisily vomiting — or cursing the world in a long, lyrical, violent stream of obscenities. Mother's silver crochet hook flashing through a delicate web of lace as she sat behind her door, her mouth pressed into a tight and final line. These things twist and hold me prisoner yet, on some nights.

Yes, it's always good when daylight comes, whether I've slept or not.

When the phone rings I'm on my knees scrubbing the bathroom floor. My hands are a bright, spongy pink and smell of sour cleaning powder. In all these weeks I've had no calls whatever, except from a peremptory woman who always asks, "C'est toi, Yvette?" and seems unfairly annoyed, not with herself but with me, when I deny it. She invariably hangs up with such crisp finality that I've named her Madame Guillotine. So I expect nothing better now and let the phone ring several times: I want to get on with my scrubbing. However, I haven't enough fortitude, of course, to ignore the call entirely.

"Hullo."

"Hi, there; is that you, Miss Doyle? Bill Trueblood here. Sherri gave me your number—I hope you don't mind my calling so early —"

(Early! It's ten after nine. And wouldn't you know her name would be Sherri.)

"No, no; not at all. And please call me Willy."

"Well, I just got back from California last night — I'm down here at Cartier now, getting through some mail and things ... I wonder if by any chance you'd like to have a bite of lunch with me. Nobody else in the department seems to have been around to look after you, so I thought you might like a chat about this and that."

"Oh yes, I'd like that very much. It's terribly nice of you to think of it."

"Well, suppose we meet at L'Escargot on St. Dominique Street. Can you find your way there all right? If we got there at a quarter after twelve, we'd beat all those stockbrokers to a good table—the place gets madly crowded later on."

"Sure, that will be fine. A quarter after. I'll be there."

(Will I not.)

"Great; see you then."

He hangs up. I sit down and try to control an exploding sensation under the ribs. Lunch at L'Escargot! And with a good-looking man! Yah to you, Madame Guillotine. But what the hell will I wear? Yesterday, in a burst of efficiency that seemed admirable at the time, I packed off every single respectable garment I own to the cleaner, in order to be ready for the opening of term. The one wearable item left is the denim dress I have on, which at the moment is covered with soapy splashes. The predicament is silly but serious. If I go down to wash and dry it in the machines downstairs, I might rouse the beast in Louis-Philippe, who tends to hang around down there in a hopeful sort of way. I'll just have to wash and dry the thing here, somehow. If I hang it outside, it should be wearable by the time I have to leave.

So I give the dress a good wash, wring it out tight, and hang it over the balcony railing in the sun. It's a glorious blue day, bright without being really hot, and all the leaves on the trees are twinkling in a light breeze.

The rest of the morning (after a final, perfunctory swipe at the bathroom) is devoted to trimming nails, shaping eyebrows, shaving legs and armpits, and applying a complicated make-up base guaranteed to conceal freckles. What an enormous amount of maintenance a woman needs. It would be intolerable if it weren't so much fun. At a quarter to twelve I bring the dress in (grand, it's nearly dry), and spread it on the ironing board. Only then do I discover that some carefree passing bird has ornamented the bosom with a large white splash.

Desperately I try to sponge it out, but the stuff is like cement, and all my efforts to erase it only seem to make the stain worse. The struggle seems to last ages, till I'm half in giggles, half in tears. Finally (it's getting late), I simply put the dress on with a large blotch over one breast, like a target. All I can do is pull on white gloves to distract attention, and clasp my large white bag over the stained patch. It will be all right. No one will notice. I hope.

Trueblood is already at a tiny corner table when I arrive; he waves to me cheerfully and rises to pull out my chair. The dress problem has made me just a little late—the right kind of late—the little restaurant is full, and he's been waiting just long enough to be really pleased to see me.

"Now, Willy," he says, his full brown eyes warm with good will, "how about something to drink? A nice cool gin-and-tonic maybe?"

I hunch over the table, clutching my bag close. "Well, the truth is I don't drink, and people hate that so much I can't face them and always ask for sherry. But would you mind if I skipped it this time? I actually loathe sherry. But please go ahead and have whatever you like."

He laughs and pats my arm. "No, let's just jump right into a shrimp cocktail, how would that be?"

A stout old woman in a black apron and bedroom slippers comes by to take our order. She appears to approve highly of Bill in his clean seersucker jacket and white shirt, and smiles at his jokes proffered in limping French. She has a lamentable set of plastic teeth, poor soul.

"Madame Le Gros is a terrific character," he tells me later. "Belgian. Went through all sorts of horrors in a couple of wars. She's been married five times — did you see all those wedding rings? She gets rid of the men but keeps the gold, the crafty old dear. Does all the cooking here herself — it's great, too — and yet this is about the cheapest place in town for a decent lunch. Um — would you like to put that bag of yours down somewhere? . . . I'm afraid it's rather crowded for you there — "

"No, no; perfectly all right, thanks; just fine. Did you see anybody today at the college? It's been completely deserted all this month; not a soul around. I was beginning to think I must have dreamed them all."

He raises his eyebrows slightly at this flight of fancy. "Well, I saw Archie for a few minutes, and he was solid enough, God knows."

"Who's Archie?"

"Dr. Clarke to his many enemies."

"Oh."

"I'm afraid you may have . . . er . . . picked up a rather poor impression of our beloved chairman, that day you had your interview. But the old boy was just having a bad day, that's all. He's sixty, you know. Arthritis bothers him a lot. So does the cussedness of things in general. There are some wheelers and dealers in the department, too — but no: I swore I wouldn't gossip. Anyhow, you wouldn't believe how completely charming Archie can be."

"Well, I can make the effort."

"Generally speaking, we all get on together pretty well in the department. I think you'll like Molly Pratt, specially if you have any Women's Lib leanings; she's down on us male chauvinists like a gorilla, but more for fun than for blood, if you see what I mean in all that mess of metaphor."

"Um. She's very attractive. Is she married?"

"Was. Her divorce just recently went through. I wouldn't be surprised, though, if she has another go at it, with someone in the department you didn't meet, called Harry Innis. He's our eighteenth-century man. American. Bit of a radical. He — well, you'll see for yourself. Sure you wouldn't like to get rid of that bag? — makes it a bit hard to cut your steak, doesn't it? All right then ... no, it isn't bad, is it?"

"Tell me more about the department. Are there other women besides Molly?"

"Oh, yes. There's little Ruth Pinsky, nice kid who looks after the Basic and Remedial courses — "

"Not Remedial English! Oh, Lord."

"My dear, you don't know our student body. A lot of it is the tired, poor, and huddled masses that can't get in anywhere else. Big contingent every year fresh from Hong Kong and other exotic parts. We even had to hire Ruthie a couple of extra assistants for this year. Then there's our Chaucer expert, Emma O'Brien. She's called Fat Emma, and richly does she deserve it."

I am enjoying all this so much that I push my dessert around the plate to make it last longer.

"And what are the students like generally? Active or passive?"

"They're quite fun, really, most of them. Not nearly as militant here as they are in some places, thank God. We've had almost no trouble, in fact. You know, occupying the building in sleeping bags, and peeing in the Principal's wastebasket — that sort of thing. Maybe it's going out of style now. But I think one reason we've been so free of it is good old Archie. He simply puts the fear of God up them. On top of that, he manages to be popular, though you may find that hard to credit. Don't ask me how he does it. Except that he can be funny as hell, you know. They had one confrontation last year, big demonstration against exams, and somehow or other he broke them up so much laughing they just went home, and that was it."

"Really?" By this time I'm so interested that I forget to hide the bosom of my dress, and finish up the last of the *crème caramel* with my bag comfortably in my lap.

"Now then, monsieur, you're not going to sit there all day, are you? — I've got other customers waiting; you see that great queue?" There is Madame being severe to the old man at the next table. Meekly he leaves half his coffee and goes while she pours us a second cup. I can't help being pleased with this miscarriage of justice.

"If there's anything I can do for you, Willy, these first weeks, I'll be very glad to help," Bill says, as we eventually surrender our table to a pair of famished-looking women shoppers.

"Thanks. I don't think there's anything just now—but I may be tempted to bother you some time . . . it's a bit hard to pry Sherri loose from the phone, I find."

We move out into the sunny day and he dons a pair of impressive dark glasses. When I drop one of the white gloves, he returns it with a gallant little bow that is amusing without being ridiculous. "It's been great fun seeing you, Willy. I suppose you'll be around the office building next week. There's generally plenty to do before classes begin — book-ordering and all that torture."

"Yes; I'll see you around. And thanks so much for the nice lunch."

(And thanks more particularly for those brown eyes, and for being in general one of the most attractive people ever. . . . What a pity I haven't had the wit to steer the conversation around to himself. How old is he, I wonder. Rather younger than . . . but it's hard to tell. He must be married, of course. Men as pleasing as that always, always are. But it would be a help to know for sure. Wonder how I could find out without seeming to care?) I ponder these angles happily all the way home.

THERE WILL BE A MEETING OF THE DEPARTMENT OF ENGLISH
AT 10 A.M. ON MONDAY SEPTEMBER 6TH IN THE COMMITTEE ROOM.
A. BENSON-CLARKE, CHAIRMAN.

This terse notice appearing in my pigeonhole might be a love letter for the powerful thrill it causes to travel through my imagination. Here it is at last, I think with delight. I belong. I am a member of a decision-making body. I am part of an institution, a group of scholars. I am involved with the forms, processes, and ideals of higher education. Like the "W. Doyle, Ph.D." on my office door, these are supremely satisfactory words, and I hug them all weekend long, like a child with a new doll.

When Monday finally puts in an appearance, it is teeming with heavy autumn rain, and unseasonably cold. It always rains on the first day of school, as every youngster knows. But today sparks of mineral glitter in the wet sidewalks, and leaves are plastered like gold stars on the black roads. The wind itself smells piquantly of stone and mould and smoke. I walk fast, enjoying the cool rain on my cheeks, and jump cheerfully over the bright twist of running water in the gutters.

"Good morning, Willy Doyle," says a voice on the stairs, and I turn to find the neat, small figure of Molly Pratt climbing up behind me. She looks charming in a hooded raincape that comes down to her heels. "On your way to the meeting? Come along with us, then. It's way up at the top of the house. Have you met Harry Innis yet? Willy's going to teach the novel course, Harry."

The thick-set young man behind her pauses on the landing to shift a damp shopping bag and offer a handshake so hearty it makes me blink. His lips are very red in a face that looks oddly narrow across the eyes, like soft fruit that has been severely squeezed. He has energetic blue eyes and a beautifully tended little beard at curious odds with the faded blue jeans that hang in tatters over his boots.

"Hi there," he says cheerfully. "Welcome to Thornfield Hall. I always think it's perfect that here at Cartier we hold our meetings in the attic. What's the good word, Billy Boy?"

This last is addressed to Bill Trueblood, now emerging from his office with several books insecurely gripped under one arm. He smiles at me and attaches himself to the group on the side farthest from Innis, in order (I suspect) to avoid answering his question—if it was a question. Up another flight of stairs cumbersome wooden armchairs wait for us around a big oak table no one has recently troubled to polish. The uncarpeted floor smells of dust. Rain darkens the pair of high-set dormer windows, and Innis snaps on a sputtering fluorescent bar overhead that turns all our countenances pale blue.

A large woman with a baby's tight and silky skin manoeuvres herself through the doorway and sinks massively into a chair. Fat Emma, without a doubt. A nervous-looking girl in horn-rims slips into an inconspicuous place beside a couple of unisex young people in trousers and long hair. They must be Ruth Pinsky and her assistants. And finally, preceded by the trumpet-blast of a prodigious nose-blow, comes Chairman Clarke, moving at an old man's shuffle behind a large blue handkerchief. To my surprise, and even faint alarm, he makes straight for me.

"Miss Doyle, I hope you've been introduced to everyone? Have you been looking after her, Molly? — good, I knew you would.

Please let me know, Miss Doyle, if there's any help I can give you at all . . . come and see me any time. We all want to help you fit in and be happy here."

"Thank you," I say, trying politely to conceal my surprise. Can this be the gnashing ogre I remember so well? His smile is cordial; it even has a mischievous twinkle of flirtation in it. His eyes are bleary with a heavy cold, but for all their pouched and wrinkled lids, they are a bright periwinkle blue. Most astonishing of all, he bestows a cosy simultaneous little squeeze on my arm and Molly's before making his way to the head of the table.

"You no doubt observe," he says to the group at large, "that I have punctually contracted my Registration Cold. It will be followed in due course by my Founder's Day Cold and my Spring Convocation Cold. You see how the academic life lends ritual and meaning even to the illiterate virus."

An obliging laugh goes round the table, but I catch a wry glance exchanged between Molly and Harry Innis, who have taken seats together across from me. I note that Innis has meticulously laid out before him a filing folder bursting with papers, a pair of ball-point pens and a large scratch pad — considerably more equipment than Sherri has, who now slouches in, yawning, and flips open her shorthand pad.

She proceeds to read out in a thin monotone a summary of the last meeting, and I understand so little of it she might as well be reciting the Koran. Harry Innis is already scribbling away busily. I wonder uneasily if I should be writing things down, too. But what things? And I have forgotten to bring a pen.

Earnestly I pin my attention to the first item on the agenda. It has to do with fire regulations in the main building. The students, it appears, routinely ignore the No Smoking signs, and there is talk of discontent in the Fire Department. Pinsky's little army, all smoking, shuffle booted feet. A very long and unprofitable argument develops over ways and means to deal with this problem. Everyone seems to have an astonishing amount to say, but no one comes up with a solution. Under cover of the table edge I look at my watch and am unprepared to discover that a whole hour has been consumed in this debate. Eventually it is agreed that bigger No Smoking signs ought to be posted up — if funds for the same can be extracted from the Maintenance Department.

We then move on to the next item. This concerns elaborate

arrangements for the entering class of students—I'm alarmed to learn there are close to seven hundred of these—to write something next week called The Inital Essay. It will provide a means of identifying which students need the Remedial English course. Students will assemble in the gym on the basement floor of the main building, where seven hundred hired chair-and-table sets will await them. All of us must be on duty to give out paper and so on; and afterward each of us will receive a large batch of essays to be read and graded at top speed. I do some laboured mental arithmetic. Is it possible I will have to deal with something like seventy-five essays? Ruth Pinsky lays all these unattractive prospects before us in a shy and diffident voice. But I soon perceive she has the situation well in hand; in fact most of the organization has already been done. She promises to put a memo in our pigeonholes tomorrow. Bill Trueblood sighs. She is a very capable girl.

By now it is close to noon, and my thoughts are beginning to wander to food. Bill has for some time been elaborating a curly drawing of a clipper ship on a bit of blotter, and Emma is sunk in her chair like a pillow, apparently dozing.

"Mr. Chairman, I'd like to call to your attention a major bit of business left over from last session." I notice now for the first time the New York twang in Harry's voice. "The question of student representation, you remember, was discussed at length last spring, but a vote was postponed. I propose that vote be taken now."

With this a palpable tension flashes into the air, almost as if he had produced some kind of threat. Emma's eyes snap open. Ruth frowns. Molly spreads out fine-fingered hands in front of her and studies them with close attention. Clarke rubs his eyes wearily and blows a loud toot into the blue handkerchief.

"With your permission, I'd like to put this in the form of a motion," Innis goes on.

"If you must," mutters Clarke.

"I move, then, that this department adopt the policy of student parity, to take effect at all subsequent meetings on this level."

"I second the motion," says Molly in a clear voice.

"I've been out of the academic world too long," I whisper, leaning near Bill. "What's student parity?"

"Equal numbers of students and staff at all meetings."

"Oh." I would add more, but he shakes his head.

"You remember that the Students' Council presented a petition for parity last year, signed by eighty per cent of the student body. We debated the question at length last spring ... I have the transcripts of tapes made then, if anybody wants to consult them. I think we're ready for the question now." Innis looks around the table with a confident smile.

"Does your motion imply full voting power for the student representatives?" Clarke asks.

"Of course. The right to hear and be heard is not enough. The right to vote is essential. Will somebody move an amendment to the motion — 'Students to have full voting power with faculty.' "

One of the Pinsky people obliges. Several people now begin to talk rapidly at once.

"But Harry, the point is that if students are going to sit on our committees — Hiring and Tenure, for instance — they'll have access to confidential files, and that raises the whole — "

"What about support people, then, like Sherri and Mrs. Barrow? They have as much right as — "

"The Students for a Democratic Society — "

"Look, that crowd is led by professional agitators up here from the States — sorry, Harry, but you know it's true — "

"Order!" says Clarke, but Molly seizes the lull to say "It's time we recognized the fact that students and faculty are equal. We're partners in the learning process. We've got to be partners in administration too." Her normally pale cheeks are flushed. Clarke stares at her. He looks both sad and angry.

"Partners my ass," mutters Bill.

Clarke draws breath to say something, but is cut off by a sneeze so explosive it makes me flinch in my chair. Then once more there is that queer element of tension in the silence. I look from face to face with curiosity. Innis places his pen down with precision and turns to the head of the table. "Perhaps you'd read us the amended motion, Sherri? Then if there's no more discussion—"

"Yes. Quite. I am still in the chair, Professor Innis," says Clarke. He is unmistakably very angry and there is something formidable about him in spite of the sneeze-bleared eyes and the blue handkerchief into which he keeps plunging his large nose. He looks so fixedly at Innis and Molly that another uncomfortable silence falls.

"We all argued the matter pro and con for many hours last spring," says Harry mildly. "I think I express the feeling of the meeting when I say we're ready for the question now." He glances briefly at the young people with Ruth, and they pipe up eagerly, "Hear, hear."

At a surly nod from Clarke, Sherri reads the motion aloud.

"Is there any further discussion?" demands Clarke.

No one speaks.

"All those in favour, then."

Molly's hand is up with Harry's, and the two jean-wearers at the foot of the table are each holding up an arm energetically.

"Those opposed."

Bill, Emma, and Ruth (looking worried).

"And you are abstaining, Miss Doyle?" growls Clarke. He spears me with an eye no longer in the least flirtatious.

"Yes, sir ... I wasn't here for the discussion, so ... "

He nods without comment, after a pause so fraught with his extreme disapproval that I feel a qualm of unease in the pit of my stomach.

"The motion is passed, then, by a vote of four to three, with one abstention. Now perhaps someone will move adjournment of this meeting." He pushes out of the room in a hurry, though Molly calls after him, "Wait a second, Archie, please — "

Harry is beaming at the centre of an arguing, chattering group which, after a second's hesitation, she joins.

"For heaven's sake, why was that so uncomfortable?" I ask, hurrying down the hall after Bill. He frowns at me, an action that sours his good looks into petulance. "Not here," he mutters. "It's a long and complicated story."

I tag after him down the stairs and linger at the open door of his office, a pleasant room with plants on the windowsill and a bright Lautrec poster on the wall. But he doesn't ask me to come in.

"Does it matter all that much, student parity?" I can't help persisting.

"Yes, it does. For various reasons. You'll see why soon enough. Sorry I've got to rush off now — got a dentist's appointment."

"But why was Clarke so furious with *me*?"

"Well, don't you see, if you'd voted no, there would have been a tie, and then Archie could have defeated the motion with his own vote. The chairman only votes in case of a tie. But as it was — "

"Lord, do you stick to parliamentary procedure as closely as that? Since when have college affairs been so political?"

"These days, ducky, education *is* politics. You'd better get your consciousness raised, Willy, that's all I can say. Now I've got to go. See you."

He hurries off, still looking ruffled. I drift homeward pensively through the rain, and reflect on my innocence, now forever lost, on the subject of department meetings.

THREE

Neighbours

I AM SITTING UP IN BED reading *Little Dorrit*, which I've put on my course reading list, when I hear a scream. It is well after midnight, and the building has been quiet for some time. No party overhead; no shouted marital argument from the old couple next door—diversions that often in the small hours form a counterpoint to my reading. This scream has an edge to it that makes the book jerk in my hands. It is followed by a silence so complete that I think I must have dozed off and dreamed without realizing it. Then the scream rings out again, this time accompanied by a thump of running feet and a crash, as if someone has fallen. It all seems to be coming from the newly occupied apartment beside mine.

Considerably alarmed, I get out of bed and pull on a dressing-gown. This is a bad old city, as I've often been warned, and by now have had some chance to discover. Recently all the mailboxes in the lobby have been rifled. There is so much burglary inside the building that the management sends out a notice urging us all to keep our door on the chain. I admit no one before identifying every caller through the little peephole, a feature of high-rise life that would give grim satisfaction to Dickens himself.

The scream comes again, muffled this time, and therefore more frightening than ever. My hands turn cold. I go and stand beside the intercom phone in the hall, my heart running fast. I listen so hard my ears ring. There is complete silence now —

except for (but it can't possibly be)—a sort of sobbing laugh. Then nothing.

"Well, if it *is* a mugging, it's over now," I think. "Might as well go back to bed." I find myself thirsty, so on the way back I go into the bathroom for a drink of water. But my hand has barely touched the tap when a voice cries out "No! No!" so close I give a little gasp of terror. It's just on the other side of the wall. Now there is violent thumping; a struggle of some kind. Gasping. Another cry. A heavy gush of water — the *shower?* Moans. They take on a rhythmic sequence: "Ah. Ah. Ah."

My God. That new young couple next door. In the bathroom, of all places. What next.

It's funny; why can't I laugh?

I go back to bed and pick up *Little Dorrit* again. My heart is still racing, faster than when I was afraid. And my thoughts, before so lucid on the subject of Arthur Clennam's frustration, dart around at random like a pile of feathers in a gust of wind. I am still thirsty, having retreated from the bathroom in great haste. My skin feels hot and dry. I keep on listening, unwillingly, but not a sound from next door can now be heard.

Later I wonder whether I really heard that episode after all, or just imagined I did. Damn Freud. Damn everybody. Damn everything, including my own extensive reading in the medical section of a good university library. Damn most particularly my own flesh, with its ignorance, its curiosity, and its automatic, mindless appetite.

I cannot stay in bed. I pace to and fro. I make cocoa, prowl up and down, look out at the glimmering island city floating in the dark. When light finally comes I go out for a fast walk in the frosty air, and it's like letting an animal off a chain.

On the day classes begin, I'm in my office at eight a.m., re-reading my notes on The Development of the Novel, and trying to overcome a tendency to swallow too often. I have not slept. The activity of my neighbours in the shower is varied by parties overhead as frequent and violent as wars, and I have not had a quiet, full measure of sleep for many nights. Instead I lie hour after hour in my queen-size bed, devoured by melancholy thoughts. The general drift of these is that I am a nineteenth-century person who has strayed by some regrettable time lag into the

wrong place and period. In fiction I would be that anomaly, a
Victorian heroine absurdly planted in the twentieth century — a
Lucy Snowe in modern Montreal. God knows, I'm glum enough
to fit the part this brilliant chilly morning. I have in fact sat up
through most of the small hours reading Charlotte Brontë, with
particular attention to her advice for novice teachers. Walk in
briskly, she advises, and close the classroom door with decision. I
wonder how much help this will actually be. All my joints feel too
tight in their sockets, and my toes itch.

Ruefully I think of the teachers I have had in my time, notably
Miss Ferguson, the ridge of whose boned corset used to show
under her clothes so that when she turned to write on the board
we all writhed in giggles. Mrs. Bartholomew, who had tufts of hair
growing out of her ears, also gave much joy. Then there was
fifty-year-old Miss Donahue, her distraught face so often crimson
with what we thought was rage. She eventually stepped out in
front of a train, poor wretch. Now she has her revenge. I wish she
would get the hell out of my mind.

"Hi," says a voice at the door, and I jump half out of my clothes
with fright.

"Oh — Molly — come on in."

She edges in, deftly nudging the door shut with the side of her
small foot as she sets down containers of steaming coffee on the
desk. "Here — I thought maybe you'd like some of this to brace
you. It's awful stuff, but it helps before a nine o'clock. At least I
think it does. Archie says hemlock wouldn't taste any worse and
would have a better effect; but you know *him*."

"Oh thanks." With trembling hands I lift my coffee. "I must say
I am terrified. Never faced anything bigger than a graduate-
school seminar. And they tell me sixty students have signed up for
the novel course. Can that be true?"

"Sounds about right. We can't all be lucky, or maybe just smart,
like Emma. She makes her course in Chaucer so tough there are
sometimes only five in the class."

She drags up one of the clumsy wooden armchairs furnished by
the college to discourage relaxation, and curls herself into it,
folding her legs under her in one cat-like movement. Her pleated
skirt at once obligingly drops into a pretty fan.

"Well, I'd be glad if this awful death-wish would go away."

"Don't worry, it will. You'll be fine as soon as you actually get in there. I was so cool the morning I first began — terribly pleased how cool — then just before the bell I had to run to the john and whoops my breakfast."

"Please don't put ideas into my head."

"No kidding, you'll be fine. Hey, did I tell you I read your book on Mrs. Gaskell, and it's really great. Nobody else in the department has written anything half that good, except Archie. Only his things on Shakespeare are so good nobody could possibly *read* them, if you see what I mean. Of course Harry's doing a book on McLuhan that'll be finished one of these years. . . . Your coffee okay? There's extra sugar here."

She reaches forward to drop a little packet near my cup, her torso twisting gracefully from the narrow waist. How pretty she is, although she looks a little tired this morning; there are faint blue marks under her eyes.

"Anyhow, the kids here are great; you'll enjoy them. Specially the graduating class. It's terrific to work with them — they're so bright, so with it and active — "

"Politically active, you mean?"

She looks mildly surprised at the question. "Sure."

The memory of that recent department meeting turns over in my mind like a restless sleeper.

"Well, I'm not sure I know just what turns them on, if that's the expression. . . . Bill Trueblood says I need my political consciousness raised."

"Billy Boy tell you that? Good for him."

"He's a nice man, isn't he? I'm sure he's popular with the kids."

"Oh sure." But her voice is colourless; she doesn't seem at all interested. Suddenly I feel cheerful, even buoyant.

"With those good looks he must have to fight the girls off. But maybe his wife protects him."

(There. That was pretty neat.)

"No, he's not married — not our Billy. Hey, it's nearly nine. — Watch that cup. Come on, I'll walk you down the street. You taking all these books?"

She gathers up a pile of them, bristling with markers, and waits for me at the open door while I wrestle into a jacket that seems to have shrunk since I last took it off. Harry Innis pauses a second on a rapid course down the hall, long enough to say, "See you after the meeting, Moll."

"There's a meeting today?"

"Not for us. Harry's Faculty Rep. on the Student Council. Actually he *is* a student—he's doing a degree at the Université de Montréal."

"Oh, is he?"

"Should finish next fall. Oh by the way, Willy, we're giving a little bash tomorrow night, just to get the term started — you'll come, won't you? Bring a bottle of wine, if you like wine. Otherwise it's good old Labatt's. Villeneuve Street, 1472, Apartment 4 ... I'll stick a map in your box. Come about nine. Here's your class: got everything? Good luck, now."

(A party! Who does "we" mean; she and Harry? Bill is sure to be there, though. Oh, lovely. What a sweet girl this is.)

She leaves me outside open double doors through which I can see tiers of seats rising in a semicircle. What looks to my shrinking gaze like several thousand students flutter and climb like swarming bees on these tiers, and the air buzzes with their voices. I swallow. With icy hands I grasp my load of books.

I walk in briskly and close the doors with decision, using the side of my foot. There is immediate silence. Rows of faces, stricken immobile, present themselves in order. I send up silent thanks to Molly and Miss Brontë, and open my notes to begin.

"Never be early for a party," my mother used to say, in her firm way. So I would sit wriggling in my white stockings and party frills through the eternity of half an hour, rebelliously wondering *why*? Even after I knew the answer, it was years before I accepted it. Why must you pretend to have many other interesting things to do? Why pretend not to be eager to go? It's like the artifice of table manners, whose main point seems to be the pretence that you're not really hungry. Mother was right, of course. On these little dishonesties civilization is built. Yes, she was always right, bless her; but what a job she had civilizing headstrong, impulsive, crazily honest me. I can still feel the tweaking pull of the satin ribbon tying back the wild hair she had so patiently brushed to a meek gloss.

"Call me when it's time to come home. Don't forget to say please and thank you. Don't eat too much. Don't tear your dress." (Don't really enjoy yourself? *Why*?) No; of course she was right. No one was ever more completely a lady than Mother. It will take me the rest of my life to be half the person she was.

At a quarter to ten, therefore, I find a parking space for the Porsche on Villeneuve, pleased to discover it's the same attractive crescent of old houses I discovered on my first morning in Montreal. It looks even more pleasing now, with the old-fashioned street lamps on, and lights in the tall bay windows. On each side of Molly's door stained-glass panels glow in a water-lily pattern. The night is dry, frosty, with a bright, white moon balanced in the thinning foliage of tall elms. A cold draught flies up my legs in the yard-wide trousers of my black satin pantsuit. I hurry inside.

Up a steep flight of stairs with brassbound treads. A door on the ground floor twitches open enough to reveal a woman with purple hair and small, fierce eyes, who watches me threateningly all the way up. The party is a cauldron of noise boiling behind a half-open door. I knock, but in the din no one hears. I try again. Nobody comes. There is a wave of laughing that escapes and boils around my knees. I am seized with an urge to turn away and simply go home. But the presence of the fierce-eyed one below deters me. I remind myself of Stein's advice, "In the destructive element immerse," and step inside. I am promptly enveloped in heat, smoke, and partynoise, all as palpable as the smell of beer, cigarettes, and incense in the place. More than ever I want to go home.

The narrow hallway I stand in is crowded with people, not one of whom I recognize. Molly is nowhere to be seen. Nor is Harry. Bill is not in sight, either. Clutching my bottle of wine miserably, I wonder whether I could possibly be at the wrong party—it's the kind of thing that could easily happen to me. Several young people are sitting on the floor arguing in French. Another group is discussing Hesse. One couple is unconcerned with any language at all; they stand so tightly intertwined against the wall they might be growing there like a vine. Near me a pair of girls hissingly denounce someone called Stephanie. At the end of the corridor a quieter group sits on steps leading to a bathroom, passing a cigarette from hand to hand. No one takes the smallest notice of me.

I make my way into a bedroom plastered with bullfight posters and add my coat to the heap on the bed. Two girls are combing and tossing back their long hair at the mirror, and one of them says Hi to me in a small, dead voice. They disappear, to be greeted with shrieks in the next room. I put on some white lipstick carefully. The black pantsuit is becoming; it pleases me because it's so *Vogue*-ish with its deep neckline and flared trousers. I have even gone so far as to invest in a long, jade-type cigarette holder. Is the V neck too deep, I wonder? Certainly is lots of cleavage there. My breasts are so high, firm, and perfect that the irrelevant attention they attract has been an embarrassment to me since my twelfth year. But after all, times are different now . . . I resist the temptation to close up a little of the V with a pin. Instead I put some more Shalimar on my wrists and load the cigarette holder. I then follow a new couple in jeans into the sitting-room.

Here I look again for Molly, peering about as best I can in the bitter smoke. How odd; there's no sign of her here, either. Across the room I see Harry Innis arguing with somebody, red lips busy in his bearded face; but he doesn't notice me. Bill doesn't seem to be here. One or two of the younger people drinking who-knows-what out of mugs may be Pinsky's assistants, but I can't remember their names.

"Nice party," I say to a tall, cadaverous child in a headband. He is wearing a large badge that says Make Love Not War; but he looks totally incapable of doing either.

"I'm Mike Armstrong," he says kindly. "I take your novel course."

"Oh, do you?"

"Eh?"

"What did you say?"

"Nothing."

"Have you seen Molly?"

"Who's Molly?"

I look up at his beardless face and feel baffled. What can I say to him? To anybody here? Tell them that Queen Victoria's eldest daughter, on her travels, wrote home about the dear Alps? Would that amuse, you, Mike Love? No, it would not. "Never mind," I say, "I'll try the kitchen." But he has already disappeared.

Once more I squeeze past the hallway contingent. The same couple (I think) is still interlocked against the wall. Somebody says bitterly, "Man, my father can't even relate to Trudeau," and somebody else knocks over a beer bottle, whose contents foam briefly over the faded carpet. Nobody mops it up.

The kitchen (what can be seen of it for a forest of people) is a catastrophe of dirty pots and plates stacked hastily in the sink. On the only chair sits a colander brimming with vegetable peel and coffee grounds. The drainboard is covered with empty crisp packets, filmy milk bottles, a sandal, and a big pot of paper flowers. Around a little table serving as bar in one corner is a crowd of eagerly chattering people, none of whom I know. Something touches my breast and I jerk away. A young man is perched on top of the fridge. His far-from-clean bare feet dangle down — it's one of them that has touched me. I think by accident, but it's hard to tell.

"Hey-hey," he remarks grinning down at me.

"Same to you," I mutter, moving away.

"Hi there, Willydoyle," calls Molly, suddenly appearing as fresh and clear-eyed as if someone has that minute invented her. She wears a long Indian dress of dull red, and her hair, unpinned, hangs down her back. She looks different like this; younger, irresponsible, vulnerable. "Where's your drink?" she demands, tugging me toward the table with a warm, small hand. "Beer or wine?"

"Oh — wine, I guess."

"Have you met everybody? Julie, Carla, Pete, this is Willy, she just joined our department. Be nice to her. She's written a book about Mrs. Gaskell." With this she turns and is at once lost in the crush.

"Fuck Mrs. Gaskell. Hi, Willy."

"Hi."

"No kidding, you've written a book?"

"Fuck books."

I see little future in this conversation, so I take charge of a bowl of peanuts and move away to offer it around as an excuse to circulate. This also gives me a welcome opportunity to tilt the muddy contents of my wineglass down the sink where they belong. After that I hover on the edge of one group after another, where pellets of argument and comment rain around me and bounce off like fragments of some code I can only partly break.

— "so I said watch it, there's fuzz — "

"He's a member of the R.I.N., what else?"

— "been busted a dozen times — "

"But she just doesn't turn me on."

—"like ask me who's the biggest shit disturber, and I've got to say Mike."

—"and one other chick went to this Stones concert—"

"That guy's been so fucked over by the shrinks that he just—"

Soon I have the feeling they are unreal, or I am. The noise and the sour smoke in the air are making me feel vaguely ill. I hide the peanut bowl on the windowsill. A slim young black cat oozes from under a chair, stretches his back, and glances up at me with golden, oriental eyes.

"Oh, come and talk to me," I coax, squatting down and holding out my hand. But apparently I don't speak his language, either. With a bound and a switch of his long tail he leaps away and leaves me hunkered down there among the crumbs of potato chips, the long, ragged skirts, the bottlecaps, and the skinny legs in jeans. For a moment I wonder, squatting there alone, whether I'm the only adult at a children's party, or the only child among inexplicable grown-ups.

A hand hoists me up by the elbow. "Hey, Wally, come on up here and join us. You look great. Smashing. Where's your glass— here, try this; it's madeira."

Trying to conceal a shudder, I recognize the taste all too well, but I return Harry's broad smile, until I see it is directed not at me but directly at the cleavage. He appears to find it something of a joke, which is disconcerting both for me and for *Vogue*. Molly in her red dress now suddenly reappears and edges into the group.

"We're character-assassinating the Principal," Harry says to me, vaguely indicating his friends. "You met him yet, Wally? He generally gives new people a little chat about the Cartier Family. The Prince of Bastards. You could put him in a book, but nobody would believe him." He thrusts a hand around Molly's waist.

"The guy is dangerous, you see, because he doesn't want anything. Only power." This from a beautiful Indian girl in a sari.

"Well, what about Archie—he's worse, because he doesn't want even that." It's Mike, the Love-Not-War boy.

"Yeah, well, the poor old guy has no balls any more, what do you expect."

"I mean even without balls, you can't be apolitical any more."

"At McGill two years ago—"

"Yeah, how do you like Clarke trying to tell us the student radical movement is over, we're like behind the times—"

"No, don't get him mixed up with those fucking Governors," says Molly indignantly. And I slip away. There is something about the code I don't like on her lips, I don't know why; it sounds both nasty and false. And for some other obscure reason I don't like Harry's hand pressed casually under her little breast.

Rock music is now blasting out of a stereo set, and there is dancing. Couples twist and sway opposite each other, fists lightly clenched, faces closed and expressionless. It is like tribal dancing, without the joy or the purpose.

Suddenly I spot Bill across the room; the edge of his curly brown head, the straight, clean line of his back in a tweed jacket. I press and shove through the crush to reach him. I call out "Hi, Bill!" and when he turns I see too late that it's a perfect stranger.

And that's the end of the party for me. I can't stay here any longer, though my watch insists it's only eleven o'clock. If I go now, quickly, I can escape and no one will notice. And if I continue to move fast enough and do no thinking about it, I can get home without remembering the empty apartment, the vacant queen's bed.

Once more I negotiate the hallway, where the same groups are squatting, drinking, arguing, smoking. The lovemaking couple has vanished, but I find them in the dark bedroom, prone among the coats. I drag mine out and hurry away, my face blazing. I am so flurried I'm halfway out of the house before I remember that I haven't thanked anyone for the party.

Well, I don't feel grateful. I even feel annoyed with my poor dead mother. It seems unfair that I've obeyed so many of her instructions and still had such a rotten time. But of course it's not her fault. I'm old enough to know by now that parties make it not better, but worse.

All the rest of that week, I see nothing of Bill Trueblood. His office door is always closed when I go by, and there is no answer when I knock. It rains and rains. The trees stand up bare as fishbones against the dark sky. Eventually, one morning on the stairs, I say casually to Molly, "Where's Bill these days?"

"Oh, I think he's having trouble with his *teeth* or something."

All the rest of the day it pours dark rain. The weekend looms up like a menace. That evening I pick up my red phone.

"Hullo, Bill. How's it going? I hear you've been having dental trouble."

"God, yes. My gums. You wouldn't believe the misery — I've been home here swollen up like a toad all week long."

"What a shame. Is it any better now?"

"Yes, much better. But so depressing."

I hesitate only a second.

"Look, Bill, are you doing anything special tomorrow night? If not, why don't you come over here and have a bite of dinner with me. About seven, maybe? Can you eat anything?"

"Willy, how very nice of you. I'd love to come. Yes, anything except maybe steak. What's your address?"

I tell him and ring off. My heart is thumping.

Saturday is deliciously busy, what with cleaning the apartment, getting my hair done, and planning the meal ... avocados, a casserole of lasagna, green salad, fruit and cheese, coffee. I've bought the lasagna ready-made from a little take-out place around the corner, so there's no need for frenzy in the kitchen, and no bourgeois smell of cooking to spoil the cocktail hour. The table looks charming with its Danish pottery and steel flatware on red linen mats. Lou's housewarming present months ago was a thick, many-coloured candle of scented wax. I light it now, but leave the zebra curtains undrawn to frame the jewelled pins of city light twinkling below. The whole effect is lovely.

At half past six I change out of my long jersey dress into the satin pantsuit. After all, this is an occasion. At ten to seven, assailed by a sudden memory of Harry's leer at the cleavage, I hastily change the suit for my blue wool dress and a string of pearls. Yes, that's better. No point in making us both nervous.

The bell rings. I clap the casserole into the oven and hurry to the door. There he is with a bottle of wine and two huge yellow chrysanthemums in a tissue cone. He has a soft blue sweater on under his tweed jacket. His face is slightly puffy in the cheeks, but he looks marvellous anyway, and his smile is warm.

"This is so nice of you, Willy. You can't think how low I got, moping at home with the mouthwash. What a nice apartment — and wow, what a view. My place is a hole next door to an all-night garage; I'm moving out right after Christmas."

We sit down at each end of the long sofa. There is a short but terrible silence. Desperately I hurry to fill it up with erratically punctuated nothings.

"Do tell me if that gin's all right, I wasn't sure what kind to get. Well, I couldn't help missing you all week at the college, I still feel terribly new there, it's hard to get used to so much all at once like computer cards. I've never had any doings with computers before, also the kids; of course they're interesting and all that, bright, some of them, too, but I never expected to feel this terrific generation gap; it's hardly fair. Because I'm not all that old, but when I hear them talk about things and people they think are neat, like Janis Joplin, I feel just exactly one hundred years old, do you?"

"Not to worry," he says easily. "We all do. Is it okay if I —" and he holds up a pipe. "Tell me what's been going on at the old salt mine this week."

I put away the glass of warm ginger ale I have been clutching and sit back.

"Well, I'm getting to know some of my students a bit. The other day a quite intriguing boy came along after class to see me . . . his name is Mike Armstrong. You know him, by any chance?"

"Armstrong . . . wait, is he a terrifically tall, thin boy with his hair tied back in a tail? Goes around with a fat girl covered in acne. He's in my poetry class; they both are."

"That must be the one. He wanted to talk about his term-paper topic for the novel course. A bright kid. He wants to trace the fathers or father-figures in nineteenth-century fiction who are corrupt or inadequate — right from Austen to Samuel Butler. Says it's the theme of the whole century. He's right, too. The only problem will be to contain it, or he'll be all over the place. A rather remarkable boy, I thought. Actually I first met him, believe it or not, at a party Molly gave last weekend. There were thousands of people there, nearly all of them students, as far as I could tell."

"Yes. Harry's twenty-nine, but he can't face it. Some sort of awful Peter Pan complex got him several years ago, and he's been in those jeans ever since."

"I suppose they're — he and Molly — "

"Oh yes, that's been on for months now. I can't quite figure Molly. After all, *she's* thirty, you know."

"Is she really."

"And I," he adds, tilting his curly head toward me with a grin, "am an old, old man of thirty-two. As you can see by my grey hairs."

"But so well preserved."

"Thanks to this" (raising his glass). "And nice people like you. What's that good smell?"

A few minutes later we are at the table, the lighted cube of the candle flickering between us.

"Delicious," he declares, tucking into the lasagna. "You can cook too, I see."

I fiddle nonchalantly with my pearls. "Nothing to it."

"Eggs are all I can manage, boiled, scrambled, and fried. Horribly monotonous."

"You live all by yourself? — do have more of the wine — one glass is all I ever — "

"Yes, my family's in Halifax. Married sister—and my mother." He refills his glass. A flick of the candlelight in a stray draught touches his face. "She re-married ten years ago."

"Oh? She was a widow?"

"No. My parents divorced when I was nine." He looks, frowning, into his empty plate. "It hit me very hard."

"Well, maybe it's worse when your parents don't get divorced. That happened to me. Better a broken home than the one my sister and I had." I'm astonished to hear myself saying this. Did I really never know it was true before now? And where has the courage come from to admit it like this now, to someone who's almost a stranger? But there's something so kind and yet so vulnerable about him . . .

"Why didn't they?" he asks.

"I'll never know. Perhaps because of Mother. She was a very high-church Anglican; called herself Catholic, in fact. But I honestly don't know why."

"Any more than I'll ever know what possessed my mother to marry this big meathead of a railway engineer. She's a woman who reads Proust, loves Bach . . . *he* likes to sit around in his undershirt and drink beer out of the can."

"I guess no one's a more total stranger than your own parents, after all. Isn't it queer."

"Isn't it. I haven't actually seen my own father for years. Or wanted to. I bore him, and he bores me. It's always been like that. He wanted the kind of son who plays hockey."

"Well, my dad was an alcoholic. You can never begin to know people like that; they're too locked up inside their own problem. But he was a funny, clever, charming man. Lonely and in his way wise. Terribly honest, with a crazy sense of humour . . . actually I look a lot like him. That's why I'm a teetotaller."

He smiles at me. "You're not a weak person, Willy. Only weak people take to the bottle." With a wink he pours himself more wine.

"I suppose you don't see much of your mother, then."

"No, visits are pretty ghastly. But I phone her every week. And we write to each other. Her letters are wonderful. I keep them all."

"Won't you have more cheese? No? Then I'll make some coffee, shall I?"

"Great. If you'll excuse me a second, I'll just—" and he goes off in the direction of the bathroom.

When he comes back, his eyebrows are high on his forehead, and I have to snort with laughter, bending low over the coffee tray to hide my hot face.

"Yes—well—next door, they—er—use the shower a lot, and the damn walls are so thin—I'm terribly sorry."

"Not a bit. Do you think it was their own idea, or have they been reading Masters? Dear Willy, you're blushing. I thought there was nobody left to blush in this corrupt old world. That coffee smells grand ... is this the sugar? Tell me, how's Archie been this week? I thought he was going to pop a gut at that meeting we had. Only a few years back he had a heart attack, you know."

"Why was everybody in such an uproar, anyhow, that day?"

"Oh well," he says vaguely. "Harry's tactics are so obvious. It insults Archie to be manipulated so openly, and yet he can't—or won't—outmanoeuvre the guy."

"But what is there to manoeuvre about?"

"The chairmanship, among other things."

"Oh! I see." (But I don't).

"Poor old Archie gets very depressed since his wife died. At the end she was completely paralysed, you know, and he looked after her all alone for months in that huge old house of theirs. Before that they used to give parties all the time, and she'd wander around in full evening dress and long gloves, with her white hair sticking up all over like dandelion fluff. She was a darling. Tiny little creature like a hummingbird. Everybody adored her. Anyhow taking care of her like that gave him something important. Dignity. Whatever. But now she's gone. . . . His career has never been what it should, when you think what a mind the man has, and the quality of his scholarship. . . . I don't know what brought him to a second-class place like Cartier, but I know what keeps him here."

"Tell me, has Archie got a drink problem, by any chance?"

"No, but he has a problem, all right, and it sometimes makes him drink, the way I might take a lot of aspirin for pain. But he's a crusty soul; won't let anybody near."

"There can't be many people dying to cuddle up, I shouldn't think."

"Willy, for God's sake it's midnight. What a wonderful evening. You can't think how you've cheered me up. It's been so wretched being all alone with my gums. Tell me, would you by any chance like to come to the theatre next weekend? The Théâtre du Nouveau Monde is doing *Tartuffe*. They're awfully good."

"Oh, I'd love to come. My French isn't up to much, but I'll read the play ahead of time. Thanks very much."

"Good. I'll see you at work, though, before then. Thanks so much for the lovely dinner, Willy." And quite easily and casually he tips up my chin and gives me a light kiss on the mouth. I'm much too surprised to respond. Long after he has gone, I can feel the cool touch of his lips. I linger a long time over the washing and tidying-up, thinking over every detail of the evening, from the moment he arrived. For once, there are few, if any, revisions I want to make in the text. Before I finally go to bed I bend over the yellow chrysanthemums and breathe up their soft, cool, spicy smell.

"Willy, I am an idiot, and I owe you a humble apology."

Bill's dark and curly head at the office door.

"What on earth for?" I ask, trying not to blush. "Come on in — I'm not busy."

"Well, when I invited you to come and see *Tartuffe* this weekend, I forgot that Archie asked me to go up to Ste. Agathe for the E.T.U.L. meetings this Saturday. Asked — well — Emma and I have practically been chained to the oars."

He pulls up a chair, sighing. "I guess I just didn't want to remember it, that's why . . . anyhow, I'm terribly sorry. Could we make it some other time — maybe in a few weeks, if you're free? The season's just beginning."

"Yes, of course. Don't worry about it. What's the E.T.U.L. anyway?"

"English Teachers at University Level. There might be a good paper or two, but mostly it's horrible meetings about money, or panel discussions with topics like 'Where Are Your Students At'. And awful people in the chair urging us all to Interrelate and Rap."

"It sounds ghastly."

He leans forward to scrape out his pipe into my wastebasket, which gives me a chance to look at his clean profile and reflect how few men have straight, neat noses like his. How pleasing, too, is the line of his strong neck with the curls on the nape touching the collar of his turtle-necked sweater. I feel intensely awake. I almost wish he hadn't dropped in, because the sight of him so soon after our dinner together is a reminder how far The Project still is from any kind of completion. Surely other people don't find such matters so difficult to arrange, so slow to arrive at the point. They seem to do it all the time with the greatest ease. And speed. Perhaps I just have no talent. After all, if this meeting is so silly, he could surely manage somehow to get out of going to it?

"And almost the worst thing," he goes on, "is that I'll have to drive up there with Emma. You wouldn't believe what happens to that mild woman behind the wheel—presto, she becomes a speed maniac, all pointed fangs and glittering eyes. Archie says she ought to put a sign on her car that says Prepare To Meet Thy God."

"You don't drive?"

"No, I used to, but it gave me an ulcer. Have you been up north at all yet, Willy? You ought to go while the trees are still out—it's really gorgeous from St. Sauveur on up; you can get there in no time on the Autoroute."

"Yes, I've been meaning to do that. . . . Maybe some Sunday you'd like to come along as guide."

(There; that was a mistake. No talent.) But he is smiling as he gets up to go.

"I'd love that. We'll arrange something soon. But meanwhile I've got to face my poetry class . . . fancy the Romantics at nine a.m. The trouble is there are days when I think Wordsworth is an *ass*. 'We Poets in our youth begin in gladness / But thereof comes in the end despondency and madness.' *Jesus!*" I laugh as he swings open the door. "Sorry again about Saturday," he adds. "And thanks for being so nice about it. *Ciao*, Willy."

I wave him good-bye with every appearance (I hope) of casual good cheer. Whatever happens next, or doesn't happen, it's vital to maintain some kind of dignity, and that can only be done by learning to be a good liar. What a queer and complicated business The Project is turning out to be, after all. I even wonder, a trifle uneasily, whether it might not be a good idea just to abandon it. But no. One of my father's contributions to me was a hopeful nature.

Late on Saturday night I sit in my dressing-gown correcting a pile of freshman essays. I've saved them for tonight because I've learned long ago how, on weekends, the nights as well as days stretch so out of their normal length that it takes all sorts of ingenuity to fill up the extra hours. I have, for instance, done all my Christmas shopping, though it's still October. The cards are addressed in a neat pile and the presents are all wrapped and tied, even to Dougie's enormous stuffed panda. Now I'm not displeased to find it can take up to half an hour to go through a single essay. This helps to reconcile me to deformities of grammar and spelling that would otherwise appal, though I am bored by their boredom with the Prioress, and sigh often as I read.

Overhead mounts the shuffle and shriek of the usual Saturday-night party. I look often at the clock. If only it were three or four in the morning when the pop records at last mercifully fade and even the distant boom of the city outside is lulled. But now it is only eleven-thirty. Hours to go before I can hope to sleep.

Just when I am thinking I might go and make myself a cup of cocoa, there is a loud *whump* in the kitchen. Startled, I put down my red ball-point. A loud, whining noise follows, like an engine in serious trouble. After some months in this building, I'm no longer surprised by any kind of noise; at least there can't be anything ambiguous about this one—it's obviously the fridge that has gone wrong. I now detect a distinct smell of burning and hurry out to the kitchen.

There, after a moment of dithering hesitation, I pull out the plug of the fridge. The noise, of course, stops at once, but a smell of scorching rubber persists, even after I open a window. The room seems very hot. There is even a faint, bitter drift of smoke in the air.

Back at my desk I try to carry on with the essays, but it's

impossible to concentrate. The smell of smoke is still acid enough to make my tired eyes smart. When I go back to the kitchen, the fridge still feels hot. At last I decide I'd better ask for help, or at least advice, and go out to the hall where the intercom phone hangs.

"Mr. Mackenzie? It's Miss Doyle, in 1204. I'm sorry to bother you at this hour, but something seems to be wrong with my fridge. A minute ago it gave a bang, and there's such a queer smell, I'm worried it may be leaking some kind of chemical . . . well, I hate to trouble you, but — yes; would you? Thanks so much."

Well, after all, it's part of his job. Somebody really should look at the thing. Just the same, I wish it weren't so late—nearly twelve now — and I wish still more that I were dressed. But there's no time now to change — already his buzz sounds at the door.

He looks as if he has dressed in a hurry—he wears no socks or shirt, only sandals, a tight-fitting sort of red jersey, and a pair of faded jeans. He surveys me with the familiar appraising half-smile, but he has a small tool-case in his hand and goes promptly enough into the kitchen where the fridge is still faintly reeking. He squats down to remove a panel and looks at the motor, whistling faintly through his teeth. Then he opens his bag and administers a few thumps and whacks here and there, in the casual, masterful way of men with machines. I go back to my desk and try to pin my mind to the essays.

"The Pioress spills her food on her clothes, this showed she had very good table manners for those times," I read sadly.

"Not'ing much," Mackenzie says at my elbow. He has come in so silently my pen has jerked across the page.

"Oh! I didn't hear you."

"My grandmother, she was pure Iroquois," he says with pride. And from the tilt of his eyes this is obvious, now I've been told. It's a queer heritage to find behind the *Bravo Expos* T-shirt, the day-old beard, and the soft little belly rolling over the band of his jeans. "I'm gon' phone the company tomorrow, they come in a few days to fix her up."

"Oh, thanks very much. I'm sorry to have troubled you, but that smell did worry me a bit — "

He takes out a cigarette packet and draws one out to offer me. I shake my head. Should I get some money and tip him? I stand up nervously. Perfectly at ease, he is lighting his cigarette in a leisurely way, and looking around the room.

"You made the place look real smart," he says genially, blowing out the first pungent smoke from his Gitane. "You like it 'ere all right?"

(I don't like *you* here, but —)

"Oh yes, thanks. It's just a bit noisy sometimes." As if to encourage me, a shout of laughter sounds from upstairs. "Specially when I'm working," I add, looking pointedly at my desk. He fails to take the hint.

"Those girls from Air Canada," he says indulgently.

"They certainly like a lively time, whoever they are."

"You're very quiet, eh?" he says, leaning one shoulder casually against the wall. "Schoolteacher? Yes, I thought so. You're 'ere since three months now, but you don't go to no parties, not even upstairs? Why don' you go?"

"I'm not keen on parties. Well, it was good of you to come down — "

"But you're young," he says, adding with what sounds like amusement, "Mees Doyle. It's no good to keep alone all the time, you know. Not for nobody, specially for good-looking woman You know that. And I know that. Eh?"

"Mr. Mackenzie, thank you for coming down." There are times when I can imitate my mother's frigid dignity quite effectively. The trouble is that this doesn't seem to be one of them. His dark, insolent eyes are not a bit daunted; his half-smile never wavers. There is something animal about his extreme stillness and his steady contemplation of me. Something almost frightening, though he says nothing and does nothing. My throat is closed; I can't speak.

"You call me," he says quietly at last. "Any time. You just call, and I come up. Only got to call." The lips holding his cigarette are half-smiling.

"Good night, Mr. Mackenzie," I say stiffly.

"Good night," he replies with perfect good humour.

To my relief he then picks up his toolbox and goes, padding lightly off in his soft-foot way. As soon as the door closes, I hook the chain. Then I open all the windows in the place to get rid of the powerful smell of his cigarette.

With grim determination I sit down and complete the pile of essays. The room grows cold, but the rich Gitane smell persists for hours.

FOUR

The Long Vacation

SO MANY THINGS SCARE ME. Dogs. Schizophrenia. Lightning. Bugs. Infinity. Dreams. Knocking uninvited on anybody's door. (Or even invited, come to that.) Not to mention people who scare me, Archie Clarke being high on that list. So when Molly tries to enroll me in a plan to swoop down on Archie's house and give him a surprise party, I have no trouble at all in saying no.

"Lord, Molly, I couldn't do that. As it is, he'd like to grind me up for dogmeat. Besides, he'd *hate* a birthday party, don't you think? He isn't the kind of man who likes being surprised, is he? Or having birthdays, come to that."

"Oh, come on, Willy. He doesn't dislike you—don't be so silly. And the poor old lamb's been so low lately, we've got to cheer him up somehow. It's just going to be women — that's the kind of surprise he's got to like—Emma and Ruth, and you and me, and three or four other girls from Modern Languages and History who dote on him. Trust me; he'll love it. We're taking along a lot of food and his favourite booze and — "

"Calling that man a lamb is like calling a bull a gentleman cow," I grumble, to cover pleasure at her "you and me". But I am already weakening, and of course she knows it.

"Right after my last class I'm rushing off to buy a huge cake, and Ruthie's home right now making pizzas, she does lovely ones. And Emma says she'll organize the drinks—we'll all chip in. And

55

you bring the coffee, will you? We'll meet at nineish . . . his house is on Dorchester, not far from Guy. Tell you what, we'll go together and I can show you the way. Pick you up at your place around eight-thirty, okay?"

She whisks out in her long raincape before I can say, "No, it's not," and either by accident or on purpose the little fox keeps out of my reach all day. At eight-thirty she rings my bell and sweeps me downstairs, saying crisply, "Right. Off we go." Meekly I trail in her wake carrying a large tin of coffee, a thermos of cream, and a box of biscuits, plus many misgivings.

"Just the same, Molly, it would be better if I didn't —"

"Time you two got over whatever it is. Stop fussing. He'll purr like a pussycat, with ten good-looking women giving him a party. Turn right here. Now left. What a gorgeous night — look at all those stars."

(But I don't like her mentioning the strain between Archie and me. That seems to make it official; depressing. Why does an intelligent girl like Molly do it?)

The Porsche noses along the curve of Dorchester Boulevard, which now suddenly loses its impersonal, multi-lane character and becomes residential in a grand, turn-of-the-century manner. The big houses are of stone, with tall windows and dignified but extravagant architectural flourishes. Some have arched doorways with stonework fruit and flowers as decoration; some have miniature towers capped in slate; a few even have crenellations. Suddenly Molly gives a gasp.

"For God's sake, the whole block's gone! Where's Archie's house? — wait, there it is. But what's happened?"

To be sure, we've just passed a large void where only a trace of stony litter on bare ground suggests that once a row of houses stood there. I turn and we cruise past the devastated area. Sitting alone on the edge of vacancy is a large brick house with a desolate but dogged air of survival. Only one of its windows is alight.

"This must be one more of Drapeau's Napoleonic schemes for the betterment of Montreal," says Molly. "Got everything? Mind that cake-box." We lock up the car, having at last found a place to park in a side-street. The night air is frosty enough to define our breath as we walk back along the boulevard. Molly's small feet in red slippers move lightly on the dark pavement. A little group of women is waiting for us under a street lamp, and as we reach them, two or three others hurry to join us. There is considerable shuffling and giggling as we balance all our boxes and bags.

"Sisters," proclaims Molly, "the hour is at hand. Everybody with it? Come on, then." And she marshals us into a cluster, hustling us up the path and into a group at the front door. I try to fade quietly into the back row, but she has my arm in a relentless grip, and I'm forced to stand with her in the front line. "'Ginevra, I wish you were at Jericho,'" I think grimly. There is no reply to her brisk rap of the brass knocker. She gives it another series of bangs. There follows so long a pause that Ruth says in a deflated voice, "He must be out. What a party poop."

"He's not," says Molly. "I phoned him and then hung up."

Sure enough, after another minute, a bulky shadow can be seen looming inside the frosted glass of the door. "Ready now," urges Molly.

The door opens. Under tousled grey hair Archie's face lowers at us. He has just time to mutter "Christ" before "Happy *birth*day, dear Archie" rises in a loud and ragged chorus. We all surge forward, me because I'm pushed from behind. He stares at us with such thunderous disapproval that I have to turn aside to hide a sharp attack of giggles.

He is wearing a quilted dressing-gown that twenty years ago must have been quite regal with its satin lapels. Now, faded and torn, it looks as if mice might easily be nesting in it. His cracked and broken old bedroom-slippers are equally disgraceful. However, in some magnificent way he manages to rise above it all, and stands aside to let us in with an air of surly dignity.

Noisily the group swirls about him to administer kisses and push gifts into his reluctant hands. Molly nips about switching on lights, her long red gown whirling. Ruthie hangs coats on an old-fashioned oak stand. Archie still stands rigid with disapproval, like some old emperor who has just detected a smell of drains.

"Emma, come and set up bar in the dining-room. Who's got the bottles? Ruth — music, please — the phonograph's over there. Something dancey. Now Archie, you come and sit right here—" Her gaiety pushes everyone into action, even our reluctant host. Eventually he shuffles, like a cross but obedient old dog, into the place where she wants him to be. Just the same, I notice that her colour is rather high, and there is the hint of an edge to her voice.

"Archie, for God's sake where have all the houses gone?" she asks as Ruth lowers the needle on Scott Joplin.

"New apartment house going up."

"What, right next to you here?"

"Closer than that, Mrs. Pratt. I've had an offer for my house. It might even be called a demand. Everybody else has sold. As you see."

"Oh well, after all, Archie, this is much too big a house for you now — I mean you'd be a hundred times better off in a nice little apartment ... "

I edge away to avoid the approach of Emma with a tray of drinks. Drifting along a hall papered in faded green flowers, I find myself eventually at the open door of a large kitchen. Old-fashioned cupboards built along two walls reach right to the ceiling. An ancient refrigerator is grinding its teeth in a corner and there's a small sink piled with dirty crockery under one window. Timidly I fumble for the switch and illuminate a single depressed bulb hanging from a very dirty ceiling. The floor is carpeted in threadbare linoleum. The cupboard shelves, which I edge nearer to inspect in morbid fascination, are crammed with every kind of relevant and irrelevant flotsam—an old typewriter, empty wine-bottles, books, tin cans ancient and modern, a parcel from the laundry, bread, unopened mail, weed killer, a pair of shoes, several pot plants, an ebony figure of a naked girl, a large bag of wildly sprouting onions ... it is chaos, but of a somehow meaningful kind. For some reason it pleases me. I find it mysteriously congenial. Certainly I feel much more at home alone out here than in the Edwardian formality of the front rooms where all those women are chittering around Archie.

One of the books is a first edition of *Mary Barton*. I am leafing through it when I get the impression someone is watching me. Rather nervously I look around. No one is there. Then by chance I glance up to meet the blue eyes of a Siamese cat draped on the top edge of the door. It opens its triangular mouth to utter a low, unearthly wail of protest.

"Sorry. I know just how you feel," I tell it.

"Quiet, Percy." And grasping a drink and a piece of disintegrating cake, the owner of the house comes in.

"You're looking for the garbage bin, I think."

"Perceptive woman. Cake and Scotch are a loathly combination." He drops the cake untidily on top of the box of laundry.

From an obscure corner he drags forth an old Windsor chair and drops his bulk into it.

"It's All Souls' Day, did you know that? Not a bad day to be born. But a ridiculous day to be sixty. Absurd, in effect, to be old. What a farce, to be trapped between Eros and Thanatos. What. A. Position."

I make no comment on these self-evident truths.

"Birthdays," he continues gloomily. He takes a very large swallow of his drink. "Depressing things. No one's left on this earth to care a damn one way or another that I was born. Much more tactful to pass the date over without pretence. Molly should know that."

For some reason, despite his gloom, I feel more at ease with him than I've ever done. He hasn't pressed me to drink. He makes no small talk. He doesn't attempt politely to conceal his depression. All this makes me feel quite relaxed. I even wander over to the sink and begin tentatively to organize the pots in order to find something to make coffee in. There is a dishpan and a large bottle of detergent on the floor beside a dictionary, so I begin to run water to wash up. He pays no attention to this.

"My mother, in fact, found my arrival highly embarrassing," he says. "She was forty, and thought herself quite safe from all that. My sisters were nearly grown up. What a shock I was, even to myself. Little, premature rat I turned out to be. Did my infant best to die with an enlarged thymus gland. Do I bore you, miss?"

"No," I say truthfully. "I was an accident myself. Nothing like it to destroy your sense of proportion, is there?"

He shoots me a keen glance from under his shelf of eyebrow. "Amazing, isn't it, the candour with which our parents reveal some things. A form of revenge, perhaps. Because they conceal so much else we'd rather know."

"How true. The only thing my mother ever told me about marriage, for instance — the physical side — was that it was 'a much over-rated exercise'."

He gives a sudden, explosive snort of laughter.

"Did she, by God. But what a lot that tells you about her, really. Not to mention her marriage."

"I suppose so. But I'm not sure what."

"Aren't you?"

I slosh a pot through the suds easily, without answering. The cat now pours itself down the door and hurries across the room to leap onto his knees. It begins to purr loudly, closing its eyes to blue slits and kneading its claws deep into the quilted gown.

"Beautiful Egypt-eyed one," he says to it richly. It gives a low yowl in reply. A second Siamese, this one cross-eyed, now materializes from under a table in the shadows and goes to sit at his feet like a monument. All three of them regard me absently.

"I like your house. It's a pity you have to give it up."

"I shall *not* give it up."

"No? But how can you —"

"Simply refuse to sell. It's a developer, you know, who's bought everybody out. Fancy being the kind of man who wants to erect eighteen floors of apartments. It will cut off all my sun. They've shown me the plans. One wall will be exactly thirteen inches from that window there. And I don't care. I won't give up. Let 'em build. This is my house. Lily likes it. The cats like it. So do I."

"Good for you."

"Move into an apartment — *pah*," he adds, with a vehemence worthy of Lear.

"My wife Lily is still living here, you know," he says, looking into his empty glass. "I see her sometimes. Hear her often. Singing in the bedroom. She has a very pretty voice."

"Bill Trueblood once told me she was very charming."

"She was. And still is. Just the same, seeing and hearing aren't enough ... any more than remembering is enough."

"Yes. It would be better, perhaps, if the dead really died. If we could let them. It's like that with my mother. She's been dead nearly a year now, and yet I dream about her nearly every night."

He looks at me thoughtfully, but before he can say anything more Molly comes swiftly into the room, her long gown bringing with it a gust of the musky perfume she wears.

"Pizza for supper, people," she announces, holding up a pile of boxes. "Can you find somewhere to put these for a sec, Willy? Where are the matches, Archie? — come on, let the oven heat up a bit, then we'll shove the pizzas in. Your *drink* is gone, love — come this minute and get a refill. And then I want to dance with you. Ruthie's found some marvellous old Fats Waller records — come on, let's go!"

She drags Archie to his feet and with a hiss the cat leaps off his lap. "Split, you brutes; he's mine," she tells them, laughing, and aims a mock missile at the cross-eyed one, which is already streaking like a shadow under the table. As she does this, I catch him gazing at her with such a look of yearning that I quickly turn away. So that's his secret. But what can hers be? I can't help wondering what really made her bring us all here tonight ... why I was pulled in and Harry left at home ...

Well, none of it really matters. The important thing is that it's nearly midnight. The evening hasn't been unpleasant, if only because for once I've escaped the apartment. I look out at the powder of white stars as I wait for the pizzas to heat. Archie, Molly, and the rest drift peacefully out of my consciousness. In the other room the women chatter and laugh and Fats tinkles his piano. I am quite content to stay where I am. Alone I can take out my anticipation and gloat over it: next week I am going to the theatre with Bill.

When I was in my teens, before anything important like an exam I used to open the Bible at random and read as an omen whatever verse my finger happened upon. "Jesus wept" could accurately predict, for instance, my results in Geometry. But as the years went on I seemed to light on only the more impenetrable verses like "Moab is my washpot; over Edom will I cast out my shoe"—a message difficult to relate to a dentist's appointment. Furthermore, I have little confidence these days that the prophets have any personal message for me. But one must look for meanings somewhere, so at lunchtime I am pleased to find that the tea-leaves in my cup form an almost perfect circle, clearly indicating (I hope) that the coming evening with Bill will be perfect too. And if I get my solitaire game out, that will make doubly sure. I sit shuffling and laying out the cards to pass the hour before he calls for me, looking hopefully into the hieratic faces of the kings and queens, and trying to forget that my throat is tickling with the first signs of a cold. The game comes out. My heart is absurdly light. When the bell rings I swing open the door and call gaily, "Coming, handsome!" as I seize my coat and bag.

Louis-Philippe stands there, broadly smiling.

"Oh, Mr. Mackenzie, I wasn't — what is it?"

"I'm collect a little something for the cleaners at Christmas, mees. A couple of dollar, maybe."

"Yes; yes, of course."

"You go out tonight, eh?"

"Yes." I close my coat to cut off his interested stare at the black satin pantsuit. "Here's your two dollars."

"'Ave a swell time," he says, still grinning. I close the door on him a trifle brusquely.

Twenty minutes more go by before Bill appears, looking faintly distraught.

"Terribly sorry, Willy — a phone call kept me, and then I had hell's delight getting a cab. I've got one waiting now, so could we just — You'll be pleased to know there's a blizzard of sorts going on out there ... will your feet be warm enough like that?" He himself is wearing sheepskin-lined boots, and the fur collar of his coat is turned up all round his curly head, on which a few melting flakes glitter. "How I hate the sight of snow, my sinuses are twinging already, getting ready to play me up the way they always do the whole winter long. I honestly don't know why anybody lives in this awful arctic city."

"Must be because it's beautiful." I look out eagerly through the cab window. Through a whirl of bright little flakes the steep streets are gleaming red, green, and gold.

"I just hope we're not going to be late," he frets. "Est-ce que tu peux te dépêcher un peu?" he asks the driver, whose reply is to leap into a gap in the traffic with such vehemence that we all nearly go through the windshield.

"Cowboy," mutters Bill.

We reach the theatre, however, in time for me to enjoy the squash of people in the huge crimson-carpeted lobby before we find our seats. The chatter of French under the ornate crystal chandeliers sparkles like confetti. "Look, there's René Lévesque," says Bill. "No — there — no, he's gone. Come on, we'd better find our seats."

We sit down, adding to the exciting pre-curtain rustle. I'm thrilled when the lights dim to the traditional three raps backstage. It's all I can do not to wriggle in my place like a five-year-old.

Unfortunately, within the first five minutes I discover I can understand only about one word in six of Molière's witty dialogue. The costumes are attractive and the acting expert, but my attention soon wanders from the lighted box of the stage. I think of Dougie's beautiful laugh on the phone last week when I called for his birthday. I think of Archie's cross-eyed cat, and the tickle in my throat, and the length of Bill's eyelashes, the curl of which are catching an edge of light from the aisle.

Gradually, but with disconcerting acuteness, I become aware of how close his knees are to my knees, his hand to my hand. I begin to wonder whether he'll take my hand in his. A faint warmth from him seems to creep through me till I feel hot all over. Strange to be sitting so close to him in the dark. Would it be nice to hold his hand or not? Horrible if my hand (or his) were perspiring. Furtively I dig out a handkerchief and dry my palm. He laughs at something on the stage and turns to me. My heart gives a jerk. Now, perhaps—but he's already absorbed in the play again. My heart is still working too hard. It's very warm, though my feet are cold. My hands are damp again. The edge of Bill's shoulder in its well-cut dark suit is just touching mine. I feel cramped, but to shift away is impossible. It would be tactless. Even rude. Only maybe he's not comfortable either, and just keeping still out of politeness? There is a faint, spicy scent from his hair. It tickles my nose. A hush settles over the theatre, and in the depth of it a colossal sneeze bursts out of me. Bill's shoulder moves away. He is trying not to frown. I wipe my palms again. Then I furtively inspect my watch. Good God, is it possible we've only been here half an hour?

At intermission he buys me an orange squash and I drink it greedily. It is warmer than ever in the jam-packed theatre bar, and we stand almost pressed together by the crowd. In spite of this he does not seem to notice the black satin suit. His eyes tend to wander away from me, and conversation is an effort.

"It's a very good performance, isn't it?"

"Yes, Gascon is always good."

"I like Dorine, too."

"Yes, first-rate."

"Have you got any Christmas plans, Bill?"

"Oh, I'll be going to Halifax."

"That'll be nice."

"Well, it won't really. However."

"I'm going to my sister's in Toronto."

"Good for you."

"Molly and Harry are going to Cuba."

"They would." He gulps the last of his gin-and-tonic. I sneeze again, and he turns away. "We'd better get back."

So we go back, the lights die, and my nose begins to run. He keeps his shoulder strictly to himself. My throat is now sore. My back aches. My hands feel both moist and cold. An hour or so later, when the curtain at last falls, I applaud heartily and think with pleasure of some cosy restaurant, a little supper, a chat by candlelight as we lean over a little table together . . .

"You'd . . . er . . . like to go home now, Willy? Or would a cup of coffee somewhere — "

"Oh, yes, coffee please."

We capture a taxi only after a confused struggle with other wind-whipped rivals. Inside it is bitterly cold; the heater is not working. We creep along white Ste. Catherine Street against a wind hissing with hard little pellets of snow. In the cab's half-light I catch Bill squeezing back a yawn with his gloved hand curled into a ball.

"I enjoyed the play very much," I say. "Just the same, I wish they wouldn't talk so fast, the French."

"You could take a course. Might be fun for you. Lots of them going at night. What ages this guy is taking . . . oh, here's the place. Let's hop out." He pays the driver, turning a crouched back to the driving wind. We squeeze into a warm little restaurant which smells deliciously of filtered coffee and Gauloises, only to find ourselves at the end of a long queue.

"Oh shit," he says half audibly. "Sorry, Willy. This wasn't such a good idea, I'm afraid."

"Look, Bill, why don't we just have some coffee at my — "

"That's right, Willy, the smart thing to do is go home and look after that cold. Sensible girl. I'll take a rain-check on the coffee this time. You wait here and I'll try to grab another cab."

I am left wondering why it is so insulting to be called sensible. Soon we are in another taxi that progresses westward in a series of swooping, lurching skids. The driver curses the ice in a low voice of intense bitterness. My feet ache with cold. When at last we reach my building, Bill gets out politely and sees me into the lobby.

"Good night, Willy. See you Monday."

"Thanks for a nice evening, Bill."

"Take care of that cold, now." He gives my shoulder a friendly slap.

"I will. Good night."

It is not quite a quarter to twelve. I unlock my door, and the stuffy air of the empty rooms makes me sneeze again. I hang up my coat and throw my purse on the bed. The old couple next door is fighting. The party upstairs is in full swing.

What went wrong? What did I do or say that spoiled it all? There can be no answer to these questions in the tea-leaves or the cards. But while I wait for water to boil for a toddy, I flip open the Bible. Under my finger I read, "Because thou art lukewarm, and neither cold nor hot, I will spew thee out of my mouth." That gives me a dry grin, the first and last of the evening.

Toronto, December 15th.

Dear Willy,

I thought of phoning you, but decided a letter would be better, you do fly up in the air so. The thing is, I'm pregnant again, Dr. Gilbert says I'm due the end of May, but am having so many miseries this time I'm not telling anybody yet. Awful nausea in the mornings the minute I open my eyes. And last weekend I started a bit of bleeding. They've had me in bed ever since, & things seem quite o.k. now, though I feel pretty seedy, as you can imagine. Now *don't* start worrying. I am ALL RIGHT. Greg is so thrilled, I just wish *he* could have the fun of this next six months. One child seems like plenty to me. They say you forget, but I remember Dougie's birth only too damn well, and I'm not looking forward.

What I'm really getting to is that G. has a client can pull strings to get us on a flight to the Barbados for Christmas, & we think a bit of sun would do me good. That means shifting your visit to Easter, but I'm sure you won't mind. It's been such a nasty grey fall, and I simply ache for a beach and some sun. Greg insists we take Dougie, & the poor kid's had one cold after another lately, so I guess he could do with a change too.

Well, this gets you off the hook of a dull family Xmas, old kid. And shall I tell a lie? — I'll be *devastated* to miss G's saccharine Mummy — I mean a woman who thinks it's cute to call her grandson Adorables — and that ghastly old uncle of his with the cough and the canes. It's almost worth being pregnant to escape all that. Now if I were you I'd buzz off to Florida—you could drive down, you get such lovely long holidays. Or you could fly to Mexico. Lucky you to be a swinging single!

Must go shopping now for some beach-type things. Take care.

Yours — Lou.

MAY YOUR CHRISTMAS BE MERRY AND BRIGHT.
— Your Paper Boy.

Halifax, Dec. 20.
Having as predicted terrible time and wish I were there. Gale force winds, twenty below zero, sinuses raising hell. I miss Montreal and you. All the best — Bill.

Toronto, December 21st.
Dear Willy,
What a nice surprise to hear from you. It was very nice of you to invite me down to Montreal for Christmas. I guess you haven't seen the announcement in the Alumnae Bulletin, but I'm going back up to the Soo to be married on January 15th. He's a dental surgeon, we met on one of my Red Cross errands of mercy. Remember our delivery runs with those horrid bags of blood? Well, I wish we could get together for a good gab. Sorry I didn't have your address in time to mail you an invitation, and sorry I can't make it to Montreal this time. Write again; it would be a shame to lose touch. Best from both of us for the festive season.
    — Marg.

This greeting comes with friendship true
And wishes most sincere,
For a very blessed Christmas,
And a wonderful New Year.
            — Madeleine and L-P Mackenzie,
            Michelle, Arnaut, Philippe, et Marthe.

"You and your DIGNITY," yells the old woman next door. An inarticulate bellow of rage rises in reply. There is a faint tinkle of broken glass.
    Christmas Eve.
    I am sitting in front of the television set trying to watch a veteran Bing Crosby film. Either it is too old, or I am. And the old couple next door with their scenario of hate on earth are both more convincing and more interesting. There's even a sort of moral value in their presence, because they keep me grateful for my personal peace and freedom, blessings that for some time I've

not appreciated nearly enough. For days now I've been sinking deeper and deeper into a bog of self-pity and depression. Squatting at the bottom of it, in fact, gloomy as a toad, till the current next-door fight broke out.

— "sonofabitching *dignity!*"

"You go to hell!"

And which way to hell, sir? It's useful, I suppose, if not exactly cheering, to know there are worse things than being alone. It isn't the fighting, though, that makes me flinch; it's the silence that follows the last slammed door. Sunday is their usual day for this recurring drama, and today is only Wednesday. It must be Christmas that's put them off schedule. Of course everything is worse at Christmas.

It was Christmas when the silence at home began. The tall tree, with its spun-glass globes and dripping silver-paper icicles, was knocked over with a tinkle of shattered ornaments by my father, jovially drunk after an office party. I laughed, but it troubled me when Mother went silently upstairs and in the silence locked her door. "My father fell into our tree, he said it tripped him," I told my best friend's mother next door. (I was six, I think.) "And then he was laughing so much he couldn't get up." Later, that got back somehow to my mother, who frowned. "Willy, you have no discretion," she said coldly. "Learn not to tell people anything about what goes on in this house. Do you understand?" I understood nothing except that she was angry with me. I cried until I made myself sick and she had to take me into her special chair and rock me like the baby I would now always be.

After that year, there was no tree put up at our house. From that date, there was no ceremonial exchange of presents, no plum-pudding family dinner, no guests. Gifts for Lou and me appeared at the foot of our beds, but otherwise December 25 was just another day — only worse, because for everybody else it was Christmas. I used to tell my friends at school that we were Jewish.

And yet, in all those years, I can remember not one single quarrel. Not one. That always seemed to me incredible, until I read about childhood amnesia. All I can remember now is that silence. And the geography of isolation in our house. Mother had her bedroom and sitting-room upstairs. The bathroom door connecting to *his* bedroom was kept bolted on the inside. Downstairs, the small study was his alone. Here he kept his supplies of whiskey and cigarettes, and sat over the radio, read the news-paper, or slept with his shoes off. To the best of my knowledge Mother never set foot in that room. All other areas of the house were buffer zones, big and empty, except for an ever-changing series of maids dusting the furniture. Silence inhabited the house from the time my father left it in the morning. Mother rocked the hours away behind the closed door of her room. My father once (it might even have been a Christmas day) stood listening in the hall to that even, regular, self-contained rhythm in the still house. "So it's come to this," he said, more to himself than to me. On that occasion he was sober.

He talked to me, though, much more freely and often than Mother did. She knew how much I loved and admired her, but she never really opened herself to me. Too proud, perhaps. Mother had a lot of pride. And not much confidence in me. "You're so indiscreet, Willy," she used to say. "You *blunder*." With Lou she could chat like another girl, but they would often fall silent when I joined them. It hurt; it made me feel not only inadequate but guilty, like the verdict of the schoolyard queen, a pink English girl called Paula, that I was "a funny little thing".

But Dad would stretch out his legs and, with his head cocked to keep cigarette smoke out of his eyes, would tell me stories of his rowdy, renegade youth, much of it spent in running away from his Rosedale origins. He told me about the trenches at Ypres in 1916, how he worked as a pest exterminator in the Depression, how he made the people in his office roar with imitations of his dyspeptic old boss, who had a chronic sniff. He rarely spoke of his marriage. Perhaps he had his own kind of pride. But once he told me, "You know what's the only real matrimonial sin, Willy? Self-righteousness. Take it from a sinner."

In my bold teens I asked him outright, "Why did you and Mother ever marry?"

He shot me a quick look out of his blue eyes. "Why, girl, you were the reason. Or the excuse, if you like. Then her family couldn't stop us, you see. I had the background, but they had all that fine distillery money. They were horrified, their treasure courted by a black sheep like me, kicked out of Ridley College, working for the c.n.r. Freight Department. By God, the whole thing literally killed them inside five years. What attracted her to me I'll never know. I only know that somehow she . . . took hold of my imagination. When that happens, unfortunately, nothing else counts. Horse sense, decency, anything. It's a form of insanity, that's not putting it too high. As you've had every chance to observe, you poor little bitch."

Yes, indeed. And yet the earliest years must have been happy enough for them, surely. My own first memory is of happiness. I sit at a long, polished table (in the dining-room, probably, before it became No Man's Land) playing with two small figures of lambs. They have black wooden legs and faces, but their bodies are soft, white, and curly. There is a record playing somewhere in the house—a thin woman's voice singing "Georgia". Was it by any chance Christmastime? Anyhow, I am intensely, deeply happy. After Lou was born, I was allowed to hold her for the photographer to take our picture, and again that feeling of perfect joy and tenderness filled me. In fact, I was so blissful when they put the warm, shawled lump in my arms that I got a violent attack of hiccups, and Lou had to be photographed propped on a cushion after all. I must have been just five then. The whole episode was a neat little forecast of my whole life, in a way.

And speaking of Lou, I wonder how *she* ever happened? A last attempt to reconcile themselves to each other? I'll never know, except that they always both adored her and approved of her without reservation, as if somehow she were the success and I the failure, though surely they can't really have felt that way. Certainly she didn't reconcile them. By the time she could sit up, the silence had fallen, a permanent verdict. Perhaps that made it simpler for Lou. She went her own way from the start. She was never involved, like me.

At eleven, Lou was pretty and already wore her clothes with an air; suddenly boys she pretended to ignore began to hang about the porch, punching each other lightly and having long, pointless arguments. To her delight, Mother packed her off to boarding-school, ignoring my blubbered tears.

"You can go too, Willy, if that's it. Again and again I've offered to send you to Harlow. It would do you all the good in the world. There is a kind of polish . . . "

But at that I only blubbered more. "No! No! I want to be with you!"

"This is not a good life for you, Willy," she said to me then, and at intervals all the rest of her days. She would press her delicate lips together, adding, "I hardly need to tell you why." Just the same, she let me stay home.

Because I couldn't leave her. Not possibly. She needed me. Or someone. In that house, every time my father came into it, there was the possibility of violence. I knew that, and so did she. One night when I was about thirteen, I saw how murder can be committed. She had left her room in the evening, for some reason, something she never did if he was home. Probably she hadn't heard him come in. I saw them meet by accident at the top of the stairs. She drew back in her fastidious way, probably from no more than his smell of tobacco and whiskey. His face darkened with an ugly rage, and his arm lifted to strike her. She flinched back in fear against the wall, calling my name, and I ran to her.

Without a word he went on down the stairs and into his study. Through the closed door I heard the clink of bottle and glass. Taking her cold hand, I led her to her room. She said nothing. After a while, she began to rock in her chair. It was my father, downstairs, behind his door, who could be heard after a while, sobbing.

No, I couldn't leave my mother, then or ever. And except for some bitter intervals in my teens, I never resented that. They owed me no explanations or apologies, after all, did they? There were no wrongs or rights, or none that I could judge. I stayed to the end, without protest. They both loved me, and in a not too friendly world, that mattered a lot. Above all, she needed me. At the end, in her frailty, her hands shrunk little, she was my child. That mattered most of all.

Christmas Day. At ten in the morning, the phone rings. I run to answer it. Is it Lou? — or Greg? Is she all right?

"Allo; c'est toi, Yvette?"

"No, I'm sorry—" (though why I should apologize I really don't know).

Clack. Season's greetings from Madame Guillotine.

At noon, another ring. I hurry to the phone. Bill, maybe? "I miss Montreal and you." Yes, he might just think of calling from Halifax. What a present it would be to hear his voice . . .

"Hello?"

No sound at the other end.

"Hello? Who's there?"

Breathing. It becomes louder.

"Who is that?" Nothing but the breathing. It scares me, for no definable reason. I hang up.

Half an hour later the breather tries again, and I drop the receiver as if it stung. After this the phone is dumb, but I am left restless, prickling with nervous energy. The sky is a grey canvas bag heavy with snow, or I would drive somewhere—anywhere— in the car. As it is, I must get out. I heave on my fun fur (ha ha ha) and boots, and stride out onto pavements crackling with ice like broken glass. It is very cold and I walk fast up the mountain slope with only the puff of my own white breath for company. The streets are deserted. Everyone is indoors overeating, confronting relatives, pouring drinks, or recovering from turkey. Though it's only four in the afternoon, houses are bright with light in the arctic darkness, and smoke rises from the chimneys like an answer to the dark sky.

I walk and walk, uphill and down, past the swaying coloured lights of outdoor pines, the bright houses and the dark ones whose owners are in Florida. The trees rattle their bare bones in a rising wind. Snow begins to whip across the zones of light cut by street lamps. An occasional khaki city bus growls past. Cars draw up and groups of people scurry into the warmth of open doorways. A dog limps past me on three legs. A solitary, bundled child wailing "Mu-um-my" drags home a new sled.

As I hurry along without direction through the freezing air I begin to feel frightened. I understand for the first time what the word alienated means. I know what it is to be without a place or purpose. My identity is a vacuum; it bounces off no other human presence. What am I doing here on this nameless street in a foreign city? Why am I on this island, and is there no escape from it? Where am I going? What will become of me? And to my keen distress, I find myself crying. Tears pour down my cold face and burn there in the bitter wind. I keep swabbing them away with an inadequate paper handkerchief, but they are as hard to stop as arterial blood.

I must think of somewhere to go. Luckily there's no one about to see me, stumbling along on feet clumsy with cold, and blowing my nose repeatedly. I must go home. No, I can't go there. There's no courage left to face that apartment. The very word makes me flinch.

Eventually I grope my way downhill toward clusters of brighter light—shops, theatres, restaurants. Mercifully, the tears stop at last. I look into all-day-open cigar stores, movie lobbies, the windows of dress shops, a chain restaurant. Maybe a slice of turkey? It's six o'clock and there's nothing to eat at home.

But when I peer through the steamy window, past loops of tinsel, I see the place is crowded to the doors, with a long line waiting to be served, and waitresses plunging in and out between the tables with an air of desperation. No, it isn't worth going in there and waiting in line just to say to the hostess, "One." There are a few eggs in the fridge after all. I won't starve. Plenty to read, a comfortable bed. The tears are dry now. What a relief to feel light and numb and quite empty of any thought or sensation whatever. It's only a question of acceptance. I turn toward home.

Snow on snow. It lashes down with quiet, malignant persistence until the city is half-buried. Bill's postcard is tucked into my dresser mirror, to be read and reread. I nurse an ugly cough, there being nothing else to do at home. The storm blows and the white hours trail slowly past. Then after two days God seems bored with the whole drama and the clouds roll away, the sky turns a brilliant blue, and all that heaped-up snow twinkles, innocent and passive as a daisy looking up at the sun.

I muffle up and climb into the car. It is the first day of the new year. My resolutions are to stop coughing, keep moving, and if possible do no more crying. In the clean new light I feel peaceful and convalescent, like the city itself, sleepily turning and tossing off its white covering. Huge, prehistoric-looking machines are grinding through the streets, spewing great clots of snow into trucks, and noisy little tanks clatter along, organizing the pavements into smooth white corridors. I am pleased with myself for having a fortnight ago had chains put on my back wheels, for the side roads are deeply rutted with ice and snow. The noon light is so blazing bright that I soon have to dig my dark glasses out of the glove compartment. Impossible not to feel a little lift of the heart under a sky as burning blue as this. I swing the Porsche briskly up the Autoroute ramp. There is very little traffic. My chains thrash out an energetic, steady beat. The frost crystals on the windows gradually melt. I find an optimistic Beethoven symphony on the car radio and knock time to it on the rim of the steering wheel.

My plan is to find some nice little country hotel up in the Laurentians and stay there for a night or two—more, if I like it.

Might even rent some skis and get out on the slopes. Haven't skied for years. Might be fun. Might even meet . . . well. My job, as I see it now, is to steer a course between that damp bog of depression, where I've wallowed so long, and the silly heights of optimism, where there are even more risks. In a few days the new term will open at Cartier. Till then, I just have to wait, and walk with care.

By late afternoon I reach the exit for St. Philomène, a little village in a valley that I discovered last autumn. Today it looks like a page from a child's picture-book, with peak-roofed habitant houses in candy colours sitting deep in snow as dimpled and smooth as cream. All round the small hotel, ancient, glacial folds of mountain shine white in the crystal air.

They have a room, smelling of woodsmoke and wax, with a rag rug on the floor and a crucifix over the bed. I put away my case, wash up and tidy my hair, and take a look out at the blue evening as it pours over the hills from the east. Then I go downstairs again. A few pairs of skis are stacked in the lobby, but no one is around. Even stout Madame behind the desk has disappeared. There seems to be nowhere I can get a cup of coffee or tea. Through an open door I can see into a quiet bar where a huge log fire is blazing. I hesitate a moment, and then go in. Why not? There is hardly anyone there. No one to care a damn whether I go or stay. Without warning I feel an ache in my throat and my eyes fill. In a kind of desperation I go straight up to the bar.

"Oui, madame?" the bartender asks.

"Ummm—I'll have a—a—(quick, the name of a cocktail) pink lady. Can you make one of those?"

"Si, madame."

A pink lady sounds harmless enough. I try a sip and am reassured to find it tastes harmless, too. On the other hand, I really wouldn't mind getting drunk, just for the experience. In fact, it might be a great idea. Already the urge to cry has ebbed away. I take my drink and sit with it at a corner table where I can see the fire. The bartender draws on a cigarette as he polishes glasses. I sip more of my sweet, bland drink. It is actually quite pleasant and warming. Maybe my father's life-style has more to recommend it than I used to think.

There is a man at the next table hunched over a half-empty glass. Perhaps it's the glass that helps, but I recognize him at once, without surprise. It's George MacKay, the real-estate salesman.

(Yes, Charlotte, of course he had to turn up some time.) At once, before I can think about it, I get up and go over to him.

"Hello, Mr. MacKay. I don't suppose you remember me, but we met on the Turbo to Montreal a few months ago. My name is Willy Doyle."

His dull eyes lift indifferently and for a second his face is perfectly blank. It's obvious he doesn't recognize me at all, but mechanically he half-rises and calls out with the greatest heartiness, "Yeah—sure I remember you—sit down, sit down—great to see you again. What you drinking; let me fill that up for you!" He has put on some weight since I last saw him; the hand pumping mine feels padded. However, he appears to be quite sober. I sit down beside him.

"I'll just finish this one, thanks. How have you been?"

"Great, just great. Maurice — sure you won't? — just another Scotch, then, sport. Yeah, that's it. Well, it sure is good to see you. I been up here for a lunch affair—head of our firm is retiring— you know how these things get you down, so I thought I'd have a quickie before hitting the road. You up here for the skiing?"

"Yes, I . . . well, it's lovely up here. Tell me, how's your family? Your son—did he ever go back to Cartier? I got that job there, but I haven't run into him. Jamie, wasn't it?"

"What a memory!" he says more quietly. His rather bloodshot blue eyes look at me with close attention now and he wags my empty glass at the bartender, one thick, warm hand around my wrist to arrest my objections.

"Nah, Jamie just gets by with temporary jobs from Manpower —could be shovelling snow right now, for all I know. But my girl finally got her head together, she's gone into nurses' training."

"Oh, that's good."

"So you came up for some skiing, eh? You . . . with friends?"

"No, I came up on my own."

' Say, that's not much good, honey. All alone up north? Hell, it's no good at all. I ought to know. May be my good luck, though." He lifts his glass to me with a knowing wink. His knee touches mine, perhaps by accident. I shift away slightly.

"How you like it at Cartier?"

"Oh, it's fine, thanks."

There is a silence. For something to do, I swallow a little of my drink. Too late to stop, I hear myself say brightly, "And how's your wife?"

He looks away, but not before I see the baffled pain in his blue eyes, looking out like a prisoner.

"Nancy? She's left me. Totally fed up. Can't blame her. I *don't* blame her. I guess she's had it for keeps now, anyway."

"I'm sorry," I say, and mean it. There is another silence. Our knees touch once more, but I don't like to move away. It would be like hitting someone already defeated. Instead I sip my drink again. There can't be any alcohol in the thing, surely; it tastes like an ice-cream soda.

"You married? Or anything?" he asks.

"No."

"No kidding."

"No kidding either," I say, and laugh. He laughs too.

"Hey, you got a great sense of humour, I like that," he tells me in high approval. "Come on — it's New Year's Day — drink up. What's it called you got there—a pink lady? God, honey, you'd be better off with straight gin, you know. Eh, Maurice — another round here. Yah, come on now, honey, you're just one of these old-fashioned gals like to say no when all they mean is yes. Am I right or am I right?"

Well, it hardly seems a point worth arguing. I finish up the pink dregs in my glass. A thick heat comes from the fire. I feel contented, almost sleepy.

"What you think about good old Quebec independence, then? You gone activist yet?"

"Not yet. There was a police cordon around our block the other day — something about a bomb in the mailbox. But they didn't find anything in it after all."

"They will. Give 'em time. Ask me, I'd get the army down here from Ottawa and — Ah, but the hell with them. Let's talk about you, honey."

"Nothing to talk about." I feel my face getting hot, and sip some of my new drink to cool it off.

"Got a room here, have you?"

"Yes."

"Look here, honey; no reason I have to rush back to town really —why don't you and me have a nice little dinner together, eh? Get to know each other better, how about it?" With this, fearing, I suppose, that he might have been too subtle, he puts his hand on my knee.

Nothing about this guileless invitation comes as a surprise or a shock. There's nothing offensive about poor George MacKay, with his greying hair and muddled eyes. In fact, as I look at him, I think Well, why not? The Project has made no headway to speak of for months. And haven't I in fact come up here with something of the sort in mind, tricking my conscience, or my mother's, with all this guff about skiing? Just the same, I hesitate; old hangups never really die.

"You know, honey, my wife says I'm dumb. But I'm not dumb enough to take a nice girl like you for a cheap pickup." His voice is warm with something almost like affection; the mechanical, sad sexuality is for the moment gone. "Only we're both alone and over twenty-one. Getting older every minute. You only live once, right?"

Under the table his warm, fleshy hand rests on my thigh. The touch is pleasant. Quite pleasant. More so than most of his conversation, anyway. Poor old George. He calls me honey because he can't remember my name. But who cares? Why worry about details? He's kind. And lonely, like me. I swallow more of my pink lady, though when I turn my head there is a sudden, peculiar sliding inside my skull, as if my brain has come loose.

"Now I want you to hold on here for just a second, honey," says George, gesturing once more to the barman while he sorts through a handful of change. "You'll have one more of these to put hair on your chest—yuk, I hope not—and I'm gonna make a quick phone call out there. Be back in just a sec."

He gives my hand a farewell pat and goes briskly out to the lobby. The barman sets down full glasses at our table, pausing just a fraction of a second to give me a swift glance from his experienced eyes. I take a large swallow of my drink to demonstrate that I am poised, in control, and perfectly sober.

This turns out to be a very unwise move. The fire advances and recedes, the ceiling moves slightly lower. With extreme suddenness, I feel ill. Is it the prospect of actually, within the next couple of hours, completing The Project? Is it the thick hands and tongue of George MacKay? Does fornication have to be such a bore? Or is it just these pink ladies, damn their bland, deceptive ways? A minute later all these questions become purely rhetorical. I hurry out of the room, blundering twice against other tables. In the lobby I look around wildly for the Ladies. There it is. But on the way to it, the floor tilts slightly uphill in a very inconvenient way. Someone takes my arm. It is George MacKay, blue eyes protuberant with concern.

"Where you going, honey? You all right?"

"No—let—go away!" And I pull free, reaching the washroom just in the nick of time. Afterwards I sit dizzily for some time on the closed lid, tapping together my cold feet and hands, and thinking of nothing at all. I remember for no reason at all my mother's lips, thin with distaste as she told me how Dad ordered two bushel-baskets of apples from the market, and the one marked with his girl friend's name came home by mistake. "Quite typical," she said.

Distantly I can hear people chatting and laughing as the bar fills up. The clash of plates and a disgusting smell of food filter in from the kitchen. Shortly I am wrenchingly ill again, and have to convalesce once more in my retreat before I can splash my face with cold water and collect my dignity to walk out into the lobby.

Windburned skiers are milling about everywhere. There is no sign of George, to my unspeakable relief. The bar is full now. No doubt he's found consolation already, if he really needed any. Furtively I creep upstairs to my room. After some fumbling with the key, I manage to lock myself in. Shivering, I lie down on the bed and pull the catalogne counterpane over me. The room gives a last heave like a heavy sea as I drop asleep. And I seem to hear my father's voice say, as clear and fresh as if he stood beside me, "Come on, Willy girl, let's be two horses laughing."

FIVE

Winter Games

$\mathcal{L}$IKE A CLEAN WHITE PAGE, the opening of term presents itself at last. Yet another snowfall in the night has covered the city and left the air clear as glass. Incredibly, after all that hasn't happened, I oversleep, and must rush directly to the classroom at ten to give my first lecture of the day. As soon as possible after-wards I hurry down the street to my office. I am so eager that it's hard not to run. The sun dazzles on the fresh snow. Car exhausts sprout white tail-feathers in the bright cold that burns like pepper in my lungs.

There is a surprising amount of activity on the walk and steps of the house—dozens of students with their clipboards are standing about chatting instead of moving off to class. Something almost like a crowd clogs the lobby, where more students are passing around copies of the campus news-sheet, and their babble of talk and laughter has an edge of excitement that puzzles me. When I spot Mike Armstrong's blond head topping the others, I push my way toward him.

"What's going on here, Mike?"

"Just a little demo," he says, grinning.

"Eh?"

"Wait—yeah—here they come. Make way, you guys; let them through."

The crowd parts to admit a mini-procession of four or five youths, all in jeans, faces still red from the frigid air outside. They carry signs reading STUDENT PARITY — RIGHT NOT PRIVILEGE. It's hard to be perfectly sure, so many of them have identical beards, but I think I recognize Harry Innis at the head of the parade. All the marchers are grinning self-consciously, but they move swiftly across the lobby and straight to the closed double doors of an ex-dining-room now used for faculty meetings. Without a pause they fling open the doors and march inside. There is a glimpse of bald, grey, and white heads turning as startled, angry, or incredulous faces snap round to confront the invaders. Then the doors close. A ragged little cheer goes up from the crowd.

"But what is the point, really?" I ask Mike. "Are those signs going to convert them on the spot?"

"Look, all the faculty brass is in there — every dean and governor in the place. They've been stalling and stalling us — now we stall them. Shit, I wish they'd open the doors and let us all in. But no, Harry wants to keep it all civilized. No mobs, he says. Keep it cool. What a guy. Did you know the Principal *threatened* him —"

"So all they're doing is disrupting this meeting?"

"Make 'em listen to us. It's the only way."

"If they do listen — you really want to be on the Board of Governors? You've got to be kidding, Mike. You'd die of boredom at those meetings."

The thickening crowd sways around us. It is so noisy that nothing can be heard from behind the panelled doors. I should go straight upstairs to work; I want to see Bill ("I miss Montreal and you") — but curiosity keeps me rooted there with all the others, while melting snow from our boots soaks the floor matting. Somewhere near the door the lame old Scotsman who is custodian of the building can be heard feebly and furiously shouting, "You yoongsters get the hell oot of it, I tell ye!"

They do nothing of the sort. Indeed, more and more of them seem to be squeezing their way into the lobby.

Suddenly there is a hush. The doors of the committee room open and a string of grim-mouthed elderly men dragging on overcoats begins to emerge.

"What's happening?"

"Where's Harry?"

"Here they come!"

" — busted it up, eh?"

"Yeah, they got the message."

The students make way with polite alacrity for the old men as they come out. All around me are young faces brilliant with a malicious, mocking glee.

"Bye-bye," a long-haired girl calls cheerfully as bald Principal Fraser passes through. He turns to direct an icy glare at her, but makes no reply. Suddenly I see Archie Clarke on his way out with the rest. Unlike his colleagues, he looks hugely amused. He lifts his head and remarks in a resonant voice that carries over the whole crowd: "'Our Playwright may show / In some fifth Act what this wild drama means.'"

"Terrific," says Mike as the crowd begins to disperse. He is evidently in no doubt that an important victory has been won. Yet when Harry and his followers come out of the room, very few have lingered to congratulate them, and they hurry upstairs with serious, preoccupied faces. Mike leans down to me.

"Hey, look, if you have no class now, how about some coffee at the Hideaway?"

"Well . . . sure. Let's go."

Normally I would have ducked out of this invitation. I will probably always find casual socializing with students awkward, even basically incongruous. But I am keen to raise my political consciousness, as Bill weeks ago advised. Besides, I like this boy.

In the back booth of a cheerfully dirty campus hangout called Harry's Hideaway, Mike dumps four spoonfuls of sugar into his mug and unhitches his duffle coat to extract and offer a crumpled cigarette pack.

"Thanks. So the demo was a success? Won't the old boys just carry on their meeting somewhere else?"

"Sure. But they *heard* from us. Now Harry can move on to the next step in the plan. They can't scare *him* off."

I look at him, frankly curious. He has a most pleasing face, with thin, clear skin, deep-set eyes, and high cheekbones. The narrow chin and hollow temples give it an almost exotic look of delicacy and difference.

"And what is the plan?"

"Oh, could be a sit-in next. Boycott lectures or something. I'm on the executive, you know, so I can't blab too much."

"Really? How can you kids get any work done with all this going on?"

"Easy," he assures me with a shrug.

"Maybe for you, boy. But I wonder how any colleague of mine can find time for it all."

"Easy there too. Harry's like committed, that's how. He's got his priorities straight."

"Has he?"

"Got it all together, too. A platform. Parity. Then we can get down to a real shake-up of Cartier. Changes in curriculum. Everything ... the dumb system of grades, exams, all that. Then all the instruction here should be in French. Going to be, anyhow, when Quebec is free."

He is pleased to observe that these remarks give me a few seismic tremors, and adds with satisfaction, "Not if; when."

"And Mr. Innis — he's all for this — an American?"

"Why not? He's up here because the States is run by a bunch of right-wing crooks. Thousands of Americans are coming up here every month now; it's like a new frontier."

"I daresay." But he appears not to notice my dryness. His hollow cheeks are still pink with excitement, and it's hard not to smile at him and thus give offence.

"Does it occur to you, I wonder, Mike, that all this connects in a way with your essay on nineteenth-century fathers? What you kids are doing here seems pretty old-fashioned to me—challenging your fathers. What you're really asking for—demanding—is attention and love, and even punishment. I'd be quite interested to know, for instance, the story of Mr. Innis and his father."

He gives me a quick, startled look. "Oh well ... I think somebody once told me his dad is some poor old bod from the Ukraine or somewhere. But you've got it all wrong. Couldn't be more so. We've all got worried, loving, overprotective dads sitting on top of our *heads*, if you want to know."

"You too?"

"Mine's an orthopaedic surgeon. Every Sunday since I could walk he spends with me. He gives time, not just money. We go hunting, games, movies. Long talks."

"Yes?"

He flushes. "All right. Lots of Sundays I'm bored out of my mind. Never much liked hunting. Don't really turn on for long talks about my grades and my future and the chicks I see. In fact, he tries to manipulate me like a piece of flesh under the knife, if you want to know."

"I see." And indeed I do, with compassion. He has no clear idea yet what forces inside himself or Harry Innis are the real manipulators. Nor, apparently, can he see how destructive they are. But he is a very intelligent and perceptive boy, and he is shifting restlessly on his bench now, as if obscurely uneasy. Tactfully I change the subject a little.

"Were you surprised to find the old man had so much blood in him?—Dr. Clarke, I mean. What a subversive *he* is, suggesting the whole thing this morning, on both sides, was a kind of charade. Mm?"

"Yeah." His face lights in a charming, almost affectionate smile. "It'll probably be his office where we sit in."

"Really?"

"Unless *you*'d like to be chosen." His eyes rest on me for a moment, still with that gleam of lazy affection in them. "I wish you'd join us," he says simply. "Because I admire you. Have you noticed that, Ms. Doyle? Or may I call you Miz?"

His smile is teasing, but I can't help being touched and amused; even flattered. In fact, I am now blushing like a fool, and this evidently gives him much pleasure. Mike may be only twenty, but he is totally male. Furthermore, I find myself suddenly aware that he is also an attractive male. Flustered by this discovery, which is both unexpected and inconvenient, I pull out change to pay the bill, and spill coins liberally all over my own lap like some inept Danae.

"We got an appointment tomorrow — to discuss my essay," Mike reminds me with a grin.

"Yes — right ... well, see you then."

"*Vive le Québec libre!*" he says cheerfully. And we go our separate ways in the bright white noon.

"Hi, Willy! Want to come for a toboggan ride?"

Molly's little face is pink inside the furred hood of her ski jacket, and her eyes blink in the sub-zero air. Harry grins genially and shifts the toboggan under his arm.

"Come on, it's Saturday. Fun time. And you're dressed for it. Not going anywhere special, are you?"

"No, just coming back from the garage. I have to leave the car there till Tuesday. The man said 'Vos rings sont loose', and I gather that's bad."

I fall into step with them and we climb the snow-clotted wooden steps that lead up to the mountain's lower flank. The sky is a brilliant blue and the white slope twinkles with children muffled in red and yellow and green snowsuits. They are dragging sleds uphill or bellyflopping on them downhill with screams of glee, or they are just staggering around like drunks in the snow. It is only three in the afternoon, but already the sun is low and red. I tuck trouser-tops into my boots and turn up my collar while Harry pulls the toboggan after us on its red cord. On the crest of the hill we get aboard, Harry, Molly, then me, hunching close. We grip each other clumsily.

"All right?" he calls.

"All systems go!" shouts Molly.

The toboggan slides, tilts, then begins to shoot down the hill. A hilarious, crazy joy sparkles in my blood. I shout with the others. My cheeks burn. I am five years old and the world is snow, sky, bright air, friends.

We clamber off, mount the hill, slide down again. Snow clots in big beads on the wool nap of my gloves. It smells wet and clean. We used to eat those beads. I am warm all over from laughing, spilling over, climbing. I pack a snowball and send it flying at Harry's red tuque; at the last second he moves, and it explodes in a crash of white spray on the broad back of an old man with grandchildren. He looks around with indignation for the criminal. Molly pushes me into the snow and I lie there weak with laughing till they drag me up. The sun is a red coal burning low on the horizon.

"Well, kids, that's it for me," says Harry. "Got to get back now and type some stuff."

"I've had enough too. My ass is cold."

I blink at them, disconcerted. They have abruptly gone somewhere else, in the arbitrary manner of grownups, leaving me to lag behind at another time of life.

"What I'd like — in fact, need — is a drink of something hot. Preferably with a lot of rum in it," says Molly as we manoeuvre the sled awkwardly down the steps. Harry's beard has snow-dust in it. My feet are numb with cold.

"Why don't you come on home with me, then. Got no rum, but I'll make some cocoa." I have no confidence in this suggestion, but Molly promptly says, "Super. Love to. You can type your old minutes later, Harry."

"No, you go; I've got to work on something else tomorrow. And we've got the Shapiros' party tonight, remember."

She makes a face. "Oh, all right. Go, then."

"Thanks anyway, Willy." He stumps off through the ruck of blue snow, and we turn into my street, where the arc-lamps are just flicking on, their light a pale green in the dusk.

The overheated apartment feels deliciously warm. We leave our snowy boots on the mat and drop our coats in the kitchen. Molly's wet mittens hiss cosily on the radiator. I pour the thick, steaming cocoa into mugs, and we clasp them luxuriously. Molly curls like a cat into one corner of the sofa. I take the other end.

"Nice pad," she says approvingly.

"It's all right, I guess. But there's something about high-rise living — I don't know — plastic. A house is different, almost any house."

"Ah, houses. They're always full of other people's footprints. I hate that."

The hot drink glows inside. The silence is compatible. It's almost easy — at least it sounds natural — to say, "I haven't laid eyes on Bill Trueblood since the holidays. Has he eloped with somebody or what?"

"No, he got back late from the Maritimes. But I saw him yesterday."

"Not sick again, was he?"

"Don't know. Only Archie wasn't best pleased. It's a bit much to miss the start of term."

"It was probably his sinuses again."

"Could be." She gives a little sniff. "Or his *mother*'s."

"Mm. Perhaps."

There is a pause. I am reluctant to say anything about Monday's demonstration, suspecting it will lead us into disagreement; but it's an awkward subject to avoid. At last I take the plunge.

"I saw the doings on Monday. Were there any reactions? From the deans and people, I mean?"

"Reactions? Are you kidding?" She looks at me almost triumphantly. "More even than we expected. Classical. Harry was summoned to The Presence. Again."

"Oh yes; one of the students — Mike Armstrong — said some-

thing about . . . he said the Principal had actually threatened him
— but that can't be true, can it?"

"God, Willy, you're naive aren't you? Of course he did. That
was way back in October, the minute he heard that Harry was
elected chairman of the League for Student Action."

"But actually threatened him?"

"Sure. In ancient *and* modern languages. Conflict of interests.
Ex officio. Responsibility. *In loco parentis. In statu pupillari*. All that
shit. 'A young man with his way to make cannot afford divided
loyalties.'" She stiffened her face for a moment into a wicked
replica of the Principal's lipless, icy frown. "In other words, Harry
baby, you are not yet a tenured member of staff. So watch it, or
the axe will drop."

"And Harry hasn't watched it. That took guts."

"And more. He *likes* Cartier. He's working for it. He believes in
this place and its future, the way that old St. James Street bugger
never has. All *he* wants is to prevent any kind of change ever
happening, so he can keep the Governors happy."

"What happened, then, when the Principal called him in this
time?"

"He made the threat definite. Nothing in writing yet, of course.
Not yet. He's too sly for that. And lots of toothy smiles, to show he
doesn't need to get mad. But it's right on the line: Harry resigns
from the L.S.A., or his appointment won't be renewed this spring."

"Really? Lord, Molly. What will he do?"

"Go right on, of course. The kids are a hundred per cent
behind him; so are lots of people on staff. So is the whole twentieth century, for God's sake. The old bugger will have to back
down."

"You think so?"

"Of course. Can you imagine anybody in the year 1969 actually
saying to a colleague that the top-level administrative system of
his college is none of his business? That's what Fraser said to
Harry, believe it or not. No, the whole department will . . . "

All at once her voice trails away and I glance at her, startled to
see that her face has suddenly turned a peculiar yellowish-white.

"Are you all right, Molly?"

"Yes—sure—it's just—" She straightens herself, taking two or
three deep breaths.

"Can I get you anything?"

"No, no." She smiles wanly, but the pallor lingers. Two sharp little lines, like brackets, have sprung out around her mouth. "I'm pregnant," she says abruptly.

I touch her arm in delight. Without thinking I blurt out, "Oh Molly, how wonderful!"

"Wonderful timing, all right."

"Well, yes; but ... "

"I can't take the Pill, and the damned coil must have slipped. After all the trouble I had even getting fixed up with that. This damned city is still living in the Pope's shadow in some ways."

"Yes, but now ... "

"You know that Harry's wife in New York won't give him a divorce. There are two kids. It's her idea of social maturity to hang on."

"Well, but ... "

"Oh, sure, it wouldn't matter all that much. We're both agnostics anyhow; and legally, who cares. But the last thing we need right now is a kid. I mean it's just out of the damn question."

"Oh. But ... "

"I would have gone to Kleber's clinic in the east end. He's a rational man and his fees are reasonable. But they raided the guy's office last week, grabbed his records, and put him in jail."

I think, 'She doesn't use the word abortion, though.' But my tongue is too clumsy to find any neutral comment.

"Well, he's out on bail at the moment, but not practising till the trial comes up. So I'll have to go down to New York for it."

I put my mug down on the end table. There is a sour taste in my throat and I swallow to get rid of it. I can think of nothing to say except, feebly, "I hope you'll be all right."

"Nothing to it. A few hours in bed. The vacuum method. I had it done once before, just before I broke up with John."

When I say nothing, she adds tartly, "Don't tell me you disapprove. A woman has rights over her own body. There can't be any woman left who doesn't agree to that."

I don't want to speak, but something pushes the words out of me. "But this is somebody else's body, isn't it?"

"Oh, Willy, for Christ's sake."

"I'm sorry, Molly. I'm terribly sorry."

But it's too late. Her pale face has twisted into a grimace of tears. She covers them with her two thin hands like a child, and I can't bear it. I scramble over to put my arms around her and rock her gently, rubbing her narrow back as I would comfort Dougie. "No, you have no discretion, Willy," my mother's voice says severely inside my head. But it's all over in a second or two. Molly finds a crumpled Kleenex and blows her nose. Her colour has come back. She gets up and smooths her hair in one crisp, neat gesture. The moment of truth is over.

"Sorry about that," she says briefly. But I am still wrung by all sorts of feelings that surprise and disturb me; I am, in fact, fighting tears myself. My voice trembles. "What can I give you, Molly? A drink, maybe?"

"No, thanks, not now; I've got to be off. Thanks for the cocoa."

"I loved the sleigh ride. It was great fun. But Molly — let me know if there's anything I can do. Please. I mean it."

"There's nothing. But thanks. Cheer up, woman. Forget it." She taps me on the shoulder and goes away with a smile.

But I can't forget it. Nor can I cheer up. Awake, asleep, dozing, working, I am haunted by that inch of humanity about to be scientifically, hygienically, rationally, vacuumed into nothingness. That human reject. While I am empty, empty.

'Bill is *avoiding* me,' I think as the weekend's night hours drain away; and it hurts like a low back pain. Not for anything will I phone him, or knock at his office door, or even ask about him. If he chooses to write lies on postcards, that's his privilege. Of course, he may be ill. Those sinuses of his. Nothing makes you feel so low. It must have been really bad to keep him in Halifax like that . . . I wonder if he needs anything. . . . Actually, I *should* call him. After all, what are friends for?

A tinny recording informs me that there-is-no-more-service-at-that-number; so next time I am in the Department building, I go straight to his office. My hand is raised to knock at the half-open door when it is suddenly pulled back and he all but walks into me.

"Hi, Bill; how are you?"

"Willy. I'm lousy, thanks." He is all muffled up for outdoors, but what can be seen of his face looks pale and his brown eyes are bleary under swollen lids.

"Sinuses again?"

"And a touch of conjunctivitis thrown in for extra jollies. Look, I'd love to have a chat, Willy, but I've got to rush home and unpack all my stuff. The movers dumped it all down this morning at my new place, then I had to go to my noon class with everything left in chaos."

"Oh, and you're feeling so rotten. Bill, let me come too, and give you a hand."

He brightens a little in a faint smile. "*Would* you? Oh you are a dear soul, Willy. Sure you want to? Come on then. It's not far, thank God; that wind is like a razor."

We crunch our icy way up the street, buffeted by a freezing wind that flaps our coat-tails and burns our eyes. Luckily it's not long before we reach a rather discouraged-looking brick apartment house crouched in the snow. On the front door a tattered Christmas wreath shivers in the pale sun.

"It's a bit of a dump," he says gloomily, "but at least I won't be driven out of my skull by all-night riveting. Come on in — never mind your boots, the floors are a mess anyway. Those movers, you never saw such animals. They looked like gorillas in clothes."

It is certainly not a very attractive place, even as bachelor apartments go. The windows are small and set high in the walls; the one room is narrow and the floor, especially in the kitchen alcove, is indeed a mess, embossed in dirt that must have fossilized there for years.

Bill looks around for hangers hopelessly and without success before throwing our coats on the striped sofa-bed. He sighs heavily as we contemplate the cartons of books, china, and bedclothes, the garment bags and suitcases that sit forlornly about on the floor together with stray oddments like shoes, tennis racquets, and a vacuum cleaner.

"All right — have they put the furniture where you want it? Bookcase going to stay here? Fine; then let's go. I'll take out and you shelve."

We set to work, Bill groaning faintly from time to time, and sneezing over the books, till I find a duster for them. Once the cartons begin to empty, the missing coat-hangers turn up, and we unpack and hang up his clothes. He has a rather large wardrobe. The afternoon light turns wan and silvery, then dims.

"Now the kitchen stuff. Nice china you have." Then I notice the condition of the kitchen shelves.

"Oh God," says Bill. "How sordid."

"Never mind. Soon fix 'em. Got a scrubbing brush?"

I roll up my sleeves and tackle the shelves. After a good scrub they shine clean and white, and I run fresh hot water to do the floor.

"Willy, you're marvellous. Strong as a horse. My back is killing me just to watch you."

Well, it isn't a romantic tribute, but it has its satisfactions just the same. While he makes up the bed and puts spare linen in the bathroom cupboard, I energetically scrub and scour the kitchen floor until some quite pleasant blue-and-white tiling emerges from under the grime. Bill plugs in a couple of lamps and throws a tartan homespun cloth over the all-purpose table. Eventually we even hang up his red curtains on their brass pole, though they are far too long for the window.

"Actually, it isn't going to look too awful," he says, "thanks to you. But do stop now, Willy, before you kill yourself. I'll make some coffee, shall I?"

"Well, if you like. It's nearly six, though, and I don't see any food — what are you doing about dinner?"

"Oh, that doesn't matter, I can eat out somewhere. At least have some coffee or a drink."

"No, there's nowhere decent around here to eat, really. Why don't I run over to that little take-out place? — did you know they make great goulash? You just have to heat it up . . . no, I'll go; you shouldn't be out in that wind." Before he can argue the point, I pull on my coat and go. Outside the sky is thick with great, bright stars that look close enough to reach up and touch. The wind has dropped and the still air is sharp and dry.

In the take-out shop I joke with the red-faced cook in his broad white apron, and choose a chicken cooked in the Basque style, with tomatoes and bay leaf, some poppyseed rolls, and four éclairs, fat with whipped cream. Bill likes desserts. Hurrying back with the big, warm box of food under those crowds of blazing stars, I have time to think, 'So this is what happiness is like.'

I find the door on the latch and Bill considerably more cheerful, having decided that a vodka martini would be more restorative than coffee. As I unpack our dinner, he says, "How good it smells. And éclairs! What a clever creature you are. And so am I, because I actually found the cutlery — with my skis, would you believe? — and the table's all set."

"Good, then we can eat right now. I must admit I'm starved."

He pours us each a glass of wine and I lift mine. "Here's to your new house, Bill."

"And to you," he says gallantly.

"Chicken all right?"

"Marvellous," he says with his mouth full.

"So I gather your Christmas wasn't very jolly, with all that sinus bother."

"Oh, it wasn't just that . . . I mean it's always pretty grim being in the same house with that redneck stepfather of mine, only this time my mother wasn't well at all. She looked all pale and drained, and then just at New Year's she had this terrible attack of pain. You never saw anything like it. She went all yellow, couldn't speak, even — it was terrifying. We got her to hospital somehow, the roads were awful with snow; and they had to give her a shot of morphine before they could even examine her. Then they whizzed her onto the table next morning and took her gall bladder out."

"Poor thing. Is she all right now?"

"Yes, but she was in awful shape for three or four days afterward. Such pain. And she is fifty-six, after all. That's why I stayed in Halifax and missed the first days of term. It was just out of the question — I couldn't leave her like that. Even now I'm worried to death. She's still in hospital, of course; but she's already itching to get home, and when she does, I know her, she'll immediately try to do too much."

He pours more wine into his glass after holding the bottle over mine with a questioning look. His hand is not quite steady and he pushes away his plate, though he hasn't finished his chicken.

"I want her to have a nurse for the first week or two at home; but of course apeman Clive can't see the point of that at all. 'I'll look after her,' he says. That's a good one. If you could see the way she waits on him hand and foot . . . "

"Never mind. I'm sure she's too sensible to overdo things. Besides, your sister lives near by, doesn't she? — well, she'll keep an eye open."

"Oh, I suppose she might, if it doesn't interfere with macramé class. Wait — I've got to take my aureomycin. Now tell me about your Christmas — was it fun?"

"Well. I suppose you could say it was about average."

"Harry and Molly got back from Cuba, I see, all refreshed from watching Fidel save the workers. Anything else new? What with moving and everything, I haven't had a second to talk to anybody."

"Well, Harry and his L.S.A. friends broke up a faculty meeting, the first day of term."

"Yes, I heard about that. Tell me more." He puts his elbows cosily on the table and pours himself more wine.

"Molly says the Principal is threatening to fire him if Harry keeps on fighting for student parity."

"I believe it. Fraser's not a guy to fool around. You don't get that shark's grin he has for nothing. I wonder what Harry will do, actually? Because, you know what he really wants is to be chairman of the department. And after that he wants to be Dean."

"No kidding! Join the Establishment?"

"Sure. Everybody knows what he's after."

"I don't think the kids do. What about the L.S.A. then?"

"Oh, that. He's just using them because student support could be a lever. Or so he thinks. But you wait and see — he'll dump them and their cause the minute he thinks they're no longer useful to him."

"That's awful if it's true," I say, shocked. I am thinking of Mike.

"*He's* awful, that's why."

"Is he really?" Now I am thinking of Harry laughing in the snow, and Molly clasping him around the waist, and her tight, white little face alone later. But out of some absurd female loyalty, I can't say anything to Bill about *that*.

"I wonder what will happen to Harry, then? He's apparently going ahead with plans for a student boycott, or sit-in, or some such thing. Or so Mike Armstrong says."

"Oh, God knows. But our department meeting next week may be interesting. Looks as if we're heading for some kind of confrontation, all right. I wonder how Archie will cope. He's in one of his depressions, I see. But what else is new? Is it true that Fat Emma's feuding with that little tiny Spaniard in Modern Languages? Hilarious if so — she could kill him with a sneeze."

"I don't know about that. But Molly took me to a Women's Lib meeting with her and Emma. At that headquarters of theirs downtown, you know, where men actually aren't even allowed inside the building? I must say that tickled me."

"So you got sensitized, did you?"

"Well yes, why not. Maybe time I got with it. The lecture was called Fifty Ways Men Put Us Down. Molly thinks I'm a perfect freak, you know. She was really shocked when I told her I didn't feel like a female eunuch, even after reading the book."

"Well, try not to let it get to you too much."

"I won't. Couldn't. I mean if your *mother* was a woman — "

"I know exactly what you mean."

We laugh. He has a second éclair. After the dishes are done, I help him put odds and ends into cupboards and stock his desk with its dictionary, paper, and typewriter. The room looks orderly and comfortable now; even home-like.

"Willy," he says as I am pulling on my long boots for the trek home, "you have been the most marvellous help, and you will be rewarded in heaven. Also on earth, because I will take you out to dinner soon. On payday, to be exact."

"Thanks. I accept. Now take care of yourself. Go to bed with a hot-water bottle and get a good, long sleep."

"I will. Good night, Willy, and bless you." As I am buttoning my coat he drops a comedy kiss on the end of my nose. It is the sort of kiss that, if anything, sets The Project back considerably, and I know it. Just the same, I walk home under the stars happy in the snowy, alien streets of Villette. I will not have to bury my postcard after all.

THE DEPARTMENT OF ENGLISH MEETING SCHEDULED FOR
JANUARY 19TH IS POSTPONED FOR TWO WEEKS, OWING TO
THE CHAIRMAN'S FILTHY ATTACK OF SCIATICA.   A.B.-C.

"There's this Special Delivery for Dr. Clarke," says Sherri, appearing at my office door as I bundle on coat and scarf for the trip home. "You live sort of near him, don't you? Maybe you could like drop it off at his place on your way?" She gives the letter into my reluctant hand. Her long fingernails are lacquered green. "Thanks," she adds firmly.

"Well, all right." The late afternoon is white with hoarfrost when I come out of the building, and the Porsche coughs and growls before it will start. But while the engine warms I look with satisfaction at the big pink box on the back seat. At lunchtime I have surrendered to overwhelming temptation and bought a long dress out of the window of a sinfully expensive boutique in Place Ville Marie. It is the delicate blue of early morning. A long chiffon scarf hangs from the shoulder; the back is bare and the skirt full and filmy. A romantic dress. Not even the lurking suspicion that my freckles may dim the romantic effect can prevent me from spending my entire supply of ready cash on this lovely gown. After all, payday will soon come around. I can do without lunch for a few days. And Bill is sure to take me somewhere nice — maybe where there's dancing, like the top of that huge new hotel on Peel Street . . . I can economize by dyeing those old white shoes of mine to match the blue . . .

Clarke's house looks stubborn and forlorn, a lonely island in its empty half-acre of snow. The wind whips at me and groans theatrically in the bare trees. Beside the steps stands a large garbage tin surrounded by an extensive litter of bottles, some of them broken. Impatiently I stamp my feet to keep warm, and knock again. Yes, or that smart Czech restaurant on Beaver Hall Hill everybody talks about . . . Where *is* the man? Can't he hear? I hammer the knocker again. My gloved hands are cold. Why don't I just push this damned letter through the letter-slot and go?

But at long last a faint glow appears in the fanlight and the door slowly opens.

"This letter came for you this afternoon, Dr. Clarke. Sherri asked me to drop it off."

He is bent almost double, grey shock of hair low, one hand pressed to the small of his back. His face is seamed, when he lifts it to me, with what looks like pure rage.

"What's that ye say? Can't hear a word. Come inside, do; no point in freezing us both to death."

I step inside and he slams the door. Without a backward glance he limps down the hall, still holding his back, and disappears into the sitting-room. By the time I have scraped my boots dry and followed him, he is lowering himself cautiously into an armchair, his lips moving in silent blasphemy.

"Here's the letter Sherri asked me to bring you, Dr. Clarke. I hope you'll be feeling better soon."

He is busy trying to juxtapose a hot-water bottle and the sore place on his back. I stand there holding out the letter with such patience as I can muster. There is a big coal fire glowing on the hearth. One of the Siamese cats is crouched on the faded rug close to the red heat. The room is dark; only one lamp is lit behind his chair.

"Where the hell are my glasses?" he asks irritably.

"*I* don't know where the hell they are," I say, as reasonably as I can. Then I spot them, precariously poised on top of a pile of books near his feet.

I hand the glasses over with the letter. "Good night, then. I'll just let myself out — "

"Ah," he interrupts me. "From my son. Bad news, without a shadow of a doubt. Wait — is that six?"

We pause to count the subdued chimes of an old tall clock in the shadows, uttered with diffidence, like an old man's tales no one wants to hear.

"Yes, it's six o'clock. I must be getting — "

"Wait, miss. Have I said thank you, at all?"

"No, sir." (Well, if he insists on being so Victorian. Actually, it suits him.)

"Well, I do thank you. And if it's six, my bread is ready to go into the oven. Take off your coat. If you'd have the great kindness, that is, to give me a hand. For some reason the kneading goes for this sciatic nerve. Come on out to the kitchen. Know how to knead bread? Well, I'll show you what to do."

There seems no way I can well refuse, so I drop my coat over a chair and follow his stooped and creaking progress out to the kitchen. In addition to its usual eclectic collection of junk, the room contains a warm, yeasty smell that is rather pleasant.

"Now the dough has to be turned out onto this board — just hold it steady — dust your hands with flour and fold the dough over on itself. Now push with the heel of your hand—no no, girl; like this. Lightly. That's it. Now fetch me those pans. Did I grease them?—yes. In a few minutes they can go in. The oven on? Good. Cover them up, then — they hate draughts as much as I do."

I set the covered breadpans gingerly on top of the stove, nearly coming to disaster as I fail to notice a dish of cat-food on the floor near my foot.

"That's Percy's. He won't eat. Poor old Douglas died, you know, last Sunday. Must have been some kind of heart attack — he just gave a sort of cough after his meal, and dropped. Ten years old, they were; brothers, never been separated. Used to fight a lot. Now Percy won't eat. Had him along to the vet, tried everything—

but he won't make the effort. So I'll be quite alone soon. Do you mind if I read my letter?"

He lowers himself by careful degrees into the old Windsor rocker. His head with its mane of grey hair is sunk over the broad chest, crookedly buttoned into a shabby old sweater. The glasses are low on his beaky nose as he fumbles open his letter. I can't help feeling sorry for the poor old curmudgeon.

"Have you got any shrimps? Tinned shrimps?"

"Probably. Why, are you hungry? Look in that cupboard; lots of shrimp there."

I push aside a pile of yellowing *Times Lit. Supps.*, open the tall cupboard door, and survey the cluttered shelves. Yes, here is a tin of shrimp. Under his abstracted direction I find an opener in a drawer bursting with old paper bags, string, candles, and small garden tools. I empty and wash the cat-saucer by the stove and arrange on it a small helping of shrimp in their juice. I take this into the sitting-room, leaving Clarke hunched sombrely over his letter.

"Now Percy, old boy. Look at what I've got. How about a bite to eat?"

I sit down quietly on the rug near him. He settles deeper into his crouch, barely opening his blue eyes in one wary glance before closing them again. His coat looks rough and his nose is dry. "Come on, old man. Nice shrimp. Just smell. Yummy." I stroke him. "Who was a nice old cat, then? There's a good boy. Come on, then, Percy, let's try. Such a handsome old man, then." Percy seems to find these remarks less fatuous than they sound. He gives a self-pitying sigh and does not avoid my caressing hand. Cautiously I dip a finger into the shrimp-juice and touch the end of his nose with it. He frowns, but his pink tongue comes out and he licks the juice away. I offer a tiny scrap of the coral meat in my fingers. After long hesitation he takes it from me fastidiously, drops it on the rug, paws it up, looks at it with disfavour, then drops it again. But he takes the next bit directly from my fingers and eats it. When I offer the plate, he looks away, pained, until I hold him out another scrap.

"Time to put this bread in, miss," Archie calls. The warm, yeasty smell floats down the dark hall to meet me as I return to the kitchen. Suddenly I feel ravenously hungry.

"He's eaten nearly half the shrimp."

"Who has?" He looks up at me from the folded letter lying on his knee as if he has difficulty remembering who I am.

"Percy. He ate some dinner. The bread's in. And now I'm off."

"Et some shrimp, did he? Good for him." He looks at his broken old slippers and makes a heavy effort to stand up.

"No, please don't bother — I can just let myself out."

"That bread will have to come out in half an hour. Take off those ridiculous boots, woman, you look like a Cossack, and have a bite of supper with me. Unless that would bore you intolerably. Can't even offer you a drink, I'm afraid. Threw out all my whiskey. Real danger of becoming a squalid old drunk, specially with this bloody back playing me up. Self-pity, it occurred to me the other day, is the alcoholic's disease. And I *have* it. So I threw all the Scotch away. But you could make us a nice little omelette, and I think I can find a bottle of Liebfraumilch to help it down."

"Well, thanks; but I'm afraid, sir, I'm no cook."

He looks at me with genuine indignation. "What—call yourself a woman and can't cook? Outrageous."

"I suppose it is, really." And I actually do feel almost apologetic. After all, men like to eat. Where did I read that food is more important than sex to ninety per cent of all men? The Project could actually suffer ... Bill loves his food, I've noticed. "As a matter of fact, I wouldn't mind knowing how to make that bread. It smells marvellous." I give him a demure look.

"Preposterous, not able to knock together so much as an omelette. Well, I propose to educate you, miss. Beginning now. Take four eggs out of the fridge; get a bowl and the whisk, and you shall make an omelette. We'll have some of the new bread with it, too, though it really shouldn't be cut so soon. Good of you to bring that letter. And Sherri's a good girl, too. Did you know she and her boy friend made a bird feeder for Lily to watch? She spent her last month with her face to the window, watching the birds. A good, kind girl. Even if I'd rather not have had the damn letter. My poor son is always being ill or bankrupt or divorced, don't know how it is; he's intelligent, he has charm; and there's no harm in him, no harm at all, and yet ... Take that bread out now and set it on those racks. Don't know what it is, but in my more depressive moods I see the poor man as another failure of my own, in the genes maybe. Or mistakes I made ... in the war, I insisted on sending him to friends of ours in America. That was in

1941. And Lily wouldn't leave me. He was just six. It was two years before we saw him again. Maybe he felt we were ... well, I've regretted it since. Very much. Have you broken those eggs? Now add a splash or two of water, some salt, a grind or two of pepper; don't hang about, girl. Ah well. Never have understood Tony, really. 'Do diddle di do / Poor Jim Jay / Got stuck fast / In Yesterday.' Eh? Must be all that aspirin that makes me so confessional. *Whisk* those eggs, don't beat them to death. You'll find a cast-iron pan around somewhere—over there, under those towels, I think. Well, perhaps my generation puts too high a value on achievement. Neurotic of us, d'ye think? But who would be a parent if he knew ahead of time all the pains and failures of it?"

"I would."

He stares at me briefly over his spectacles. "Don't get that pan too hot—you're burning the butter. No, no—here, give it here, I'll do it. You shake the pan like this, d'ye see—slide the mixture till the whole thing folds over. Oh Christ, my back. Fancy not knowing how to make an omelette, a woman of your age. Are the plates hot? Well, why aren't they? If those loaves are cool enough now, you can cut a slice or two. Pay attention, now. The knife must not be too cold. Crust not too dark? No, just right. You know, in sixty years I've achieved absolutely nothing, except a dim perception of Shakespeare's genius. A third-rate émigré scholar who's achieved the total obscurity he so richly deserves. But I can, by God, make magnificent bread. And do you know what I am going to do for you, miss? You have been good about Percy. And there may even be other qualities in you worth cultivating. I am going to teach you how to make good bread. You will present yourself here at nine o'clock in the morning this Saturday, in a clean apron, for the first lesson."

I look at him. He stares back (can it be hopefully?) and pulls himself straighter, one hand still pressed to his back. Excuses, evasions, form on my lips; but I say meekly, "Yes, thanks. I'll come. Sir."

Department-meeting day is cheerful with flashes of sun and snow dry as powder sparkling in the bright air. Sherri's heels tap smartly up and down the hall; phones buzz; people pop in and out of each other's offices with an air of energy and purpose. A supercharge, perhaps just of static electricity in the air, stings my fingers whenever I touch a metal doorknob or wastebasket. I keep looking at my watch, but the meeting is not due to begin for fifteen minutes yet.

Suddenly, to my surprise, Harry Innis appears at my door. He is carrying that plastic mug of coffee without which no one at Cartier ever seems to move.

"Come on in, Harry. Can I do anything for you?"

"Yes, Willy, as a matter of fact you can."

"Really? What can it be — Molly's all right, is she? I mean, she's been off work this last week ... "

"No, she's fine," he says, as if surprised at the question. After pushing the door shut, he drags up a chair and sits back in it, cocking one bent, jean-clad leg over his knee. "It's a small deal, just. Ruthie is going to nominate Mike Armstrong to the Hiring and Tenure Committee, and will you second it? He's a student of yours, isn't he?"

"Yes. But—is that what today's meeting is all about? Hiring and Tenure?"

"Not on the agenda, no. But now we've got parity, the H & T has got to double in size, and now's the time to set it up, before the spring when it gets to work. Used to be just Molly, Bill, and Archie. Now we need three students. Mike, Leo Bernstein, and Mary MacGregor ... it had better be people we know."

"Well, yes, I suppose so. But Mike is —"

"Mike is what?"

But I can hardly say, "Mike is in your pocket. Is he really right to serve on a committee that may soon have to decide on your future? — Even if we concede he's the right person to decide on any departmental business ... " So I wriggle uncomfortably and mutter "so young".

"Not a federal offence, is it? He's a smart kid, Mike."

"Yes. Oh yes. He's smart."

Harry's eyes pin mine, though his red lips are still smiling. "It's important to get the right people on this committee, Willy. You've got to see that. Hell, your own job will be on the line next year."

"Yes, I realize that. But can you be sure who are the right people? I don't think *I* can."

"Why not? Bright people. Socially mature. Reliable. The kind that don't skip meetings or get fooled by a lot of bullshit from Administration. Right?"

"Sure, as far as it — "

"You don't sound convinced."

"No — well — it's only that — " Irritated by my own silly diffidence, I add in a rush—"It just seems pretty contrived, somehow.
Arranging who'll nominate and who'll second and all that."

"Contrived? Of course it is. That kind of thing is plain common
sense, Willy. Or self-defence, if you like." His good humour
seems unruffled, but under his blandness I sense the flick of
something like anger. He takes a swig of coffee and the sun pulls a
gold flash out of his signet ring. He has surprisingly small hands,
with clever, narrow fingers. "No," he goes on, "I know what's
bothering you, the idea of rigging the committee. Christ, as if this
whole place wasn't — but here. Have a look at this and you may
lose a few of those delicate scruples."

He plucks a folded letter out of an inner pocket of his jean-
jacket. It is dated this week, from the Principal's office. The
message is only four lines long. "The Principal and Board of
Governors regard as irreconcilable your professional commit-
ments and your leadership of the League for Student Action, and
inform you that resignation from that post is a necessary condition of your renewed academic appointment at Cartier College.
Faithfully yours, Fergus M. Fraser."

"What price manipulation now?" he asks.

"Ugh. It's a horrid letter, all right."

"Well, I intend to get legal advice and all that, and it's not that
I'm personally worried. Shit, if it comes to that, there are other
jobs. But you can see — well. The thing needs no comment.
Incidentally, Molly's turning in her resignation today from the
H & T Committee. Is that contrived, do you think? She has her
scruples, too. Well, forget I ever proposed Mike — no hard
feelings, kid. Come on, it's time to get upstairs."

I shift unhappily in my chair. He will not forgive me now, but I
say, "Harry, wait. I'll second Mike for the committee."

He shies his empty cup with one fast, accurate slam into the
metal wastebasket, and it raps out a loud, sharp, peremptory
clang — applause for one hand.

"Good girl," he says. "Let's go."

Dougie has to go into hospital and have his tonsils out. This news
so darkens the whole day of my date with Bill that I can hardly

think of anything else. Yet Lou on the phone is so crisp and sensible about the whole thing that she makes me feel both silly and guilty about being silly.

"Nothing to it," she says firmly. "They just keep them in over-night — not half long enough, if you ask me. Of course the day he's booked, Greg's off to Goderich, so guess who will have to carry the whole can."

"Oh, the poor baby. Is he scared?"

"Scared! What of? He can't wait for the ice cream."

But I remember the total, the overwhelming desolation of being left among kind strangers in that white, strange-smelling place. I remember having no real belief at all that I would ever see my familiar world again. And my mother's departure was abso-lute. As final as death. My grief when she died last year was easy, the tears flowed—but not then; I couldn't cry then. At four years old I had to bear a sorrow too numb and huge for any comfort whatever. How could Lou possibly — how can anyone — forget what it's like?

"Won't they let you sleep in with him?" I ask, my voice coming out in a stiff croak.

"Oh, of course not, Willy."

"Well, do they at least have rocking chairs beside the cots?"

"Rocking chairs? Good Lord, *I* don't know. Anyhow, at this point I've got no bloody lap to rock him *on*. It's barely February and I'm like a Mack truck already ... it would be just like God to sentence me to twins. What did you say?"

"I said tell Dougie I'm sending him a little surprise. Lucky thing I called. I'll get it off today. It should reach you before he goes in. Mind you keep it wrapped, Lou, and don't give it to him until the minute you have to leave. You will remember, won't you? That way it might help him over those first few minutes."

"Yes, sure. Thanks, Willy. Now I've got to rush off. Nice to hear from you."

I sit down immediately and begin the construction of a picture story on squares of cardboard from the laundry. With quantities of coloured ink I portray our favourite invention, a thumb-sized fat lady called Mrs. Carstep Jamwaddle. She sits up in bed with one curly hair springing from the crown of an otherwise bald head. On top of the icepack round her throat is her friend and part-time furpiece, a yellow caterpillar called Wallace. She tucks into a large mound of purple ice cream. Then her mother comes in, arms outstretched. And then they all go home, Wallace undulating behind, with his suitcase on the end of his tail.

By the time I have sewn this epic together with a length of red ribbon, wrapped it all up, and rushed out to get it into Special Delivery, it is late in the afternoon, and I recall distractedly that I haven't yet dyed my shoes. In haste I spread out newspaper and apply the blue, pleased to see that the colour spreads on smoothly and looks well. To speed the drying process, I set the oven to low and put the shoes inside.

It is not until I'm stepping into my bath that I notice the blue blotches on my hands. Soap, the nailbrush, soaking, all prove futile. Desperate, I scrub with cleanser from the tin. All that accomplishes is to turn the skin red, where it is not already blue. Oh, it just isn't fair. Do these crazy things happen to other people, or just to me? And why to me? Why do I always seem to be the butt of some cosmic but not very good joke? I mean, if the Great Author wants to make us tragic victims, that's one thing—it even has a certain dignity—but playing straight man to a low comedian is something else. What do you do then? Laugh, I suppose — if you can. But a couple of angry tears are plopping into the bathwater and all I can manage is a disconsolate sort of snuffle. Eventually, though, I remember a pair of long white kid gloves at the back of my drawer, and as it turns out they heighten the elegance of the new gown to an almost imperial level.

Bill's face when he first sees me is a study in lightning adjustment from utter dismay to extravagant and gallant admiration. Too late (of course) I realize that his own outfit of cashmere pullover and tweedy trousers indicates he probably had a movie and barbecued chicken in mind.

"Bill, I could pretend I only put it on to show you. It will only take me a second to change — "

But he catches up my gloved hand and raises it to his lips with a superb Rupert-of-Hentzau bow.

"You'll do no such thing. That dress shall not be kept from a waiting world. No kidding, Willy, it's gorgeous. Turn around and let me see the back. Mm. Lovely. Wait—here's a little hook open." Deftly he fastens it, while I wish there were more of them. "Yes, it's really super. The blue makes those blue eyes of yours jump right out of your head. Now lead me to the phone and let's see if we can get a reservation somewhere nice. I wonder whether the Porc-épic ... or the—no, I've got it. You know the Boule-de-Suif near the CBC—we'll have to line up, they don't take reservations. But with all those producers there dressed up as anarchists, nobody will notice I'm not in your class."

"Oh great. Hold on a minute while I take my shoes out of the oven."

"Eh?"

When I explain, he throws back his curly head to laugh and says, "I do like you, Willy!"

All this gets us off into the snow with a dash. In the cab I confess the reason for the long gloves, and he laughs again, which makes the sad face of mid-Europe at the wheel split open in a sympathetic grin. I am so warm with happiness, even while we wait in a chilly queue outside the restaurant, that instead of running forlornly through my mind Dougie sits in a quiet corner of it, patient and resigned.

"Look, there's Archie — see? Up ahead."

"Good heavens. Fancy him being here. His back must be better, then. Who's that with him?"

"Some old trout or other, I can't see too well."

But just then a group between us drops away, abandoning the line-up, and Archie notices us.

"Join us later for coffee," Bill mouths. After a truculent stare at me over his long cigar, Archie nods.

Dinner is a lively affair because of the vivacious, French-speaking crowd, most of it from the nearby CBC studios. They have come not to eat the food but to devour each other in long, simultaneous conversations, in hostile stares, in kisses, in high shrieks of laughter, in head-together murmurs. As Bill promised, they are in every possible bizarre kind of dress, and some of them keep their dark glasses on, though the room is dim with candlelight. "Otherwise, you see," Bill explains, "the tourists might not know they are producers."

After dessert, an obliging waiter takes orders for espresso coffee, and conjures extra chairs to our table for Archie and his lady. While the introductions are in progress, I have time to hope no mention will be made of my recent cooking lesson, during which I dropped an egg on the floor and was denounced: "*Slut!*"

" ... my sister from Jamaica, Jessie Tort," says Archie. He seats himself with caution, but he looks much better; there is, in fact, a high colour in his cheeks.

"It's great fun to find you here," says Bill pleasantly. "I'm always surprised, even after years here, to find what a small town Montreal actually is. You hardly ever spend an evening out without seeing someone you know."

I think proudly how clever Bill is with easy small talk, and how agreeably he stood up to greet Archie's old sister, a lean and formidably erect old lady of about eighty, whom he's given one of his best smiles. And I wonder why Archie's bush of eyebrow is knotted in that scowl. It surely can't be his back.

"You and Molly used to frequent this place, didn't you?" he asks, gazing at Bill and pointing the cigar at him like a challenge. To my surprise, Bill flushes a little.

"No, not really." The cordiality has faded slightly from his voice, but he adds, "Who's having a brandy with coffee — Willy? Mrs. Tort? Archie?"

Once all that is settled, Bill turns to Archie's sister with his engaging smile once more on duty.

"Is this your first visit to Montreal, Mrs. Tort?"

Only then do we discover that either the lady's teeth are a poor fit, or she considers herself too old to bother with the finicking details of enunciation, for she chops up words with the abandon of a manic butcher whirling his cleaver.

"Oh no, thissame fourteen visit, be exact, to Monorail. First time was in '19 when the Prince of Whale was here. Though half a mo, wasn't I here in time for the flu picnic? — or was that later, Archie? Yes, that was the time Windy my Peke bit the Trades Missioner, such a sensible doggie, he was an awful bore. I don't know why gobber ficials must always be bores, never matter what country, all dread creatures capable writing dull books like Hill-er's *Unkempt*. Must be that round ficial fairs they have to tend, dulls their nits or something. Good brandy." And uttering a baritone laugh, she pats Bill's arm.

He avoids my eye with some care. I stir the black pool of my demitasse industriously. When I do glance up, I catch Archie in the unmistakable act of looking down the front of my dress. I am the only one to blush.

"Nice that your sister is here," I say, trying to make it sound true. But no one ever believes me when I speak platitudes. Archie transfers a gloomy gaze to the end of his cigar.

"Jessie is trying to persuade me to go and live with her in Jamaica when I retire."

"Oh, really. Well, I hope that won't be for ages yet." But to this blandishment he returns only a cross grunt.

"Yes, pearly ridiculous spend old age in a city same climate as Linengrad. Come and get some topical sun, never have another tinge of all his wizaries then. I always tell people the first Bishop Erect lost his romantics for ever first year he came to Kingston, no place like it, look at me I say."

We all do, with some awe. I have been in minor but sharp agony, however, for quite a few minutes now, and Bill, perceiving this, begins at once to bundle us off. He creates a bustle paying the bill and making our farewells, and then almost runs us out of the place. Once safely outside we burst out laughing like a pair of escaped lunatics. People turn in the street to stare at the two of us holding each other up and guffawing explosively.

"Come on," he gasps, "they'll come out and find us here — let's grab a getaway cab." And we collapse into a taxi, still laughing.

"Oh God, she can't have any roof to her mouth — "

"The Bishop — the Bishop — "

"The Peke was from Peter Pan and Windy, I suppose — "

"That bore *Unkempt* — "

By some happy accident I find myself folded inside his arm, which he now settles more comfortably around me.

"Poor old Archie," he says. "Fancy spending your twilight years with a companion like that. Well, you have to feel sorry for him. Did you catch that crack about me and Molly? It's not that there ever was a real thing with us, you know. It's just that he has this patriarch complex or something. He'd like all the women in our department to be nuns. A queer old boy, and that's the truth."

"Would he?" I think of him looking down my front, but say nothing, because that aspect of the evening no longer seems of the faintest interest. Bill's arm and shoulder are comfortingly warm in the cold taxi. He feels relaxed. I rest my head against him. Eventually, as we draw near my apartment building, he leans over me and my arm slides up around his neck. Our mouths bump together shyly, part, and meet again. Table manners now, Willy. Must not seem too hungry. But his lips are soft and fresh and feel lovely.

The meter ticks. The cab has stopped.

"Well, well. We're here," says Bill. "Hold on, driver; just wait here a minute, I'll be going on. I'll see you in, Willy — mind that ice. Thanks, love, for a grand evening. Call you soon."

Oh Dougie, my poor baby, are you there? But I am so happy. Forgive me, I can't help it. . . . I haven't forgotten you. It's just that right now I believe as simply as you do in happy endings.

SIX

Generation Gap

"I DON'T WANT TO KNOW THAT," protests Mike.

"Now look. It's part of my job to ask Socratic questions. You may call 'em questions I don't know how to answer either; maybe nobody does. But I have to ask them."

Moodily Mike takes a swig from his container of coffee. "Yours is getting cold," he points out.

"All right. Now I'm asking whether Theobald Pontifex is a bully because he's a clergyman, or because that's simply his temperament, and he'd be the same kind of father if he were a ballet dancer or a botanist."

"Yeah, but my whole thesis is that it's got to be because he's Establishment."

"You remember that scene where the children choose a hymn — 'Come, come, come; come to the sunset tree' — ?"

He frowns.

"Oh, you must. When Ernest got a beating for not being able to pronounce 'come'."

"Oh. Well. Yeah."

"Doesn't that scene suggest to you the old man is a natural sadist? The hymn and the Sunday background and the dog-collar make it much nastier; but are those the basic elements, or is it just old Theobald's glee at the spanking?"

Mike blows out air patiently through his nostrils.

"The Church bit is basic. That's my thesis, man."

"But is it *Butler*'s, Mike?"

"Hell, how do I know. I'm just a crazy, mixed-up senior, trying to screw a degree out of this place."

My mouth twitches dangerously. I take a large gulp of tepid coffee to keep it out of mischief. *The Way of All Flesh* lies on my desk in a puddle of late afternoon sunlight. In the little silence that drops between us, I can hear the ticking of my watch.

"Well, all I'm asking is that you consider these situations not just from a sociological point of view, but as illustrations of human behavior. Butler's portraying people — complicated people, not just Victorian stereotypes."

"Yes, ma'am. I'll remember that."

"You say you're not going to do anything with Dickens? Seems rather a pity to waste Gradgrind and Dombey."

"No, too much been done. It would just be rehashing Johnson and Taine and all that."

"Well, maybe."

"No, Trollope and Hardy next."

"This thing is going to run to the scale of a full-length thesis, then."

"Looks like it." His ingenuous smile is full of pleasure.

"Anyhow, it sounds pretty good so far. I'm really interested in it."

"Then why won't you come with me to the Carnival Ball?"

"Now Mike, we've been over all this before."

"You haven't explained, only made excuses and run like a rabbit. You're hiding behind a whole lot of clichés, admit it. You act like being human could be fatal. We're just two *people*, Miz."

"Mike, I —" Certainly the quarts of coffee I drink every day at Cartier must account for the recent tendency of my heart to race, my hands to perspire. Yet my reactions are thick and slow. I am not quick enough now to prevent Mike from rising, coming around the desk, bending his tall head swiftly down, and dropping a kiss on the side of my neck.

"Well!" is all I can find to say, and highly ridiculous it sounds, to both of us. But I seem to have no breath for any more effective comment. That delicate little kiss has shot like a bullet right to its target, and my face is burning like other areas, and well he knows it, too, the mischievous young warlock. Once more bonelessly draped in his chair, he eyes me with a sparkling kind of glee, and all that saves my dignity is that his own cheeks are bright pink.

"Now see here, Mike. The answer is *no*. You have a girl. I've seen her around with you — that big dark girl. She's the one to take to your dance, not a prehistoric monster like me."

"Val isn't my girl. She just hangs around."

"We're not arguing about it, Michael."

"Huff, huff, Miz. Have it your own way, then. Only it would've been fun. Shake 'em up a bit. Your peers and mine. A good thing all round."

"Not good. Or wise."

"Don't you ever want to try something unwise? Dangerous, even?"

I pause, thinking of the undoubted folly of The Project, so far, in all likelihood, from being a wise or good plan, even if it—even if Bill —

"You see? You can't fool me, you know. Because you're real, not a non-person, like so many faculty types in this place." He pauses, stretching out still farther his long legs in their skinny, tie-dyed jeans. The room is growing dusky now. I switch on my desk lamp.

"You ever feel you have to do something crazy just to prove you're really alive?" he asks me.

"Sometimes," I admit with reluctance.

"Me too. I took some kind of stuff last month on a sugar-cube — the guy sold it to me didn't even know for sure what it was. Anyhow, my father's spelled it all out for me, Christ, you can imagine in what detail—all the kinds of genetic and other damage you can get from the hard stuff — so I knew exactly what *could* happen. That's why I took it, really. Just what the hell, why not."

My stomach knots. "What did happen?"

"Nothing much. It was probably cut. Sometimes what they sell is nothing but detergent or whatever. Anyhow I just felt a bit dizzy and my eyes went sort of funny for a couple of days."

"God. I hope it's the last time you do that."

"Probably won't be. The thing is, while I was waiting for something to happen with it, I was alive all over, every damn cell. *Alive.* You see what I mean?"

"But aren't there other — "

"What other ways? You tell me one, Miz. The lever's stuck —

what turns you on? Even bed's a big bore half the time, admit it — booze ditto — and there aren't many books as good as *Dracula*. You know what I do sometimes, just for kicks? I steal stuff from the department stores, or bookstores, or whatever. Sometimes Val helps. How does that grab you, Socrates?"

"I'm shocked," I say helplessly.

"Why?"

"You could be *arrested* — "

"Sure. That's the whole point."

"But — " I look at him, baffled. "You have all the money you want, surely? Your parents — "

"Ah. Ah! My father! Here we are again, eh? Now we're at the point! Mystery solved!"

His repressed but intense excitement disturbs me so much that I have to get up and pretend to look for cigarettes in my coat hanging behind the door.

"And sometimes," he goes on more quietly, "I unlock the drawer in the library where my father keeps this Mauser he got in the war. I open it and look at the two bullets inside. I think about it. I can sit there and think about it for two hours sometimes. Just looking at it." He watches me intently, but I am under control now.

"Rather a silly thing to do, isn't it?"

"Depends whether you think death's silly, or life is. Right?" In one swift movement he is on his feet and slinging on his battered duffle jacket. His face is totally blank, closed, bland.

"Wait, Mike — don't forget your notes."

"Thanks."

"It's going to be a good paper, you know. I'm keen to see the finished product."

He smiles gently. "What a pity you haven't got more guts, Miz. We could have had fun at the dance."

"Sorry, Mike. I know I'm right."

He opens the door without farewells and has already stepped outside when suddenly he turns and comes in again, holding out a folded bit of paper pulled from his jacket pocket.

"Here," he says. "I wrote this for you last night." The door closes behind him. I am left staring down at a foxed bit of lined paper. Written on it in his delicate, spidery hand is a small poem:

She is like still water, shy and cool.
I am aching, thirsty, dry —
And her eyes are gentle as moonlight.

I put it away quickly in a drawer. Reading it again would be unwise.

Archie's broad belly is draped in a linen dishtowel gaily printed with pink and blue mushrooms. Through his half-glasses he directs a menacing glare into the pan where I am sautéing chopped green onions in butter. Since my arrival for the weekly cooking lesson, he has been one great glower, an occasional grunt his only comment on my existence. Apparently I have in some way given offence, though I have no idea when or how. Or at least no intention of letting him know I have.

"I made bread yesterday. Turned out well. I thought your sister might still be here today — I almost didn't come, but I was keen to learn more."

"Went back Wednesday," he grunts.

"Oh."

"Turn that down. Peel the mushrooms. No, no; with your fingers. Now add 'em to the pan. Salt and pepper. Not too much, imbecile."

I have some ado to hide a smile, partly because I am irrationally happy in this crazy kitchen with blue-eyed Percy sitting on top of the door, and partly because, in spite of Archie's histrionic scowl, I suspect he is also enjoying himself. The mixture sizzles in the pan, sending up a delicious smell. So does the browned steak and kidney waiting in a chipped blue bowl. A beautiful red winter sunset looks in at the snow-crusted window.

"Do you often go to the Boule-de-Suif?" I ask.

"Of course not," he says crushingly.

"I enjoyed it. All those people working at being picturesque."

I reach over to turn the heat up and am at once rapped smartly over the knuckles with a wooden spoon. *Wait*, he says fiercely. "Picturesque, indeed. Was that your idea, in that outrageous dress you wore? Or almost wore?"

"Well ... didn't you like it?"

"Like it! Why no civilized man could like such a preposterous rag, miss. Brazen. Shameless. Vulgar. Yes, in extremely bad taste, like everything Picturesque."

"Oh, do you really think so?" I rub my knuckles and try to look suitably crushed.

"Might as well have flaunted yourself in your nightgown," he adds indignantly. "Really, I was surprised at you. Thought you had more sense of — of — "

"Propriety?" I suggest meekly.

"Yes, propriety. Well, what are you standing about for like a weed in a thunderstorm? Add the meat here, and the stock, and let them simmer while you roll out the pastry."

"You know I'll never be able to make pastry."

"And why not, pray?"

"Too much of an idiot."

"Ah. I see you have the common delusion that the word 'idiot' means 'fool'. Hand me that dictionary. No, it's right there, don't ye see, beside the catbasket. Now here we are. From the Greek root *idios* meaning 'own' or 'private'. Hence an idiot is simply a private person, and in that sense of course you're an idiot. Mind you, God knows you're also sometimes a fool. Like most of humanity. Now cut this butter into the flour until your bits are about the size of peas. And furthermore, even a fool can make good pastry if she's got me to teach her how." He claps the big dictionary shut with an air of finality. I bend industriously over the pastry board. After a brief silence he adds, "Well, possibly vulgar was a rather strong word. The — the colour was not entirely unbecoming."

"Thanks," I say, letting the smile bound off its leash. My cheek then receives a floury pinch. Evidently I am now forgiven — though savouring the nature of the crime makes me grin even more broadly than before.

"Now when you've rolled that out and covered the dish—put in an eggcup first to hold the top up—you can stick the whole thing into the oven and come have a nice little glass of chilled rosé by the fire. I've got a new recording of Vivaldi we can listen to before we toss the salad."

A little later, while I blend oil and vinegar with a pinch of mustard at the bottom of a wooden bowl, I judge him in a sufficiently mellow mood to open a subject on the top of my mind.

"Archie, do you find the generation gap a problem between you and your students?"

"Of course I do. And a good thing, too, on the whole. Without the generation gap, what would protect us from each other?"

"Yes, but just the same, the way they think and feel . . . it's so baffling. So different . . . Whatever happened to the idealism of youth, anyhow? And the enthusiasm — the way *we* felt?"

"It's still there, you know. Only in a different shape. Perversely disguised as boredom, more often than not."

"Sometimes it almost scares me, I feel so out of touch with them — so old. Other times it scares me because I'm so involved. Can't be objective. That's not right, is it?"

He darts me a quick blue glance over the top of his glasses.

"Involved, eh? You mean emotionally?"

"Well . . . up to a point." (I judge it far more prudent not to reveal or even hint at what point.)

"Hrumph. Of course it isn't right. Otherwise we'd be seducing the young right and left."

"Or they'd be seducing us."

He gives a brief guffaw that convulses the pink and blue mushrooms. "'If it were easy to be good / And cheap, and plain as evil how' — yes, Auden knew all about it. Oh, I've had female students that kept the old Adam rampant, I can tell you; and they still do, sometimes—though I find those jeans rebarbative—little witches with their long hair . . . oh yes." He pauses, looking reminiscently into space. "Molly was a student of mine, you know. Peculiar relationship, teacher and pupil. Nine parts parental discipline and pride, and the other one pure fire-and-brimstone torture. One of the aspects of pedagogy Charlotte Brontë understood all too well, eh?"

This particular literary reference brings the blood up hot to my cheeks. Damn it, has the old walrus been reading me all along, while I fancied myself so enigmatic? It would be more than disconcerting if he ever broke my private Lucy-code, and began to see the analogies that so absurdly haunt me. However, I find myself unable to resist saying,

"Yes, don't you think—I always have—that the nun Lucy and Paul saw — or thought they saw — was the spectre of their own celibacy. That's why it scared them witless, poor intelligent, scrupulous things."

"Quite right," he says, giving me an approving professorial

look. "And how marvellous, in the end, that the true identity of the nun should be an amorous suitor. And yet you find cretins who claim that Charlotte had no sense of humour."

"Well, in her line of business, she didn't dare let herself have much. Sometimes I think the whole ridiculous business of sex is a bad joke on God's part. Just think how serene and dignified our lives would be without all that."

"And how dull."

"All right, maybe. But there are times when I'd settle for that. Gladly."

"You are telling me either too much or not nearly enough," he grumbles. "Here — where's your glass? — have more wine. That pie is beginning to smell grand. I wonder whether it will turn out to be eatable." He sloshes his own glass generously full, bracing himself just in time to save it from Percy, who has chosen that moment to jump down from the door to his shoulder.

"It's just that the most wildly unsuitable people seem to be attracted to each other, generally. Hardly ever any suitable matches." I think sadly of Louis-Philippe, and George MacKay, and wistfully of Mike with his little poem. I think too of Bill, who, when he came last weekend to the apartment for Sunday brunch, fell asleep with his mouth slightly open while I was washing up; and then went home, yawning drearily, because the antihistamine he was taking for an allergy made him so groggy. It is becoming painfully clear that this kind of thing will always be there to menace The Project. And where does that leave me? — not that I want an answer to that question.

"Just possibly you are wrong about who is suitable," Archie says carelessly. Percy is purring into his ear. The long, dark Siamese tail hangs down the back of his old grey sweater, twitching slightly at the tip, as if in private amusement.

"A nice philosophical point of debate," he adds. "But at the moment, it's time to take the pie out." Just then the front doorbell peals loudly. He moves off to answer it, complete with Percy, the mushroom apron, and his wineglass, declaiming floridly as he goes,

> "Will his name be Love,
> And all his talk be crazy?
> Or will his name be Death
> And his message easy?"

A moment later Molly comes into the kitchen, followed by Harry, with Archie and the cat bringing up the rear. Molly's cheeks are rosy under the white fur of a pretty winter hat, and her grey eyes are sharp as a bird's.

"Well, what in the ever-lovin' world is going on here?" she cries.

"Archie is giving me cooking lessons," I explain, with a demonstrative gesture at the rolling pin and other clutter on the table. But I am aware this really explains nothing.

"And is that what you call it, by all that's wonderful!" she says, looking at him.

"Yes, Lady Teazle, by all that's damnable," says Archie. "Stay and sample the product, why don't you? Plenty for four."

"No, thanks, Archie; we're on our way to Emma's for a meal. And thin pickings it may turn out to be—have you heard she's on the grapefruit diet? We just dropped by to borrow your copy of Pacey, if you don't mind—I can't seem to find mine anywhere at home—though it's probably right there, buried under all those *mountains* of Harry's mimeographs."

"All my fault, of course," says Harry patiently. He holds out a mittened hand to Percy, who promptly stalks away from him in the insulting way cats have, with his tail straight up in the air.

Archie bestows a glass of wine on both of them, and then with a casual air of mastery produces Pacey's book from under a potted fern on the windowsill. I make a few ineffectual attempts to dust flour off my crumpled apron and out of my hair. Molly as usual looks immaculate as a new doll in her long, crisp green dress. An extravagantly long white muffler is wound around her neck and hangs down nearly to her heels, accentuating her littleness and her beautiful, narrow shape. Her face is smooth and fresh, but for some reason her gaiety seems to fade as she looks around the warm room and sips her wine.

"You really ought to taste this pie," Archie is urging, after he has broken off a bit of the crust and munched it critically. "This woman actually has the root of the matter in her, I do believe. The pastry is positively quite edible."

"'The edible woman'," says Molly. There is mockery in her voice and in the glance she throws me, and it stings like a light slap. I thought she liked me. I like her . . . admire her; but she . . . I turn away to hide my ridiculous face in a busy tidying-up.

"Thanks, Archie, but we've got to run. Come on, Harry, we're going to be late. Thanks for the Pacey—return it on Monday. So long Willydoyle." She hands me her empty glass and, tossing back the trailing end of her muffler, makes an effective exit. I busy myself scraping up pastry-scraps and try to push off a cloud of motiveless depression; but Archie comes back from the door briskly, whistling, apparently in the highest heart.

It snows again on Department-meeting day. White chalk flakes dropping thickly from a blackboard sky. The grey February snow piled below in the streets receives them with resignation. The light is wan in our chilly attic room, where the one radiator knocks and spits irritably but gives little heat. Yet when we're assembled around the oak table, with all the student representatives there in force, we form quite a crowd. Mike is there with his heavy-faced girl, who looks bored. Emma arrives, enormous in a muskrat coat (the grapefruit diet has had no visible effect). Bill hurries in late, nodding apologetically to Archie at the head of the table, and takes a chair near the door.

The first item of business concerns some complicated entanglement of the exam schedule. I find it hard even to follow the problem, much less contribute any helpful solution. My mind persists in wandering off to focus on irrelevancies like Archie's new and florid neckscarf, or the silver bangles tinkling on Molly's wrist as she slides a note across to Harry. Ruth Pinsky is falling asleep. Her dark eyelashes droop lower and lower; her head sinks, showing the curly whorl on the crown; she leans more and more perilously to the right, where Bill's tweed shoulder looms. He is shading a series of profiled faces on an old envelope and notices nothing. Just as Ruthie is nearly on him, Emma prods her sharply with a pencil and she sits upright abruptly with a comic little snort. I have a brief coughing fit into my handkerchief.

The hands of my watch crawl around. I mentally write another Jamwaddle story for Dougie, who now has mumps, to the keen exasperation of Lou — as if the poor child could easily have avoided mumps if he weren't bent on being difficult. She has not mentioned my coming up to Toronto for the Easter break. Probably it would be a bad time for a visit: she seems to be having a very uncomfortable pregnancy, poor thing. I wonder whether I could afford to go south for a few days ... all this eternal snow does weigh down the spirit.

The meeting, when I tune it in again, now seems to be about delegates to some conference or other in Winnipeg. Nobody wants to go there, including me. Ruth is dozing off again. It's nearly four-thirty. My left foot is buzzing with pins and needles. Now we are discussing funds for a student literary magazine. Mike is very alert and vocal in the discussion, though I wish he would learn to address the chair properly, and avoid beginning sentences with the word "like". Still, he is full of ideas about the student quarterly, some of them extremely practical and constructive, and he is listened to with respect. His square-built girl watches him worshippingly. I can't remember her name — Sandra?—no. Victoria? Virginia would be lovely in April, and the Porsche is running well ... wouldn't it be wonderful if Bill ... I wonder whether by any chance he might ...

Two or three of the students slip away. It's after five o'clock, and these hard chairs begin to numb you after the second hour, in the most fundamental way. But Archie is pawing through papers, muttering to himself as he looks for something. Evidently the meeting isn't over yet. Molly, who has slung on her shoulder-bag and half risen, now sinks back with a sigh. Harry is deep in a murmured conference with one of the students and does not look up when Archie at last produces the paper he's been looking for, and addresses us.

"Ladies and gentlemen, I have received a directive of some interest from the Board of Governors, relating to Hiring and Tenure."

All the restless shuffling immediately stops. Harry turns his head quickly to face the head of the table.

"It reads as follows. 'All matters relating to Hiring and Tenure at Cartier College, in those departments where full-time staff exceed seven in number, will from this date be dealt with by a committee consisting of the Vice-Principal, two members of the Board of Governors, the Deans of both Faculties, and the Chairman of each department directly concerned, plus one of his immediate colleagues, to be chosen by him.'"

"*What!*" bursts out Molly incredulously.

"Departments with more than seven — that's only Maths, French, and us. Surprise, surprise."

"It's a hatchet job — "

"Archie, would you be good enough to read that again," asks Harry, cutting off with authority the rising tide of voices.

Archie reads it again, without expression. No longer at all

tempted to wander, my attention is focussed sharply on Harry's bearded face. It is hard to be sure, but I could swear I saw relief in his eyes when the directive was first read. There is now a brief silence. The radiator gives a light hiss, like the serpent in Eden.

"Well, that's that," says Harry bitterly. "I presume there's nothing to stop them legislating a monstrosity like that, to choke off student power." His voice is calm, almost satisfied.

"There *is* something to stop them," says Mike fiercely. "*Us.*"

Harry shakes his head. He looks heavy with shock; yet I can't forget the look that flashed into his face a moment ago when he was off guard.

Ruth Pinsky, with an apologetic glance at her watch, quietly leaves the room with one of her assistants. They have evening classes to meet soon.

"Cunning of Archie to keep this little item to the last," mutters Bill, leaning close to my ear. "He's learning."

"Why can't we just inform the Board we have our own Hiring and Tenure Committee, duly elected — the question is actually a legal one, isn't it — does anybody know where we can get expert advice?"

"Yes, the college must have a constitution or something."

"It's the most shameless set of brass knuckles I ever — "

"Somebody ought to get hold of the press."

In all this, Harry takes no part. He sits there in silence, his face quite impassive, only shaking his head from time to time like someone teased by flies.

"I must admit I see no way we can refuse to recognize the authority of the Board," says Archie, frowning and rubbing one hand through the mane of his grey hair.

"Like it's perfectly simple," says Mike urgently. "We just refuse. They can't ram this down our throats. We'll paralyse the place. Boycott lectures. Sit in. All of us — we're all in this, right?" He looks eagerly at Harry, who lifts one shoulder in a shrug. It is disturbing to see the shadow of doubt fall across Mike's eyes.

"Look, man, you're *with* us, right?" he demands, his voice cracking into an adolescent treble. "You can't for one second be thinking of *giving in*? After all you've done to get student parity this far? We're right behind you — you can't be going to quit now, for God's sake."

"Mike — not now. We can talk strategy later. There's no point, really, saying any more now."

"I quite agree," says Archie. "Novel as that may seem to some of you. Motion to adjourn, anyone? Right. The quondam Hiring and Tenure Committee may want to meet informally soon—shall we say Wednesday at five, in my office?"

The meeting then disintegrates noisily. Molly is silent; she looks depressed and tired; but everyone else is loud with talk as they scrape back the heavy chairs and get into their coats. Mike and the two students who are left, all talking excitedly, are close at Harry's heels as he leaves.

"Poor bugger," Bill says quietly to me as we go downstairs. "He's got his confrontation now, for sure. I wonder what he'll do."

"Well, as he said himself, there may be nothing he can do."

"He could maybe save himself here, if he drops the student cause now. Question is whether he actually *can* drop it."

"You think he really could? Save himself, I mean?"

"I said maybe. God, I wouldn't want to be him."

For the rest of the week, a portentous air of underground political activity pervades the building. People huddle together having low-voiced conferences in a secretive sort of way, as if they are afraid a spy might read their lips. Even a visit to the Ladies can become fraught with significance: I find Emma and Molly in there one morning having a hissing quarrel.

Most of these negotiations tend to be suspended as soon as I appear. Perhaps my colleagues share Mother's view that I have no discretion. Or perhaps I'm thought to be already committed to either the radicals or the reactionaries, though the truth is I'm uneasily on the fence. Bill is perched on it with me, though far more comfortably. "I simply refuse to be involved," he says firmly. "I haven't got the energy."

But one way or another, all my biorhythms seem to be in a state of agitation. I actually *lose* a large batch of test-papers. (They turn up later at the bottom of my Out tray; but not till after I've spent a frantic day searching for them.) I stumble on an icy curbstone and twist my ankle. It swells. Lou gives my nerves a further twist by phoning on Sunday night to demand without preamble, "Are you all right?"

"Sure I am. Why? Aren't you?"

"Willy, for God's sake the papers here are full of Quebec — it sounds as if the damn place is about to blow up in some kind of crazy revolution. It's only a matter of time, according to the *Globe*. And we were at a cocktail party this afternoon where we met this chap from Montreal, he's a Q.C., and when I asked him about the situation there, he took a huge gulp of vodka and said, 'I *think* the police will stay loyal.' Well, I mean it's not exactly reassuring, is it? What a place to be living! Of course I *told* you at the time, only you never listen. And that poor night-watchman that got blown up by terrorists; that Army place is right near your apartment, isn't it?"

"No, no; it's at least a mile away."

"But aren't you terrified?"

"No," I say in some surprise, because if anyone has a talent for being terrified it's me. "Nobody here is. Nobody I know, anyway. The other day, it's true, I came into the lobby downstairs and there was a cop talking to our janitor. But they were having a big laugh. Afterward I asked Louis-Philippe what was going on, and he said, 'They're try to fin' these guys that plant the bomb at the recruiting centre. Looking for a frien' of mine, in fact, he belong to the same . . . club. They'll never find him, mees.' He seemed to think it was all a joke."

"But the watchman died for real, Willy. And they keep on phoning in bomb threats, don't they, to schools and things? And you're at a school. It's awful. I'd be worried sick, in your shoes."

"Well, I'm not. I tell you, there's nothing to worry about. It's only a little band of nuts. Everybody tells me the French Canadians are ninety-nine per cent middle-class conservatives. Don't believe all these alarmists. The trouble with us Wasps is that we're too nervous."

I don't bother to tell Lou that Louis-Philippe, after the cop left, rode up with me in the elevator and made me nervous, though not politically. He leaned a hairy wrist on the Stop button at my floor to keep the doors shut while his eyes slid over me in that lazy, arrogant way he has.

"Your — fridge okay now?" he asked.

"Yes, thanks. Perfectly okay."

"Maybe I better check."

"Don't bother, thanks. And open the door, please."

He grinned. "You got your fridge built in, mees. Like all *les Anglaises*. Or you pretend. Eh? I think you pretend."

"Would you like me to press the Alarm button?"

He laughed. "Okay, mees. *Au revoir*." And the doors slid open, allowing me to bolt like a rabbit into my own hole.

But none of this has a soothing effect. Far from it. Later that evening, when the weekly fight erupts next door, I face the wall and yell at the top of my lungs. "Cut that out!" There is a balm-like quiet for the rest of the night. I'm impressed by my own daring, but I still can't sleep till daybreak.

I go to my office at eight-thirty to correct papers. But even at that hour, the corridors are full of sibilant whispers and furtively closing doors. When I go to class, the students are restless, and their muttered ground swell of private chat runs through my whole lecture on George Eliot.

Wearily I plod back to the office after lunch, my ankle throbbing. There is still a pile of work on my desk to get through. It is a brilliant day, with a sky smooth and blue as fresh enamel. Here and there a little snow has actually melted, leaving a wet patch of earth to look hopefully up at the sun. Yet the pavements are still sealed under inches of black ice, and spring seems like only an unfounded rumour.

At the desk I pin myself to work. Gradually the building hushes and empties. The sun drops low. I switch on my gooseneck lamp. After the papers are done, I get some coffee and begin to make notes on *Felix Holt, Radical*, thinking with satisfaction, 'How's this for Relevance, kids, to use one of your favourite words?' The office is quiet and cosy in the lamplight as I scrawl away.

But suddenly I become aware of a confused and growing uproar outside—banging, shouts, many voices—and I jump up in alarm to peer through my window. My office faces a side-street, and all the narrow angle of vision reveals is what seems to be a ragged sort of procession passing the front of the building with banners. A motorcycle cop putters along at the rear, but the sight of him is not really reassuring. The noise swells until it seems to be actually inside the building. "*You're* in a school," says Lou's voice. My heart begins to thump unpleasantly. The house is invaded; feet are thundering up the stairs and pounding along the halls. A nearby blast of sound like the brass voice of a trumpet makes me jump. Voices shout to each other in French. I stand near my closed door, wondering what to do—lock it? Pull on my coat and run outside? What on earth can they be doing — what is it all about? "Aren't you terrified?" Yes, Lou, I am.

A random kick lands against my door, but the running feet, after discovering that this corridor is blind, now recede in the distance, thumping their way to the top floor. Apparently they are not looking for me personally, which is some comfort, though not much. A moment later I hear the whole cavalcade pouring downstairs again and outside.

Back at the window I glimpse the dishevelled procession on the move again. By now I have recovered enough of my scattered wits to notice that many of the marchers wear the blue tuque of the Université de Montréal. A moment later there slides into my angle of vision a group flourishing in triumph the orange flag of Cartier College that normally flies from the absurd little cupola on top of this house.

Taking a deep breath, I sit down. A student prank. This is Carnival Week. But oh, those biorhythms.

Next morning I wake up with a headache for which I hold the Quebec separatist movement entirely responsible. All day long the pain nags with mounting insistence. By three in the afternoon, when my last class of the day ends, my skull feels too tight, my eyes itch, and from time to time all my skin roughens with goosebumps. I make the best of my way home, thanking God, for once with genuine fervour, that it is Friday. Archie has earlier cancelled our weekly cooking lesson in order to straighten out a tax problem downtown—"with someone in Infernal Revenue, as my sister would call it".

I spend Saturday in bed, full of aspirin, the headache still throbbing like jungle drums. By Sunday morning it has vanished; but when I reach out a bare arm for my slippers, the morning sun reveals a dense rash of red pinpoints from wrist to shoulder. A year ago I saw the same tattoo on Dougie's silky cheeks. Measles. It's been going around among the students. How ridiculous. And uncomfortable, as I continue to discover.

"Hullo, Bill. Are you feeling okay?"

"Yes, why?"

"Because I've got the measles."

"Christ, Willy."

"Temperature's a hundred and two," I add, not without pride. Bill is always impressed by medical details.

"How long does it take to incubate?"

I know what's worrying him. A few days ago we spent the evening together, parting after a modest kiss and cuddle. This agreeable (and I trust, hopeful) habit is gradually becoming more or less regular with us. And who could possibly regard it as the least risky, in the normal course of things? But for us, it would seem, nothing is really easy.

"Oh, I wouldn't worry about it if I were you. Surely you had measles as a child. Nearly everybody does."

"I can't remember. When I call Mum tonight, I'll ask her if I ever had it. God, I hope the answer is yes. Measles I *don't* need."

Shortly after this he hangs up, as if afraid the virus might somehow get to him through the telephone wires. No use mentioning to him that there's little to eat in my fridge except a frozen pizza and a tag-end of bacon, neither of them even remotely tempting. He will not come near the apartment until it and I are purified, and well I know it. "What can't be cured must be endured," Mother used to say, and that goes for our friends as much as our diseases. Just the same, I feel better after talking to him.

When Lou hears my news, she giggles unfeelingly. "How silly, at your age," she says.

"Well, it's not all that damn funny. I'm covered with this hideous rash. It's even between my toes. Itching like hell."

"Oh, it will be gone in a few days. Cheer up."

I would if I could; but it isn't easy. Monday, Tuesday, crawl away. On Wednesday I disguise myself in dark glasses and a large headscarf to shop for groceries and calamine lotion. My legs feel hollow and the light hurts my eyes; I'm glad to get home. On the way in, I help myself to the top copy of a pile of *Stars* that has accumulated on my neighbours' doormat. The old couple must be in Florida, or perhaps in a pair of His and Her straitjackets.

For something to do I stretch out for a skim of the news. And there on Page Two is a headline that brings me bolt upright in a hurry. "Power Struggle at Cartier. Instructor Fights Dismissal Threat." There is a pop-eyed picture of Harry Innis, looking either terrified or militant, it's hard to be sure which. According to the article, he has hired a lawyer and intends to take the college to court for attempting to restrict his civil liberties. He is quoted as saying that the principles of academic freedom are also at stake, threatened by "bigoted, arrogant, and fundamentally ignorant men like Principal Fraser, a puppet of St. James Street". The last paragraph of the article describes student support for Harry and his cause as "an almost crusading enthusiasm". Mention is also made of widespread faculty sympathy, and the support of "his devoted wife, Molly".

"Well!" I say seconds later to Bill. "Have you seen tonight's paper?"

"Heady stuff, eh? That reporter is just a part-timer — a kid himself—but I wonder how on earth the thing ever got by, it's so terrifically pro-Harry. The Principal has issued a statement, you know — we all got a copy in our mail this morning. It will be in tomorrow's *Star* for sure. Announcing that Harry is fired, by unanimous vote of the new Hiring and Tenure boys. So there'll be lots of fireworks. By the way, Mum says I had measles when I was six; but you can get it twice. She's got a touch of phlebitis; I may just fly down there this weekend to see how she's getting on. You feeling better? Good. Be in touch later."

I am restless after this, and long to get back to work, but the rash lingers and I have to accept my leper's isolation over the weekend. On Sunday evening I'm surprised to receive a phone call from Archie — my first. He regards Mr. Bell's device with truculent suspicion and dislike.

"I hear you have contracted a children's disease." His resonant voice crackles out of the receiver with such energy I have to hold the phone away from my ear.

"Yes, but I'm over it now."

"Back to work tomorrow?"

"Oh yes."

"That's why I called. You've been following this affair of Harry's, have you? The fact is, I hear we can expect trouble here tomorrow. The students are planning to boycott classes. Or so the rumour goes. I'm phoning to ask everybody in the department to meet classes just as usual. If so much as one student turns up for the lecture, he should see you there. But of course if any attempt is made to interfere with you—heckling, let's say, or some attempt to lock or bar you from the room — of course in such a case you will just withdraw with dignity. The point is I'd like everybody to report for work as usual, to make it quite clear we won't accept intimidation. As for me, I very much hope somebody will try to restrain me from giving my lecture on *Macbeth*. It would give me

the liveliest pleasure personally to dislocate anyone so misguided
as to try. I boxed for my college, you know."

"For pity's sake, Archie. What happened to withdrawing with
dignity?"

"That," he says, "is my advice to you, not me, miss. You are
aware, I presume, of the difference in our age, if not our sex."

"*Vividly*," I assure him through a wide grin.

"I'll probably see you tomorrow. In any case, the lesson in Eggs
Benedict can take place Friday evening, if you like."

"I like. In fact, nothing could keep me away."

It must be my father's genes that make the idea of a real scrap so
stimulating. I am dressed at seven and ready for any amount or
kind of confrontation at Cartier. Dad was as combative as a
terrier, though not much bigger than one, and his best stories had
to do with various colourful hand-to-hand combats. One was with
a coal carter beating his horse on a steep hill. Another, less
altruistic, was a punch-up with an Irishman in a tavern who said
something uncomplimentary about Winston Churchill. But my
favourite was an encounter with a pompous little department
manager (in the days when Dad sold paint). On that occasion he
lifted up the manager by the coat collar and seat of the pants and
dropped him into a large wastebin. That's the way he told it,
anyhow. And I'm quite willing this morning to believe him. How
difficult it must have been for Gerald Wellesley Doyle, when you
think of it, to be married to a Quietist like Mother. It almost makes
you wonder whether things would have been better between
them if she could have brought herself, just once, to have a low
brawl with him. Maybe refinement, dignity, and restraint are not
as wholly desirable as they might be — not in life, anyway, as
distinct from in fiction. Perhaps Mother and I both read too much
Trollope and Thackeray. It's a rather disquieting thought.

The snow crunches underfoot as I walk briskly up the street to
the classroom building. I am ready for anything—revolutionaries
at the door — security guards — riot police — but rather to my
regret, I find everything absolutely normal. The halls are quiet.
The students circulate as usual. The doors of my classroom stand
open wide. A quick survey from behind the lectern shows that
most of my students are present, though Mike and his big-
bottomed girl are not there. The class sits more quietly than usual,

clipboards laid out, pens at the ready. They eye me demurely. My rather dull lecture on George Eliot and the concept of Duty proceeds in respectful silence, without incident of any kind.

Much deflated, and inclined to be rather cross with Archie (and even Dad), I gather up my books and set out for the office. On the steps I fall in with Ruth Pinsky and we walk uphill together in the blaze of a cold sun. But as we come nearer to the house, she touches my arm with her gloved hand and says, "Look!"

Then I see that the doorway is blocked by a solid knot of students hoisting placards. These have been professionally printed, in big red letters on white, with slogans like "Sit-In for Civil Liberty", "Students for Democracy", and "Back Innis and the L.S.A.".

"For God's sake," says Ruth. "They're occupying the building. All that stuff about a lecture boycott was a blind."

"Come on," I say, pushing with energy through a loose group of spectators. "Let's find out the score."

"Not me," she says, and drops behind. But I march vigorously up the path and face the group barring the doorway.

"What's going on here, lads?" I demand with academic severity.

One or two of them, whom I know, smile at me cheerfully. Several are chewing gum. They are all eager to provide information.

"We're sitting in. The L.S.A. occupied the building at six this morning."

"Yeah — we stay till Innis is reinstated. Nobody goes in till Fraser gets his head together. They got food, sleeping bags — we got shifts set up — like we can stay here for months if we have to."

"Lots of sympathizers in there from faculty, too, you know. And one of the Math professors just sent in fifty coffees for us."

"I suppose Mike Armstrong is in there with the other colonels?"

"Yup. We can put you down for a shift or two?"

"You can not."

"Then do you mind getting out of the way here. Look, you guys — look — photographers! Christ, this is great. Please move out of the way, Miss Doyle. Hold your signs up high, guys."

I decamp without delay, having no ambition to see my picture in the papers. The loose aggregate of onlookers has by now thickened into a small crowd, and it grows as the pressmen level their bulky cameras at the house. As I edge away from the path I suddenly find Bill beside me among the spectators. His head, all but a heavy frown, is retracted behind the wings of his turned-up coat collar.

"Hi, Willy. Better now? What do you think of this caper? They won't let me in to my office. Damn it, they're so hot on human rights, what about mine? Well, up to now I've been neutral. Now I know who I'm neutral *against*."

"Come on, let's get some coffee at the Hideaway," I suggest. But at that moment a little whirl of excitement boils through the crowd. Five police cars have turned into the street and pulled up opposite us. A score or so of large men, thick in their winter uniforms, get out and hitch up their holsters in a businesslike way. Their brass buttons wink in the sun. They group together briefly, and then, at a signal from one of them, march heavily up the path to the front door. Necks crane to see the action. Someone pushes me. A brief and quiet colloquy takes place at the door. We can hear voices, but not what is said. Then suddenly a scuffle breaks out. A student shoves violently past me, hurling his placard like a lance into the deep snow. Several others are then escorted down the path, each in the firm grip of a policemen. They are put into a police van that has just parked behind the patrol cars.

"Fascists!" a young voice yells.

"Pigs!"

"Come on, you guys — get those doors!"

But support is wavering and scattered. The police now have control. They disappear inside the building, leaving two of the burliest posted at the entrance. Swaying, fascinated, the crowd watches in silence. The pressmen, who have been clicking away avidly, wait too. A mobile TV unit has now drawn up to add to the congestion in the road. There is a long pause. "Oh, the hell with it; my feet are cold," says Bill. "I'm going home." He disappears.

All the rest of us linger. It's as close as most of us will ever get to watching history happen. And before long we are rewarded. A straggle of students with backpacks begins to file out of the front door. They are not under escort; the police at the door barely glance at them, and they seem in effect to disappear without trace among the crowd. Last of the group is a young woman in a long, hooded cape. She comes out alone and walks quickly away — surely it must be Molly, but she has kept her face hidden.

Another pause follows. Then a pair of uniformed men emerge

abreast in the doorway. Slung between them like a hammock is a big, dark girl in jeans and a maxi-coat that drags on the snow. Yes, I recognize the bottom. Mike's girl. One after another of the students is hoisted out of the building in the same way, and deposited in the waiting van. Mike's long legs dangle, awkward as a lamb's, and his jacket is torn, but he looks gloriously happy: his face is one huge smile. The others hang limp in the grip of authority, their faces impassive. The police who carry them pant and perspire. In the still crowd I can hear their leather accoutrements squeak and their big boots crunch the snow.

Dramatically last of all, Harry Innis is carried out, arms and legs spread-eagled in the grasp of two cops. By some triumph of character or conviction he manages to appear dignified in spite of this ludicrous posture. I stare at him curiously. In his bearded face there is the calm look of a man fulfilled. All round him the cameras whirr and click. One of the policemen carrying him stumbles and mutters *"Calice!"*, but he and his colleague wear indulgent half-smiles. This is a day's work to them, not destiny unfolding. A sort of dim and perhaps ironic cheer goes up from what is left of the crowd, which has already begun to scatter as people do when a parade is over.

SEVEN

Theft

WHEN MY BUZZER SOUNDS, just after nine in the evening, I am startled; even mildly alarmed. I'm not expecting anyone. And since yesterday's episode at Cartier, my appetite for combat has somehow quite disappeared, and the idea of a stranger at the door puts me into a silly flutter of indecision. Shall I answer it or not? In the end, however, I can't bear to be left wondering who is there; so I go and squint through the peephole, feeling ridiculous. At first, owing to a poor choice of angle, I can see nothing but the opposite wall of the corridor. Then I see the top third of someone's head in a white fur hat. Molly Pratt's grey eyes meet mine. Hurriedly I unbolt the door.

"Come in, Molly. Sorry I was slow to answer ... "

Without smiling, Molly pulls off her boots and steps inside shoeless, in which state she looks no taller than a child. As she moves past me, taking off the fur hat, I catch a whiff not only of her musky perfume but of whiskey. With my experience I know that odour of demolition only too well.

"Come in and sit down, do. I'm so glad you're here. What can I get you?—coffee? A drink?" She says nothing at all, but makes for the sofa while I grope for small talk. "Nice of you to drop in," I add, wondering even as I say so whether it really is or not. Her face, usually so alight and alive, is sombre, almost grim. And I notice with a little shock that she has had all her lovely long hair cut short, cropped like a little boy's, with a fringe falling across the

128

forehead. It makes her look startlingly different — bolder, harder, older, though not less attractive.

"Rye, if you have it, with a bit of water," she says economically.

Luckily I have recently acquired a small bottle of rye; Bill sometimes prefers it to gin. I bring in a tray with two glasses, the stiff ginger-ale being for me, and she at once takes a long swallow from hers.

"Tell me what's been happening, Molly."

"Well, I've had a somewhat mind-bending day."

"Yes, I suppose.... How's Harry?"

"In jail."

"Really? But it said in this morning's paper they were all released on bail."

"He wasn't. Do you know what those bastards set his bail at? Fifteen thousand dollars. That's Fraser's work, of course. They know damn well we can't raise that kind of money. Not in a hurry, anyhow. Furthermore, Harry's being awkward. Says he won't accept bail money: he'd rather wait for trial in Bordeaux. I saw him this afternoon. He's got a huge bruise on his cheekbone and one eye swollen tight shut."

"Oh, Molly."

"He told me how it happened. 'I called one of the fuzz a bugger for shoving me, and immediately after that I fell downstairs.' That's what he said, with this big meathead cop sitting right near us picking his nose." She pauses to take another thirsty gulp of her drink. "Well, of course none of this is doing Harry any particular good. He's talking now about getting right out of the western world, going to China. He says it's the freest country in the world. And of course he's just asked for a lot of this mess. I mean, letting that reporter quote him about Fraser being ignorant and bigoted—I begged him not to do that, but ... And then his father calls up last night from Utah and cries over the phone, as if *I* could have prevented it all. Well, I wasn't even able to get much *sense* out of Harry today, and that's the truth."

"Oh, dear."

"Well, being beaten up by the arm of the law doesn't help anybody to think straight."

"No, I'm sure it doesn't."

"Of course he's been moving farther and farther left for a long time now. Ever since the start of term. It's really been getting to him that freedom or justice simply don't exist here, whether it's on campus, or in Quebec, or in the whole of North America. And the smug hypocrisy of the Establishment is enough to make anybody vomit that knows how they really operate." She puts down her empty glass with a clack. "Thanks, I'd love another. Christ, I'm wound so tight I could take off like a rocket. Where's your john? Be back in a minute."

Off she goes, slim as a boy in her tailored white shirt and black trousers. I have never seen her dressed like this before. The trousers are very becoming.

"Then I went downtown to see our lawyer. One of those French Canadians who speak better English than we do. Brilliant guy. He's the one who won that big case for the waterfront union — you know — I forget their name — last year. He says Harry's got a perfect case against Cartier. They'll have to give him his job back or pay a big whack of compensation money. And of course he also promised to raise hell about Harry's black eye, though I don't know what good that'll do."

"Well, it's something, I suppose."

"Sure. But the point is, can you see Harry getting another academic appointment after this? Like hell you can. There's the c.a.u.t. of course; but by the time we get his appeal through their committees, and his actions vindicated, and all that, he'll be *forty*. I mean, who's got forever?"

"Nobody," I murmur soothingly. She is indeed very tightly wound, and the rye seems to be having anything but a tranquillizing effect. Her hand trembles so much as she lifts her glass that the ice in it rattles.

"Trouble is, I don't really like LaSalle," she says. "The lawyer. I don't even, actually, trust him. How can you trust a guy who wears a bow tie?" With a malicious little smile she stretches out her legs to prop her feet on the coffee table. "No old girl of Miss Edgar's ever trusts a man in a bow tie. Best boarding school in town. What training. Never trust *any* man in *any* tie. They're only any good with their clothes off, men. That's what we didn't learn at Miss E.'s. Only this guy LaSalle has little tiny eyes and he takes your pants off with them — you know."

"I know."

She draws a long sigh. For a moment there is silence.

"Will you try to raise bail for Harry, then?" I ask.

"Yes, I guess so. He can't stay in that awful place out of sheer bloody-mindedness. I guess we can raise the money somehow. His people are farmers, poor as fleas; but my father might help a bit. Only, he remarried last year and they're living on pensions in a little apartment in the Bahamas. They haven't got much, actually."

"And your mother ... ?"

"Mum cancelled herself with a lot of sleeping pills when I was fourteen."

"—Look, Molly, I could help. I've had a lump of cash just sitting around ever since last summer when I sold our old house in Rosedale. So don't hesitate — I'd be glad — "

She looks at me. "Willy, do you really mean that?"

"Of course, or I wouldn't say it."

Her hand slides across the sofa and slips into mine. It is a cold, small hand, with frail little bones, and it grips as if it wanted help, though exactly what it is asking for is difficult to say.

"Can I have another drink, Willydoyle? Rich Willydoyle?"

"Sure." But out in the kitchen I make it a very weak one. And I set the coffeepot on the stove in readiness. Some of her tension seems to have transferred itself to me, and everything I touch rattles and clatters. When I get back to the sitting room, I find she has stretched out at full length on the sofa with her hands behind her cropped head. Her eyes are closed, but she is still talking too much and too fast.

"Thank God for now, anyway," she says. "For being a woman now, and not fifty years ago. I am *completely* happy, you know, Willy."

"Are you?"

"Of course I am. No frustrations. No hangups. I've got my freedom, my own salary, my profession, my status as a person ... "

"And on top of all that, you've got Harry."

I intend no irony, but she frowns.

"Yes. Well, actually — for a while there, I had quite a thing going for him—but lately, I don't know, it's been wearing off a bit. Don't know why, really. He's pressuring his wife for a divorce. He wanted me to have—I mean he wants kids and all that. In a few years. Only I don't know—I think I'll hang onto my freedom. I've sort of *had* marriage. Last night, for instance, I ran into an old friend—actually a guy I lived with for a while after John—and we went dancing. I mean, you must admit it's great to be free."

"Great," I agree, trying to sound enthusiastic.

Her glass is empty again. "Just one more little smash, please, and then I'll go home. You probably go to bed at ten and get up early to eat wheat germ."

"What makes you think that?"

"Oh, Bill's influence, maybe." She giggles briefly. "He's very hot on wheat germ, Billy Boy."

I would like very much to ask, "How do you know?" but before I can say it she has gone on.

"What I'd like to do this summer is go to Greece and see all those gorgeous islands. There are some good, cheap tours, you know. Maybe you'd like to come with me. More fun than clammy old Cape Cod, which is Harry's idea of bliss. Wouldn't it be great, all that sun and old stone and the blue sea ... " She sits up to receive the new drink. This time I have made it almost non-alcoholic because dark rings have formed under her eyes and her voice has slowed down as if it weighed too much to move easily.

"We could do any damn thing we wanted to, Willy. I don't think you realize that. You have to use your freedom. Live it. Right? We don't even really need men any more."

I knit my fingers together and frown at the floor. Without wanting to, I think of my mother's imprisonment by convention, and of my own "liberated" life, sealed inside a loneliness without date or boundaries. Molly leans forward, her dark head in her hands. What has she come here for? Does she know, herself? Do I dare to guess? The newly exposed nape of her white neck looks tender and vulnerable. I would like to touch it. To —

"God, I'm really exhausted. Also stoned out of my mind. Forgive me, Willy; I've got to go before I pass completely out. Could you be an angel and call me a cab?"

"I'll do better—I'll run you home. Come and get your coat and things." It turns out that she cannot negotiate her feet into the boots until I sit her on the floor and put them on for her. She puts her own hat on, after a fashion, muttering to it, "St. James Street puppet." In the car she falls asleep and I have some ado to get her up the long stairs to her apartment and open the door with her key. She leans against the wall watching my efforts with a drowsy smile.

"Now can you manage?" I ask, steering her inside.

"Yes, yes, yes. I can manage. You're a good man, Charlie Brown."

"Give me a ring, Molly, whenever you like, about that bail business."

"All righty. Bye-bye."

She is still smiling when I close the door; but I don't feel much amused. Nor did Lucy find much to laugh at when she played a man's role but kept her skirts on. In fact, she wisely resolved never to act the male again, on the grounds that she enjoyed it too much, and it might prove dangerous. And how right she was.

Returning from a brief sortie to the library the next afternoon, I am somewhat taken aback to find my office door ajar, with a pungent eddy of smoke drifting through the aperture. In my swivel chair sits a large masculine form, tilted back at a perilous angle.

"Oh, it's you, Archie."

"Do you always leave your office door open, miss? Have you never heard of theft?"

"I have nothing anybody would steal."

He sits up, drawing a faint shriek from the chair, and eyes me searchingly over the stub of his cigar. "Depressed? So am I. It's the weather. First thaw always does it. Sit down. Have you got your exam paper ready for the novel course?"

"Afraid not."

"Today's the deadline, you know. Now we have all these clever machines it takes them much longer to print the papers. Why aren't you ready?"

"Sorry. It's been hard to work lately."

"Well, you're not the only one to find it so," he says with severity. "Whole department's by the ears. Emma's not speaking to Molly. Harry is still incarcerated. Bill thinks he has shingles. As for the old man — 'He wept that he was ever born / And he had reasons.' Eh?"

"Shingles! Poor Bill."

He directs a fierce scowl at me. "I have just had the verbal equivalent, namely a monumentally unpleasant interview with the Principal. He appears to feel that recent developments can all be directly traced to my mismanagement. My evil influence. My incompetence. He touched at length on all these points."

"Well, that was damned unfair of him. To put it mildly."

"Of course he's loathed me for years. He's a profoundly dis-
honest man. Whereas I, whatever else can be said of me, am at
least honest. God knows I have my sins, but trickery, treachery,
fraud, and deceit are not among them. Every word Harry was
foolish enough to say about him for publication is true. And of
course you realize that Harry's case is sound. His judgement is
quite another matter. There I can't support him. Nor do I *like* the
man. But I believe he's acted within his rights — his legal rights.
When I told Fraser so, he bared his teeth at me in that vulpine
smile of his, and said that loyalty to a junior colleague was no
doubt highly commendable in a chairman. Freely translated, that
means my own appointment as chairman will probably not be
renewed this spring." With a gloomy flourish he stubs out the
cigar and throws himself back in the chair again.

"But that's outrageous!"

"Ah well. I don't really care, you know. Never really liked
administrative chores. And I'm getting near retirement. It's time
somebody younger took over." He eyes me sidelong.

"Oh, rubbish," I say briskly.

"Not at all, miss. But it cuts rather near the bone, just the same,
Fraser's view. As a father-figure I've certainly been a bit of a dud
lately. I've had many talks with Harry, you know, particularly
during this year; but I've completely failed to convince him some
of his more radical views are unsound. If I'd managed even to
moderate some of his actions, I could have averted the crisis we're
in now. No, it's right to replace me. I'm a spent match."

"Come off it, now, Archie. You know there's nobody in this
place more respected than you are. By *everybody*." The evening
star has just tentatively emerged behind his head in a sky the
colour of blue ink. I am hungry, and burrow into my purse for
some toffees I keep there. After tossing over one that lands with a
plop on his waistcoat, I put another into my mouth. He eyes his
gift broodingly, then tears off the wrapper and eats the toffee,
breathing noisily.

"I am ... rather worried about Molly," he says after a pause.

"Yes."

"It's extremely difficult for her, all this. You know she was here
among those sitting-in last Monday. But when the police ordered

them all out, she went with those who left voluntarily, instead of choosing the martyr's crown like some of the others. Now, poor girl, she's come to me for help in raising bail for Harry."

"Has she!" I say with interest.

"Just yesterday. No real difficulty there. My bank is willing to put up half of it on my surety, and she's found the rest among friends."

"I see." And why it should hurt that my offer of money has been passed over would be hard to explain. And it's even harder to know the reason why.

"She is still with him, you see," he says sadly.

"Yes."

"And you?" he suddenly raps out, staring at me with his keen blue eyes. "Whom are you with?"

"You," I say without hesitation. A smile of immense sweetness touches his pouched, lined, weary face. Clumsily brushing cigar ash off his waistcoat, he gets to his feet with a glance out at the one bright rivet of light in the sky. I button up my jacket for the slushy walk home. Rather to my surprise, I find the depression that has dragged at me all day has now vanished completely. Still faintly smiling, Archie stands at the door waiting for me to pass him. In his florid voice he rolls out,

> "In farm and field through all the shire
> The eye beholds the heart's desire;
> Ah, let not only mine be vain.
> For lovers should be loved again."

I leave the office galvanically. My bottom has been pinched, by an expert.

"It wasn't shingles after all. Only dry skin."

"I'm glad."

"Just the same, it's no fun. You should see these big welts on me like hives. The skin man told me half his patients are in the teaching profession, which doesn't exactly cheer the heart, either."

We are side by side in my little galley of a kitchen, preparing a late supper after seeing an old Jeanne Moreau film at Bill's favourite French movie house. He is poaching eggs while I stir a pot of hollandaise sauce. A heavy rain is sluicing down the windows. He leans over for a greedy sniff of the lemony tang rising from my wooden spoon.

"You *are* clever. I always thought only great chefs could make hollandaise. Doesn't it go queer on you—curdle or something?"

"Oh yes. It's doing that now. But all you do is just—" And I demonstrate by casually tossing a little cold water into the sauce-pan and stirring briskly. The rich sauce at once becomes smooth as yellow velvet. Trying not to grin with triumph I silently call down a blessing on Archie. How is it I never knew what fun cooking is until he showed me?

"Are the buns toasted yet? Well, could you put the ham on them, and then the egg on top—good—then we pour on some sauce, and *voilà*."

Each with a smoking plate and cutlery hastily plucked from a drawer, we hurry to the table in the next room and begin to eat. Far below the city sparkles black and gold through heavy rain. It streams down, drumming arrogantly on the entrance canopy twelve floors below, but whispering too, in a hurried, heavy way, like a voice telling secrets.

"Thank heaven spring is coming," I say fervently.

"Marvellous, this," Bill says with his mouth full. "Yes, but by the time bloody spring actually gets to Montreal, we're all too pooped to enjoy it. Completely run down with igloo fever. Did you know February had only eleven hours of sun? No wonder everybody has that corpse-like pallor."

"Good time of year to be somewhere else, all right."

"What are you doing over Easter, Willy?"

My heart gives a startled little jump. "Oh, I don't know. I did think it might be nice to get away . . . maybe drive south for a few days, to Washington or somewhere . . . "

"Yes, the trees will all be out down there."

"They say Virginia is lovely, too. All green and balmy. And Richmond doesn't look all that much further on the map."

He sighs. "And when you think the snow will still be piled up in corners all over Halifax . . . "

I sigh too, and get up to make coffee. While I move to and fro clearing the table, he settles in a corner of the sofa to perform the complex ritual of pipe-lighting. He looks almost like a curly-headed boy in his open-necked blue shirt, but the flame of the match shows how deeply the lines are cut across his forehead.

There is a comfortable domestic silence while I pour the coffee and pass over his cup; black with half a teaspoon of sugar.

"How's your mother these days, Bill?"

"Oh, the phlebitis cleared up finally. But she just hasn't got her strength back the way she should. I don't think her doctor is really with it — one of those old-fashioned G.P.'s that wait around for nature to cure everything. I wish she'd go to a younger man. If she had some of these liver injections they'd lift years off her. But I can't persuade her. And of course that clot Clive . . . last time I was there he wanted her to go *curling* with him, if you can imagine. And her barely on her feet again."

"Tch tch."

"Well, I suppose I worry too much. But you know how it is . . . I mean your mother is . . . you can't help being terrifically involved, can you?"

"No, you can't."

"Of course I tend to be a pretty heavy worrier about quite a few things. Anxiety. Actually, I've had two breakdowns, you know. The one ten years ago — I was in the Douglas for five months. The last one wasn't so bad, only a few weeks. The shrink has helped a lot. You ever had therapy?"

"No. Though I daresay a few sessions might do me no harm. I was very attached to my mother . . . well, even though she died over a year ago, I'm still — I haven't come to terms with — with being alone."

I steal a cautious look at him, but he is puffing smoke abstractedly and gently scratching his calf. He seems barely aware I am there at all. Suddenly he says, "Willy, do you think I could have a little nightcap of that nice rye?"

"Of course you can." I jump up to get it.

"Cheers," he says, raising the glass. He downs half of the drink at one gulp and then slides down low against the cushions with his long legs stretched out. Yet he does not look really relaxed.

"You've never been married, have you, Willy?"

"No."

"Neither have I. Do people try to make you feel *odd* because of that? Weird? I know it's true nearly everybody our age is married and breeding kids, or at the very least shacked up with somebody; but just the same — "

"You think I don't know? A woman completely on her own

might as well be some kind of *monster*, the way some people ... "

"But it does make you wonder sometimes if you aren't missing something. I mean, look at Emma. You know, she used to be *thin*. Very uptight, sad girl. Then she got married and instantly had four kids, and now she's fat and obscenely happy."

"Is she?" I say, trying to sound suitably detached.

"But surely it's possible just not to be the marrying *kind*, isn't it? I mean, what's so peculiar about that? Anyway, I've never wanted to get all tied up in that particular knot. In fact I've never—well— it isn't that woman don't *attract* me. No, they attract me like mad. *You* attract me. I even got engaged once. But I was just a kid ... it didn't work out." He frowns into his empty glass.

"Like another one?"

"Please."

This time he takes only a discreet sip while I settle back in my corner. The pipe lies abandoned on its side. His hands are jammed deep in his pockets. The air is charged with something he wants to say, but he can't seem to get it out.

"Willy — "

"Hullo."

"Would you be—would you consider—I mean what would you say if ... What I mean is, how about us going off to Washington together or wherever, for a few days at Easter. Share expenses and ... and all that."

I look at him carefully.

"I'd say yes."

"Would you really? Oh, that's marvellous. You are a dear, Willy. It will be such fun."

He has flushed a little. In fact he seems so elated that I have to smile, even while I wonder why, now that at long last The Project seems (as it were) in the bag, I am not more elated myself. Perhaps it's the note of gratitude in his voice that bothers me. Now when he swings around to arrange himself cosily with his head in my lap, all I feel is a mild surprise at how heavy it is. But I touch his greying curls gently and try to smooth away the deepest line in his forehead. He draws a long breath and closes his eyes in contentment.

"You know, Willy, I may be an awful square, but I don't suggest this kind of thing lightly. I mean, you're not that kind of person either. We're quite a lot alike, in fact. But you're so nice. Kind is what you are. Generous. Mellow, somehow. You're wise and experienced."

"Well, no, not really — " I begin. But he has already gone on without a pause, his eyes still closed. "Surprising as it may seem, you know, I have actually never — I mean it's fairly unusual in a man my age, but — Oh, I've messed around and messed around . . . women attract me, they always have, but — Well, Molly for instance. I suppose I'd better admit it, we did go around a bit together, just after her marriage broke up. But not for long. She was too aggressive, or something . . . it put me off."

"There's nothing to worry about," I say soothingly. A muscle in my leg is twitching. His head is really amazingly heavy. I wonder in dismay why this is all I feel. Where is all the joy, the excitement, the pleasure? The other evening I felt more delight than this when Percy the cat pushed my nose with his whiskered, velvet face.

"As a matter of fact," I say resolutely, "— I'd better tell you this — I'm not really experienced either. Not . . . well, after all what does it matter? But as you said before, we're a lot alike."

"Really?" he says. Is it disappointment in his voice? Chagrin? Sympathy? Whatever it is, it makes me restless. The rain is still gushing down with such primitive force it frets my nerves. Bill reaches up to fondle my cheek gently.

"Give me a kiss, Willy. As you say, what's to worry about? What's the difference? No problem. None in the world. So that's agreed: we take to the road at Easter and have ourselves a wonderful time. Okay if we take your car? I can spell you a bit with the driving. It's only cities that get my ulcer roused. A week together in the south . . . oh, won't it be nice?"

"It will be lovely." And now for the first time I begin to feel a cautious little flutter of happiness. But the weight of his head is making both my legs prickle and twitch and I can't help being relieved when he suddenly sits up.

"Half past twelve — God, I must get home. Nine-o'clock class in the morning. See you around tomorrow, I expect, Willy dear." And almost before I can get to my feet he drops a kiss on my hand and lets himself out.

Alone with the coffee cups I think of a dozen things I would have liked to say, and to hear him say — a dozen questions to ask and answer. Still, there's plenty of time for all that. And yet, for some obscure reason I'm not sorry to be alone now. It's actually a relief to be by myself. What a baffling and contradictory creature I am, to be sure. I don't understand me at all. Just when I should be listening, entranced, to the horns of Elfland faintly blowing, I am suddenly giggling instead at the memory of Archie yesterday switching off a broadcast of the Montreal Symphony, growling, "Dieu que le son du cor est triste."

And yet, after a night's sleep I come up buoyant, warm, tingling— the way you're supposed to feel after champagne, but generally don't. I lie in bed savouring it. And the more I think about last evening, the better I feel. A week in the south . . . you're a dear . . . won't it be lovely? Yes, it will. Perfectly lovely. Marvellous. The urge to talk to Bill is irresistible. I jump out of bed and ring his number, but there is no answer. Strange that it was so hard to talk to him last night, while this morning I'm brimming with things to tell him. But maybe love is like that?

The window frames an excited day full of wind and blown cloud and gashes of bold blue sky. Great stretches of pavement have been hosed bare by the rain. A million tight little knots of bud swing on the trees. I eat a large breakfast (Emma, is this how it begins?) and after a little cursory housework cannot bear to stay indoors. It is Saturday; why not do a little shopping downtown?

You see, I say to Bill as I swing energetically downhill, it all depends on what you mean by experience. Because in a way, a sort of way, I've had quite a lot. Even too much. With a jump I dodge a bright puddle flashing and puckering in the road. Nobody's untouched, so to speak. There's more than one form of virginity. Let's cut across this little park, threading past all the birds, children, and dogs hopping in the sun. An old woman in a battered coat and running shoes is ambling along the path ahead of me. She stops abruptly, stoops with caution, and straightens again. In her hand is now a big blue glass alley. I grin at her cheerfully as I pass. Poor old thing.

I'm heading for that old-fashioned department store I enjoy because, unlike its rivals, the staff is middle-aged and the stock attractive, instead of the other way around. Furthermore, on Saturdays a kilted piper walks through the main floor skirling his bagpipes, which always tickles that five-year-old Willy permanently in residence within your colleague Professor Doyle.

Am I sentimental, do you think? A revolting thing to be, but I can't resist this huge bean-bag caterpillar in Toys — it's Wallace himself — and Dougie will love his winning embroidered smile and little black-bead eyes. No, I promise not to tell you or myself that *my* broken engagement (or almost) was a shattering emotional experience. Because it wasn't. I can hardly remember now exactly what Dieter looked like, even though we walked together right up to the idea of marriage. He was in my Middle English class at graduate school, a brilliant German boy with a neat, small, straight body and soft brown eyes that always looked wistful, though in fact he had a character tough as old rope. We saw a lot of each other, making full use of institutions like parks, libraries, and museums, because he was on a scholarship and perpetually broke. For several months we walked the city and the campus hand in hand, more companions than lovers, perhaps because it was only being lonely that we had in common. But there was a streak of tenderness in him that touched me so much I thought at the time I loved him. Because he soon learned I preferred it that way, he never pressed me to accept more than kisses. Acute shortage of cash and opportunity simplified things, so that a constricted bit of necking at the movies was the extent of it for us. Perhaps he had his sentimental side too. On my birthday he gave me a single, perfect white camelia. Yes, I suppose I almost loved him — so far as that was possible, in my peculiar circumstances.

"You see, I can never go out in the evenings," I told him.

"Why not?"

"My mother needs me at home. I have to be there . . . my father drinks . . . he might — I can't talk about it."

"Then we won't talk about it," he said. "You shall stay home in the evenings. But there are eight hours in the day, yes?"

So there were, and as time went on we used them all. Eventually he took off a little signet ring he wore and put it on my hand. Mother tried to smile when she saw it. "If you really like this boy, dear," she said, "bring him home to lunch one day." Oh, my poor mother. Never confronting the actual problem directly, because he and I both must have known it was insoluble, we talked about teaching jobs after graduation and even looked at ads for cheap apartments. He and Mother seemed to like each other. I liked his sister, the only survivor of his family. In the spring, that season of illusions, I almost persuaded myself that Mother would agree to come away and live with us. . . .

Then one day Dieter told me he'd found an ideal apartment for rent—three big rooms near High Park. It would be vacant in the fall. The landlord would show us over it at eight that evening.

"But Dieter, I can't be away from home in the—"

He looked at me squarely. "How long with this, Willy? You can be away. You must. We've got to face this some time."

"I don't know ... "

"You must know. Right now."

"I'll phone her," I said miserably. The landlord showed us the apartment. I can't remember a single thing about the place now. When I got home soon after nine, I closed the front door quietly (G. W. Doyle sometimes dangerously prowled the lower hall, glass in hand), and stood for a moment, listening. The house enclosed its usual silence. Or seemed to. Then I heard the faint sound from upstairs. I had not heard it, not from earliest childhood. My mother, sobbing.

She never told me what had happened. It could have been almost anything. Or maybe nothing. I ran up the stairs to her, and it was hours before she stopped crying. All the rest of that night I seemed to hear it. I can hear it now. The next morning I met Dieter at the library and gave him back his little ring. As I say, he had a very strong character. Or a well-developed sense of reality. He never tried to get in touch with me again.

On display in the Lingerie Department there is a set of baby-doll pyjamas in black lace—bikini pants of minute proportions and a sheer top cut like the surplice of a depraved choirboy. So I attract you, do I? Wait till you see this, man. After buying the pyjamas, I find a short rose-coloured nightgown with ruffles that I must also have; and minutes later I come upon a dark blue pantsuit too attractive to refuse. Luckily it's on sale. And that leads to a mini-dress in pale blue, printed with clusters of little white flowers ... do you know that silly old joke, Bill? — "and that's why my trousseau tore so ... "

Well, don't let the word make you nervous. After all, people do get married all the time after capers like ours. There must be something encouraging in it. This happy, hopeful feeling—have you got it too? As if the mistakes, the frustrations, the failures of the past never happened, or don't count. One of mine was a chap called Graham Foster. Shall I tell you about him? It's not every day you hear about somebody whose first real sexual experience was with a Latin professor, now is it? Well, there you are, you see. If that wasn't experience, nothing is.

I was nearly eighteen, in my first year at university; he must have been, I suppose, about thirty. He taught Latin I, a course obligatory in those days for anyone planning "to proceed to graduate studies". How the stately prose of the college calendar does bring it all back! The very first day he came into the lecture room in his gathered black gown and looked intently at us through his horn-rims (all us girls wearing the pearls and sweaters mandatory in the fifties) I tumbled into a schoolgirl crush of really violent intensity. It was so acute I worked like a fanatic over my translations, and soon he knew my name because I topped the class. (It's not that women's brains are different from men's; just their priorities.)

Anyhow, he took up permanent occupancy of my mind. Stalked through it on his long, thin legs like the Lord through Eden, reciting Catullus and taking off the horn-rims occasionally (oh, what that did to my personal syntax) to look at me with beautiful, myopic dark eyes. But week after week, no matter how often he said thrilling things like "Can *you* translate this sentence, Miss Doyle?", nothing else happened. No progress made. At last I failed the Friday quiz.

"What on earth happened to you?" he asked. "This isn't like your work at all."

"Well, I just don't understand this business of *oratio obliqua*."

This was, of course, a lie. But a functional lie. He suggested I come along to his office after class. Which I very primly did. This led to a number of further meetings when I had difficulties with the ablative absolute and my circulation; and after that we drifted into the love poetry of Catullus. Not long after that he offered one rain-soaked afternoon to drive me home. We proceeded to Rosedale via a web of wet country roads completely empty of traffic. He stopped, removed the horn-rims, and took me in his arms.

"What gorgeous eyes you have," I said.

"My mother is Portuguese."

"But you were born here."

"Right here in Cabbagetown."

His lips began to travel from place to place on my cheeks, neck, forehead, in delicate, exploratory kisses that gave me a new and intense pleasure. It never occurred to me with any clarity at all that there might be more pleasure even than this. Not even when, on subsequent journeys out past muddy Mormon farms, he extended the field of his research as far as the removal of my sweater and bra. This added nothing to my happiness. In fact it made me both uncomfortable and uneasy. But I felt it would be impolite to stop him. Besides, if it made him happy, I was perfectly willing. Are you wondering what, if anything, I expected all this to lead to? Why, I no more expected it to lead to anything for me than algebra had. Like most educations, mine had prepared me for everything but the basic realities of life. The cautious Sex Education part of my instruction consequently seemed to me to have not the remotest connection with these long kissings and fondlings in Graham's car, his glasses carefully put aside in the glove compartment and my sweater folded up with some of my inhibitions. I was quite sure pregnancy could not result from any of this; there seemed no other consequence to worry about. What with my reservations and his, we might almost have been a pair of celestial beings with wings, arms, and heads, and no lower parts whatever.

Until, that is, one May afternoon with the sun warm on the windshield and thin young leaves of yellow-green shining in a gusty wind. For the first time his hand slid up between my legs. I shifted away, startled. Then he pulled my hand over and pressed it to a part of his anatomy whose condition very much surprised me.

"It's all right," he kept saying. "Don't be afraid. Don't worry. I won't hurt you. Just touch me. Touch me."

"But you're married — " I remember saying like a fool.

"That has nothing to do with this."

And a minute later the blind, thick column spurted a jet of clear fluid in an arc smelling of the sea. His face was buried in my neck and he breathed as if he had been running. A searching, terrible sadness like nothing I'd ever felt before crept through all my ignorant and foolish flesh. My eyes were sore with tears that could not fall. How strange that I should have thought about Ronnie all the silent way home. He was the little boy at the end of our street who shared a secret cave with me when we were five — a buggy and decrepit big-city grape arbour smelling a little of cats. There we retreated occasionally to eat bootleg candy and explore each other's most interesting differences. Yes, as I drove home through that green day with my professor of Latin I remembered the tender little bud of Ronnie's maleness and the lordly way he straddled to pee, while I had to squat. We agreed that his was a handy thing to have for a picnic. Our milk teeth were just beginning to loosen. We sometimes kissed, and laughed at the matching wobbles. We were not sad with this terrible sadness.

Until the day his mother caught us, literally with our pants down. I was marched grimly home. I felt only bewildered. Then — and only then — guilty. My mother looked at me with cold disgust. "Never again, do you hear me—never again do anything so filthy," she said. "I am ashamed of you."

Now I knew a climax of shame so bitter I could hardly look at Graham.

That was the last time we drove out to the country. I refused to go again, though he tried several times to persuade me, and once, in a brief scuffle in his office, broke my string of pearls. They popped loudly onto the floor and rolled derisively into every corner. He collected them all with care and poured them into my hand. "Don't want the janitor to find them here," he said, with the rich Portuguese eyes looking into mine.

And after that I never went to his office again.

I got a First in Latin. He left abruptly at the end of that academic year; there was some scandal about a student—gossip about her pregnancy. From that day to this I've never seen or heard of Professor Foster, any more than I remember seeing Ronnie again. The two of them might have been made to vanish by a spell.

Oh, my feet are giving out. Let's catch this elevator down. Unfortunate that my parcels are so numerous and bulky; it's hard to squash into the little cage already full of portly Westmount dowagers who like this store as much as I do. They glare at me, their hats trembling with indignation.

It's all very well, and perhaps preferable, for some men in one's past to disappear; but it can be a problem when they don't. Greg, for instance, didn't disappear. He lived two doors down the street from us—actually he's a second or third cousin of ours—but he was away at boarding school a lot of the time, and we didn't notice each other till one hot summer when we were both about nineteen.

I was intent on getting a tan that year, though all the sun ever did for me was bleach my hair and fuse all my smaller freckles into large ones. But in my scanty bathing suit I lay for hours on a rug in the garden, religiously anointing myself at intervals with sun oil. A clock (to check when it was time to turn over), books, dark glasses, lemonade, a small portable radio to bleat out Hit Parade tunes—all this was necessary equipment, and getting settled was an elaborate business. Among other things, I had to move with the angle of the sun, and make sure my nose was covered (it got red and peeled otherwise).

One afternoon I caught a glitter from the bushes of the garden next door but one. Surely it was the rims of a pair of opera glasses. Quietly I slipped into the house and from Dad's study got his big pair of racetrack binoculars.

Back in the garden I put the glasses to my eyes and focussed the lens. Into the twin circles jumped a boy's face, cheekily grinning behind a pair of binoculars.

A cracking laugh came from behind the bushes. I laughed too, though I was hot all over with blushing and sunburn.

"Can I come over for some of that lemonade?" he called.

"If you leave those glasses at home."

Though I hurriedly put on my clothes before he arrived, Greg and I from the start seemed to have known each other for a long time, in a basic and simple sort of way. He was a highly attractive boy with a zany laugh. We thought the same things funny — always a great bond. One of our mutual great-uncles died that fall, and Mother sent me to the funeral. I think she thought it would be educational for me. And so it was, though not quite as she planned. My first experience of the kinship of love and death. As the flower-heaped coffin waited beside a square of plastic undertaker's grass, Greg whispered to me, his breath tickling my ear, "Uncle Wilf used to pinch girls."

"Did he?"

"Well, he was ninety-six. Too old even to play chess."

I might have been able to cope with these footnotes to mortality if just at that moment one of Uncle Wilf's ancient brothers had not boomed out in a theatrically solemn, biblical sort of voice, "Good. Bye. Wil. Fred." Then the awful struggle not to laugh made me choke and gasp hysterically. I doubled over while perspiration came out like rain on my forehead. "That girl feels faint," some aunt or other announced. "Push her head down between her legs." Someone else mercifully said, "Take her back to the car." And Greg, looking stern and solemn, very stiff in the shoulders and back, took my elbow and escorted me to the limousine, where we collapsed helplessly, stuffing our mouths with handkerchiefs.

Just weeks later, Greg met Lou, home on holiday from the Harlow Academy for Girls. And that was that. I don't know whether they ever laugh like that, or ever did. Perhaps it doesn't matter. I'm very fond of Greg still, and I think he likes me, if anything, better than Lou herself does. No passion or anything messy like that on either side, of course. Just liking. Nothing the Prayer Book could possibly object to. And if you ask me whether I'm glad of that or sorry, I honestly am not sure.

So you see, Bill, it really does all depend on what you call experience. You didn't think we had so much in common, did you? But now that you know, you've got to be as cheerful about us as I am.

EIGHT

Sounds & Sweet Airs

MONDAY IS A MOROSE DAY, with snow leaking down from a sulky grey sky. Everybody at Cartier looks grim, or put-upon, or annoyed. I feel very out of place with my bright face beaming. On my way to class the caretaker detains me with a long and bitter complaint about student litter in the classrooms. He is a sad, crumpled, whining little man in a cotton jacket who looks rather like a bit of litter himself. I give him a pack of cigarettes and a pat on the arm before rushing off. The lecture fails to stimulate my class, which sits in apathy twirling its hair or gazing sadly at the floor.

On my way to the library I pass bulletin boards posted with the exam schedule. Students mill around these, groaning and trading their favourite four-letter words. At the library I am in a hurry to get away, but Mrs. Salvatore, head of Circulation, keeps me there interminably, grumbling about the students who steal and vandalize books. She has an incipient beard which rivets my eyes, and her harangue goes on until I begin to feel like vandalizing her. Climbing the stairs at last to the haven of my office, I meet Molly coming down, her face squeezed up in a cross frown.

"Having a hard day, love?" I ask her. "Cheer up. So is everybody else. Mrs. Salvatore has been gibbering away to me about vandals."

"I'm on my way to the library now, damn it. Trying to track down a plagiarist. Stupid bitch in my class has turned in an essay on Grove that I know damn well she didn't write. I know because

148

I've read it somewhere. That means pawing through back issues of *Canadian Lit.* for hours, just when I'm up to the neck in other work. Do you know a girl called Valerie Peterson? Great big cow with a heavy face."

"Val Peterson — yes, isn't she the one that hangs around with Mike Armstrong?"

"That's the one."

"Yes, she's in my novel course. Not a very bright star."

"Too right she isn't. Just wait till I get hold of that article she's pinched. I'll massacre her."

"Well, good luck on the hunt. Harry all right?"

"Home with a cold, but okay."

"That's great." She doesn't look as if she really agrees, but goes on her way with a harried nod. I pull out my office keys and finish the climb up, whistling.

A quick glance along the corridor shows Bill's door closed. Thanks to everybody, I've missed him. He'll be in class for the next two hours. But something has been left on the floor close by my door: a small potted plant enclosed in a plastic puff tied at the top with red string. I take it inside, smiling with pleasure. There is no card with it, but only Bill could think of such a thing. What could be lovelier than live white violets on a grey March day? Bill, you are a sweet man. Carefully I give the sandy earth a little drink. I am touching the furry leaves fondly and counting the half-hidden green buds when a rap at the door makes me turn. Mike stands there with snow melting on the shoulders of his jacket. He is frowning. What on earth is the matter with everyone today?

"Can I talk to you for a minute, Miz?"

"Yes, of course. Come on in. Something wrong?"

"Yeah, sort of. Not with me."

"Oh?"

He shoots a cautious look at me as he closes the door. "Like I'm here as a friend, right? Everything strictly off the record, okay?"

"If you like. You look worried, Mike."

In fact, however, he looks not so much worried as highly intent; even excited. I steal a quick look at my watch. Over an hour yet before Bill gets out of class . . .

"Well, what's the trouble, then?"

He has twitched round one of the heavy chairs and folded his tall, thin frame by stages down into it, legs over the arm, torso turned so I can see only his profile. "You know damn well what worries me," he mutters. "You, that's what, all the damn time worrying hell out of me. But that's not really why I'm here. I think. Only some days I don't know why I really do anything, if you see what I mean."

With some difficulty I keep my mind on this diffuse set of remarks and my eyes from wandering to the pot of violets. What was that Molly was grumbling about — an essay on Grove —

"Has this got anything to do with Val, by any chance?"

He looks slightly startled. "Sharp. How did you know?"

"Want to tell me about it?"

"So the word's out already, is it? Look, can I trust you?"

I hesitate. "Well, it depends a bit what — oh well, all right. Everything off the record."

He takes a long breath. "Well, Val's mother moved out a few months back to bed down with a guy ten years younger than she is. But she keeps on seeing Val for lunch and telling her what a baddie her *dad* is. Get the picture?"

"Go on."

"This makes it very tough on Val."

"Yes, it would."

"She's been on sleeping pills. They zonk her out so much she's been messing around with uppers — benzedrine — to help her study. Not the best scene."

"No, indeed."

"So her grades drop, she can't concentrate. Right now she's way behind, and the exams are almost on our necks. This is her final year. Panic situation."

"I see."

Suddenly he flashes me a smile warm as the sun. His eyes linger on me and his fresh lips shape the ghost of a kiss.

"Dear Miz. You — "

"All right now, Mike. Is that it, then? Because you know the Student Counselling people can probably help Val. Once they know the situation they can notify her instructors that she's under a lot of stress. Maybe get permission for her to write the exams later this summer. Can you persuade her to go and see them?"

"Well," he says, shifting in the chair, "you maybe know already, it could be a bit late for that to help much. Val's done something dumb. She — sort of used an essay, on that prize pill Frederick Grove. Rewrote some of it, like; cut some parts out. But it isn't her essay."

His cheeks are a trifle flushed. Frowning, he jerks and tugs at the laces of his grubby sneakers, with bony fingers that are not quite steady. My heart goes out to him. He cares more about that big-bottomed girl than he knows. I look at the plant to give him time, and in the silence we can hear big snowflakes patting the window-glass.

Finally I say, "Mike, the best thing she can do—if I can offer a bit of advice—would be for her to go right away to Mrs. Pratt, and tell her the whole story. All of it. And hope for mercy. You understand I have no idea whether—well, the rest is strictly up to Mrs. Pratt and perhaps the Chairman."

"Yeah. But you see, it's her pride. Having to spill the whole thing. I mean it's like you say, asking for mercy. That's tough to do."

"No doubt. But theft is theft, right?"

"If you want to call it that."

"Well, what would you call it? Plagiarism is theft. Fraud. Dishonesty. Deception. I don't like those names any better, do you?"

"No. But you're so terribly pure, Miz." He is grinning now. The frown is gone. His feet dangle, relaxed. The bell sounds to mark the hour and he jumps up cheerfully.

"Anyway, thanks. It helps to tell somebody. I'll see what I can do about getting Val to see the counsellor. She's pretty spaced out right now, but I'll try."

"That's all you can do. By the way, how's your own opus coming along? Will you have it in this week?"

"If I can get the Hardy section done."

"Good. Come and see me if you need to."

"Right. Will do. So long for now." But he puts his head back inside the door to add, "Nice plant you have there."

"Mike, wait a minute. Did you — "

But he has gone. Damn! I make a face at the violets.

A day or two later, at a spot in the corridor where a fluorescent tube has died, producing a Gothic sort of gloom, I nearly collide with Archie in full sail, his large form made larger still by the billows of his academic gown. He is the only faculty member at Cartier to cling to the monastic scholar's garb, and a venerable garment it is, the sleeves hanging in picturesque rags of faded serge that flutter as he speeds along with his impatient stride. No one seeing Archie could ever possibly mistake him for anyone else, which is no doubt exactly his intention.

"There you are, miss," he remarks, stopping short.

"Yes, indeed," I return mildly.

"Dark here as Dido's cave." He moves closer and his hand closes firmly around my arm as if to prevent my escape.

"Going anywhere in particular?"

"Just to—my office." (Actually I was on my way down the hall to Bill's; but there's no need to mention that.)

"Well, aren't you going to invite me in?"

"Sir, you do me too much honour. But I would be infinitely obliged."

He turns me brusquely into the office, still gripping me by the arm, and in the better light there turns upon me a long and suspicious scrutiny.

"You're looking very glowing today, miss. What's been happening to you? Eh?"

"Nothing at all," I say lightly, hoping he'll mistake my blush for simple health. Well, it's partly true. I've not seen Bill for more than a couple of seconds all week. A scribbled note left in my box at lunchtime promises equal austerity for the next few days: he's snowed under with end-of-term essays. But Archie's eyes are full of a truculent suspicion that I find both amusing and touching. "It must be just the spring," I add disarmingly, and edge away.

"Spring," he growls, glaring with disapproval out at the delicate brightness diffused by a pale blue sky. "Much it does except add to the confusion for most of us. Must admit I don't welcome it this year. Would it surprise you to know that I miss my wife as a lover does? Would it?" I wish he would sit down. He looks unnaturally large against the light.

"No, it wouldn't."

"At the same time, there's that feeling of release . . . freedom. Even though I loved her. Queer, isn't it."

"Yes. It was a long time before I stopped feeling guilty about that after Mother died. There was nobody to explain to me it's natural to feel relieved when someone you love dies. I had to find that out for myself. Sit down and have an apple."

A grim smile twitches at his lips. "What I so adore about women is the way they combine irrelevant ideas. And you, miss, are supremely female. I wonder whether you're fully aware of that."

He casts himself into a chair, which utters a faint scream of protest. His blue eyes are intent on me, very much as Percy's would be on a mouse. The place where he gripped my arm still seems to feel his hand. In fact, as the old stallion stares at me, I perceive he is deliberately trying to make me aware of him. I resent this very much, because he is succeeding. It couldn't be more highly inconvenient and ill-timed, not to say potentially troublesome. Surely the man can't really be interested in me in that way. It's absurd. No, he is just being mischievous. He couldn't seriously ... But how annoying of him to make me uncomfortable like this. It's not as if I could ever — poor old man — and yet once or twice lately he's made me feel ... what? half frightened, I suppose, in a not unpleasant sort of way. He *is* a wicked old sorcerer. Poor old thing. Just the same, I wish it were somehow possible to have Bill with Mike's tenderness and this impossible old man's magnetism, if that's what it is ...

"No question about it, you have that moonstruck look. You are in love," remarks Archie, still staring at me.

This is so nearly true that I say quickly, "Not a bit of it."

His reply is to take a ferocious bite out of his apple, and get to his feet munching. He sweeps the ragged gown about him with a regal and ridiculous gesture. The scowl has gone from his eyes; he might even be smiling behind the apple.

"Not that I expect to be thanked — but you haven't mentioned the violets," he says. "Is that because you're shy? Or just being female?"

Before I can reply, he winks at me broadly and whisks out of the room. And I am left to look ruefully for the second time at the potted plant. This time I put my tongue out at it.

My fingers are trembling so coarsely I can hardly fit them into the dialling holes. Twice I call a wrong local before I get through to the campus newspaper office.

"Is Mike Armstrong there, please? It's Miss Doyle in the English Department."

"Hey, Mike around?" yells the young voice at the other end. One or two muddled replies drift back. "Nah, he's gone for coffee." "He's taking a leak." — "Yah, he's here; hold on."

"Mike? Will you come around to the office right away; it's important."

There is an almost imperceptible pause, but his voice is clear and fresh as he says, "Sure. Ten minutes be okay?"

"Right. I'll be expecting you."

But it is half an hour before he appears at the door. During that time I sit in silence looking at the folder on my desk. Once I get up to ease a sharp muscle-pain in my back. The sun of a bright day moves silently on the wall. Bill's office is closed—he's gone to the bank. I sit there and think about things like responsibility and involvement and vanity. There is a brassy taste in my mouth.

"Hi, Miz. I'm all excited, getting a call from you. Rushed home to change my shirt."

"Close the door, Mike. And sit down."

He does so, his smooth face expressing nothing but cheerful inquiry. Just the same, now that I'm looking for it, I can see a little flick of awareness in his eyes, even as they smile at me.

"I've just been to the library. Maybe you've heard about the trouble they've been having lately with theft and vandalism. This morning Mrs. Salvatore showed me this binding for a thesis. It was found in a library wastebin several weeks ago. The typed pages inside have all been very neatly removed, maybe with a razor-blade. All except the title page. "Studies in Paternal Authority in Some Nineteenth-Century Fiction", a thesis presented in partial fulfilment of the requirements for the degree of Master of Arts at Cartier University. By Anthony Joseph Adams. 1957."

There is a silence.

"What you've submitted to me is simply Adams' thesis. Same paper, typing, everything. Well, what have you got to say, Mike?"

"Nothing," he says simply.

"You have a carrel over there. I suppose you saw this on a shelf months ago and just . . . took it."

"The subject interested me."

I look at him incredulously. "Is that your only comment?"

"Well, what is there more to say? Why waste your time with a lot of excuses or psychological crap about pressure and all that. I took the thing. That's all."

"But *why*, Mike?"

"I just thought — why not?"

"But you know how well you did in the Christmas exam, and in any quiz I've ever given . . . There was no *need*! You could have had a First without doing this. You haven't got Val's problems.

Any of them. I don't understand. I really don't."

He waits till I've finished. His air is politely and patiently attentive, as if he has heard all this many times before.

"It doesn't really matter why, does it?"

"It does to me." I grip my hands together on the desk-top. They are very cold. His composure, though, is helping me toward anger, and safely away from other kinds of distress. His face is turned to me, but it is absolutely expressionless, except for a slightly brighter colour than usual over the high cheekbones.

"I suppose it was like that sugar-cube, and the shoplifting you once told me about. Just for kicks."

"Maybe."

"The thing I find hardest to take is . . . well, that you could lie to me like that. This kind of cheating is a lie. You've been playing a kind of game with me. A con game. And quite apart from . . . that case of spring fever you've had, I thought we were friends."

To my angry distaste, I can't entirely control the tremor in my voice.

"All that part of it was straight," he says quickly.

"Do you expect me to believe that? Surely you knew . . . oh well, there's no point in going on. Only it just baffles me how you could do this—not to me, to yourself. What went on in your head? For one thing, discarding this folder in the library itself was just asking for discovery, wasn't it?"

"Tough things to destroy, those binders. But you're right. I didn't specially want to get away with it."

I try to relax the tight muscles of my back, which ache as keenly as if I've been digging a ditch all morning.

"Well, the situation is this. Freshmen who try this kind of thing are sometimes let off with a warning the first time. But for a senior, you understand, it's a different — "

"I know. It's expulsion."

"I've got to take this to the Chairman and the Dean. It's going to be — it will be hard. But I have no choice, Mike."

"That's all right."

"Unless you can find strong grounds for some kind of appeal, I'm afraid they'll — and how can I possibly defend you?"

"Yeah. I know. Don't worry about it, Miz."

He gives me a gentle look, almost as if I were the errant one to be comforted, punished, and pitied. And the devastating thing is that I know myself to deserve that look.

"I don't care if they fire me," he says. And it sounds like the simple truth.

"Your family is going to care. Plenty. It's your whole university life down the drain."

He shrugs. "Maybe that's the best place for it."

Loudly through the building rings the inexorable hourly bell that packs our learning and teaching lives into prefabricated fifty-minute boxes. I have a lecture to give. To the class taking the novel course. The thought of facing them makes my backache spread all over. But with exam pressure building, they will all be there in force. And this is no time to flinch from responsibility. Or to let myself remember I have yet to face Archie with this sorry tale.

"Well, I'll be in touch with you later about this, Mike. You'd better get your parents ready for it somehow."

"Like just one thing—" he says. "I'm not really sorry about this crap—" and he gives the folder on the desk a contemptuous little flick with his finger. "But about the rest of it I am. Really sorry. If that's any use to you."

It isn't. But with a cold qualm I remember that loaded Mauser he likes to look at in the drawer of his father's desk, and I say nothing.

"All right, Mike. Go home."

He goes. I close the door after him. After a few minutes I blow my nose fiercely and go to meet my class.

"*What?*" says Archie. "What's that ye say? Speak up." Maddeningly, he is having one of his deaf days.

"One of my students has plagiarized a thesis. He stole it from the library and turned it in as his own work."

"Ah. I thought you said pulverized, in which case we could perhaps congratulate him. Well, don't look so glum, my dear. It's not the end of the world. What student is it?"

"His name is Michael Armstrong."

"Armstrong?" The shaggy eyebrows give a twitch. "You don't mean old Doctor Armstrong's grandson? He's just been appointed to the Board of Governors. No, tell me it's a different Armstrong."

"This boy's father is an orthopaedic surgeon."

"Oh God. That's the one." Breathing hard he crushes out his

cigar and rubs both vein-roped hands through his grey bush of hair, which causes it to stand up like the mane of a worried old lion. "Well," he says grimly. "Tell me about it."

I give a brief, dry outline of the facts. The cool sound of my own voice gives me some satisfaction. I am able without difficulty to omit the central truth of the matter — even, for the moment, to forget it. I allow myself instead to be glad I chose this morning to wear my becoming new mini-dress of plum blue, which generously demonstrates how handsome my legs are. To them Archie has been dedicating a small but gratifying proportion of his attention. Now, however, he interrupts me, frowning.

"Just a minute. Of course I know this boy; he's one of the student representatives. Comes to Department meetings. And haven't I seen him a number of times hanging around your office?"

"You may have done. As I say, he's enrolled in the novel course."

"Seems to have needed a lot of consultation. What?" He levels the blue eyes at me pugnaciously.

I manage to make no comment. Though his gaze is focussed on me like a laser beam, I am able by an heroic effort of will to keep from blushing.

"And how long ago did you discover this theft?"

"Yesterday morning. I called him in and he admitted the truth right away. Now I'm turning over the evidence to you—here's the paper he submitted last week, and the thesis cover he cut away from it."

"And you had no suspicion at all — no sense before yesterday that he was up to all this?"

"None. There was no reason to suspect him. He's an unusually intelligent boy."

"It's a matter of character, miss, not intelligence. What's the boy *like*?"

Mike's face, with its slightly exotic eyes and sensitive lips, drops like a coloured slide before my mind's eye.

"Well, he's very—he's—I'd say he had a very pleasant personality. He always seemed perfectly open and honest. Once or twice he's mentioned things that suggest he may be rather . . . well, not exactly disturbed, but—There's been at least one experience with hard drugs. And it seems that relations with his father are pretty strained."

"Told you all this, did he? You've been quite confidential and chummy with him, eh?"

"Not more than . . . I mean students quite often tell one things like that. It's not really unusual."

"Let's put it this way," he goes on, intolerably like a prosecuting attorney with a reluctant witness. "You know him extremely well. Is that correct? Well enough to be aware he might do something erratic. Eh? You must have had some inkling before yesterday, surely."

I furtively tug my skirt down to deflect his now disapproving glare, and I wish with some ardour that his parents had never met.

"Well?" he demands.

"Well, no. I had nothing remotely like evidence till yesterday morning."

"I'm asking about perception, not proof."

My face is burning now. Of course he's rooted out the truth. And he knows it. I've been hiding a nagging little suspicion about Mike from myself for weeks, pushing away doubt for a long time. When did I first . . . was it the day when we first discussed that Butler chapter, and Mike didn't seem completely familiar with the text? Or even before that, when he told me about the bookstore thefts? Or was it just the other day when he came to me about Val? Surely I knew then. I did know then.

"Once this winter you spoke to me about the problem of emotional involvement with students. This boy was in your mind then, wasn't he?"

Honesty forces the words out. "Yes. He was."

"So you've been — you actually — "

"Wait a minute. He's had a schoolboy crush on me. And I found him an attractive boy. That's all."

"That's all! By God, miss, it's more than enough."

My hands are trembling now and I lock them together. When I can trust my voice, which is not immediately, I can only say, "None of that had any connection with what he did. Or how I've handled it. Or I wouldn't be here."

"No? A debatable point. You won't deny that it had every connection with your own actions? Or lack of them? If this boy had been any other student, you would have suspected him far sooner, wouldn't you? And taken steps to protect us all from this?

You could have confronted him in such a way he would in all likelihood never have presented us with this ugly—evidence, as you call it. Is this the truth or not, miss?"

By now two large tears have spilled down my cheeks. But if I imagine these might soften him, or make me feel better, I soon discover how wrong I am on both counts. With an angry heave he struggles up out of his chair and turns his back to me. He stands there looking out at the traffic below through a spatter of frozen rain, and enjoys the advantage of not seeing me or letting his own face be seen. There is a brooding silence. I mop my cheeks dry quickly. "I'll go now," I say, catching with gratitude at this chance of escape. "There's really nothing more to say."

"But there is," he says without turning.

"What's that?"

"Put aside for the moment the uncomfortable thought that this matter hasn't been handled with objectivity and therefore the lad's whole future . . . But never mind that. What's done is done. But the Dean and ultimately the Principal are in the picture now. I've got to report this. I've got to justify your . . . passive attitude."

"There's no need for you to justify anything, Archie. I'll speak for myself."

"You will have nothing to say, miss, d'ye hear me? Not one word. I will take over from here. Embarrassing as it will be. And painful."

"I'll take it to the Dean myself."

"You'll do no such thing!" His voice is so loud I dart an involuntary, frightened glance at the door. He glares at me. But now the truculent set of his shoulders and the histrionically flung-back head suddenly begin to make me angry.

"Look here, I think you're forgetting that I've done nothing unethical. I'm not guilty of anything except reluctance to suspect the worst about Mike till I had proof."

"You know what your reasons were for that," he says loudly. "And how to judge the results."

"It's not a crime to be human!" I shout. I am so furious all at once that it is a kind of ecstasy. "How dare you try to make me feel like a criminal because I'm—because I have emotions? You know damn well, or should, that that's no crime!"

His face darkens with something that is not rage. I have struck home.

"So you'd like to excuse yourself because others are guilty?"

"I'm making no excuses. I only — "

"It's self-defence, is it, to taunt an old man because his heart is still green?"

'Shame on you for such fourth-rate dialogue,' I think with scorn. I get as far as the door before his voice stops me. It is so hot with anger it stops me in my tracks like a bullet.

"Just one minute, miss. I will have Sherri make an appointment for us to see the Dean as soon as possible. I will be present, because it's my duty. But I will say as little as possible. If you want to submit any special appeal for Armstrong at that time—and I daresay you will—then it's your privilege to do so. I shall say nothing whatever about that. Or about your personal ... er ... reactions."

"Thank you, Professor Clarke," I say with extreme politeness. And I close the door between us with exquisite and elaborate care.

Back in my own office, I am still exalted with anger. A hot, powerful, dangerous rage fires my blood. There is no room for any other feeling whatever, thank God. It's fortunate my classes for the day are over, or the sight of me would literally petrify my luckless students. I have no impulse at all to find Bill and pour out the whole story. For the moment, he seems totally irrelevant. I fling on a coat and boots and set out walking, on long, fast legs, up the mountain slope. The sky has cleared to a pacific blue. Rags of black ice crunch underfoot as I speed along, feeling eight feet tall. Other pedestrians instinctively edge to the side of the pavement as I pass; and well they might. A stiff wind from the west drags my Medusa hair out stiff, and I breathe up the cold air fiercely.

Never again will I speak an unnecessary word to that man. Him and his monastic gown. Poverty, chastity, and obedience, indeed. With his smiles and his winks and his pinches! Shameless old hypocrite; he's far more venial than Mike.

It's gradually calming to think with contempt of both of them, the old man and the boy, reduced to equally insignificant stature. My rage cools. I turn toward home. For the first time in many weeks I feel supremely simplified, purged, and calm. Free.

During the next forty-eight hours I sail on this smooth, euphoric wave. I houseclean the apartment. I write to Lou, postponing the Easter visit. I balance my chequebook. I sew on buttons, sort gloves, mend slips, and polish shoes. And then, right in the middle of making a suppertime omelette, serenity wears off like a shot of novocaine. The silent apartment closes around me threateningly. My heart beats so hard it hurts. The smell of eggs and butter turns me queasy. There is a sudden rumble of thunder from outside and I shiver.

I hurry to the phone. My voice sounds high.

"Bill? Are you doing anything special? Would you by any chance like to come round and share an omelette?"

"Oh thanks, Willy, but I've just eaten. Now I'm sitting here getting indigestion over this huge pile of essays. God, how I hate the end of term — everything falls in on you at once, just when you're most exhausted."

"It doesn't matter. I just thought maybe you — "

"I know. We haven't spent an evening together for ages. But you must have piles of work to get through yourself. Hell, isn't it? But never mind; it'll soon be over. Only ten more days to Easter."

The sound of his pleasant voice is blessedly comforting. I grasp the receiver tightly in my damp hand.

"No, I've hardly seen you all week. That's why I called . . . you don't mind, do you?"

"Of course not, Willy."

Must think of something to say. Keep him talking.

"Any news your end?"

"No, not really. I had to see Archie today about a report on that conference up north last fall, and I must say he was about as much fun to be with as a flamethrower. In fact, I've never seen him quite so totally bloody-minded. Gnashing and growling away about taxes and radicals and women. If this is what giving up drink does, lead me to the bottle. What's the matter with him, anyway— that Armstrong business, is it? How did your meeting with the Dean go?"

"It wasn't as bad as I thought it would be. Archie hardly opened his mouth."

"Well, that makes a change. Ruthie says he's talking about resigning as Chairman. Has he mentioned it to you at all?"

"Not really."

"Sherri told me he had an appointment with his doctor this afternoon. Maybe the poor old guy is ailing."

"Maybe."

"Well, it'll be ghastly if he quits on us. Can you imagine Emma in the Chair? She's a good scholar, but I know for a fact she thinks south is always downhill, and 'budget' means the basement floor of Eaton's. But she's next in seniority to Archie."

"Um. Well, maybe we could do worse, even so. At least Emma doesn't eat people."

"True. But the Principal will probably bring in somebody from outside. Some American, most likely. He just loves a chance to weigh in with an appointee of his own, you know. Some bastard like himself who'll be properly grateful, and take orders without any fuss."

I hook a chair near by with my foot and sit down in it. Bless him, Bill does so love a gossip. That nasty feeling of panic has begun to ease.

"One sure thing, Harry won't be the new Chairman."

"No, and that's good news. Have you heard the rumour going around that he's been offered $50,000 compensation?"

"Compensation for what?"

"Well, that smart lawyer of his; it seems he can prove that Harry had a perfect legal right to belong to the L.S.A. Something in the Constitution. Fraser made a bad tactical mistake giving that as the reason for firing him. So it looks as if Cartier will have to shell out compensation all right. It's just a question of how much."

"I'm glad for him and Molly, then. Because it won't be easy for him to find another post."

"No, it won't. Actually, he's talking about getting right out of the profession. Going into newspaper work or something. But I can't see that working out. Harry's such a McLuhanite he can't write a line in straight English."

"Is it true they're moving? Molly said something the other day about them wanting to live among Francophones on the other side of town. To be in touch with the new Quebec, she said. Do you think Harry might get on the separatist bandwagon next?"

"It wouldn't surprise me a bit."

I sigh. Soon I will have to let him go. The night is waiting for me, long, dark, and solitary. Rain has begun to fall again, hissing against the windows like buckshot. I think of Lucy crouching out on the roof in rainstorms when *her* novocaine wore off. But I live twelve floors up, stranded in the twentieth century.

"It's lovely to talk to you, Bill. I am *not* feelin' groovy tonight. But your voice makes me feel ... better." I wonder sadly why it seems so necessary to be careful what I say to him. Surely two people with our plans shouldn't have to be so cautious, so timid. What am I afraid of, anyway?

"Cheer up, Willy," he is saying, on exactly the same safe and cheerful note as I have chosen. "You've just got the end-of-term blues. This too will pass."

"I suppose it will."

"Sure it will. Just think, we'll soon be on our way south, won't we? You aren't going to change your mind, I hope. God, the sun. I can hardly wait."

"Me too. I'm taking the car in for its checkup tomorrow. Oh, it will be fun, won't it? I've never been farther south than Niagara Falls, have you?"

"Well, I went to California and Mexico last summer, and I didn't get much out of *that* except the most awful dysentery. This is sure to be different, and better." But he is politely holding in a yawn. "Well, have a good night, Willy. If you're around tomorrow, steer clear of Archie is my advice."

"No fear."

"Maybe we can get together for coffee some time."

"Yes, let's do that."

After hanging up, I scrape the omelette into the garbage bin. I drink half a glass of milk and pour the rest away. The old woman next door yells "Go to hell." To a drum-roll of thunder the rain lashes down harder. There is a faint sound of running feet from the young couple's apartment on the other side. I resolve to buy a newspaper tomorrow and look at ads for flats or even houses to rent. This place is haunted, though not by any nun. I switch on the TV, and three minutes later switch it off. At last I go into the bedroom and try on the new black baby-doll pyjamas. This has a distinctly cheering effect. They look spectacular. Only ten days to wait. Surely I can hang on for ten days.

Before Bill and I leave, however, one important matter has to be attended to, and it costs me many baffled hours of thought. What am I going to do about contraception? I used vaguely to think that information and supplies would be the easiest things in the world to acquire, in these permissive days; but it begins to appear I was wrong. There is nothing easy about any of it.

The obvious person to ask is Lou; but how can I? That dear sister of mine would immediately ask, "Why do you want to know?" She would then add, "What are you up to, Willy? Who is he?" And the next thing she would do is tell Greg all about it. No, asking Lou is out. For various (though different) reasons, I can't ask Molly either. I don't know anybody else well enough ... except maybe Bill himself. And that would be quite impossible.

That leaves the printed word. But here the annals of literature, usually so helpful to me, are peculiarly empty of any really concrete help. In my favourite nineteenth century, all I can remember offhand is poor George Eliot's request to a friend for birth-control information, before she set off for France with Lewes. As for the more unfortunate Charlotte B., she seems to have lacked the wisdom even to ask. I recall Anna Karenina's dilemma; but when I look up the relevant passage, I'm frustrated again. Dolly *whispers* her contraceptive advice to Anna. It was all very well for impulsive girls like Juliet or The Fair Yseult, who appear never to have given the problem a single thought. But much more mature and up-to-date heroines like Lady Chatterley seem equally blithe and unconcerned. I get no help from any of them.

Of course there are those women-oriented magazines intended for reading under the drier; but even here there is less help than one might think. They all agree the only reliable methods involve seeing a doctor. And I flinch from that. He (or she) would probably want to investigate me in a personal and uncomfortable way. Then I might well get not a simple prescription for the Pill, but a moral lecture, or some kind of fitted device; and both of these possibilities repel me strongly.

The pharmacy and its products seem to be my only hope. I go along accordingly one morning, choosing not the little neighbourhood drugstore where the fatherly old chemist knows me, but a large downtown place lit by green fluorescent bars. Unluckily the counter here is served by a remarkably handsome blond young man. I flee. Halfway down the next block there is a smaller shop. It seems quite deserted. I edge up to the counter where boxes of sheaths and tubes of spermicidal jelly are cheerfully on display. A white-jacketed man with grey hair and a severe frown pops up from nowhere.

"Madam," he says forbiddingly.

"Some—toothpaste please," I manage to ask, blushing down to the soles of my feet.

But time is passing. The next day I try again. One of the big discount places this time, where you serve yourself. Just as I find the relevant products on the shelves and stretch out my hand, an old priest in a long soutane looms up behind me. It is Lucy's confessor, Père Silas; I recognize him at once. What in the name of all that's papal is *he* doing here? I've never told anyone my love secrets—here at least I've been tougher than Charlotte. In panic I seize a packet and hurry to the checkout counter, where a gum-chewing girl rings up the sale in blessed indifference. Only when I get home do I discover that what I've bought is a box of extra-strength condoms.

Well, I don't feel quite equal to going back *there*. But I visit a similar establishment and come away, triumphant at last, with a tube of jelly rather coyly labelled Familiplan. I feel greatly relieved with this in my possession. Now, with just a little luck and accurate calculation of my cycle, there should be no problem. It would be grand, I suppose, to be made of the epic stuff that boldly conceives, bears, and brings up a child in single blessedness. But such an enterprise would bring my poor mother stalking out of her grave, more distraught than ever Hamlet's father was. Then there is the thought of Lou's face . . . no. The allure of motherhood fades before these prospects. Far better the Familiplan.

Unfortunately, all this anxious forethought makes me feel tense, apprehensive not so much of disaster as of anticlimax. I wonder whether Bill feels this too? It may turn out that he and I are too much alike for comfort. I've seen very little of him lately, and when we do meet, for some reason we are careful to avoid those friendly embraces we used to enjoy so much. We are shyer with each other than we were that first day when we met in Archie's office. Odd. Oh well, these qualms are all no doubt perfectly normal and common as headcolds. It will be perfectly all right once we get away. I still have the warmest confidence in the sheer black pyjamas.

The night before we're due to leave, my sleep is crowded with a swarm of anxiety dreams. It must be a mistake to plan things like this such a long time ahead. Builds up too much pressure in the psyche. My mother's door is locked against me, though I can hear her rocking inside. I knock and call in rising desperation. She needs me, she is weeping, but I can't reach her. I unpack to find I have forgotten something vitally important. Panic. It must be there. But the suitcase is empty. What is it that is missing?—*Anna Karenina?* — my alluring new nightclothes? I don't know, but I wake up gasping, with a sense of calamity. Louis-Philippe is in the kitchen. He is completely naked, though his genitals are blank as a Ken doll's: my censor evidently never sleeps. He says, stopping the elevator with a sickening jolt, "Be very damn careful about rape, mees." The police are running after Mike and me with guns. We run and run up the mountainside, desperate for breath. "How silly, at your age," says Archie. "Embarrassing. And painful."

These absurd nightmares cling around me even as I drink my coffee and dress. It is a cool, silvery day. The new pantsuit looks fresh and smart. I put the last items into my suitcase — checking with great care to be sure everything is there. At seven-thirty (we've agreed on an early start), I put the key into the Porsche, drive over to Bill's street, and park outside his door. When he comes out, coat over his arm, suitcase in hand, I have a queer feeling of unreality. Is all this really happening, or am I still asleep? How strange that wide-awake I seem to have no emotions at all, of pleasure or fear or anything else, whereas in those dreams —

Bill looks rather pale. I notice with complete detachment that before putting his suitcase into the trunk he darts a quick glance around, as if afraid someone might see us. Does he think that old man with the poodle is a plainclothes morality detective? Or that Molly is hiding somewhere in the bare shrubbery, waiting to jump out and denounce him? I rub my eyes and try to wake up. None of this seems to be actually happening.

"You're right on time," says Bill, inserting himself sideways into the seat beside me. The cold breeze has ruffled his hair.

"Yes. Don't sit on the map."

"Not going to rain, is it?"

"I don't think so."

"You had breakfast?"

"Just coffee."

No, I'm awake, all right. The dialogue in dreams is never so banal. The doors clunk shut. We move off. The engine hums us across the long bridge heading south. "Off the island," I think with satisfaction. I have cleaned the car inside, and washed and polished the white chassis so that it looks positively bridal in the pale morning light. A sweet, spicy smell of shaving lotion comes from Bill. He is troubled by a persistent little hacking cough as he studies the map.

"We can get down as far as Albany by lunchtime," I say. "Then we pick up the freeway southwest . . . see it?"

He throws me a glance almost of alarm. "I'm pretty hopeless at maps."

"Not to worry," I tell him soothingly. His nervousness makes me feel calm and capable. "I hear signposting is very good in the States. Let me know when you'd like to drive."

"Oh, not till later — much later. I'm a zombie till noon. Maybe we could stop for coffee in a while, that might wake me up."

"Sure."

"I might have a little doze now, if you don't mind."

"Not a bit. Go ahead."

He closes his eyes. The miles slide past in silence. We might have been married for years.

At lunchtime we reach Albany, and Bill, apparently much refreshed, sits up and runs a comb through his curly hair. "Let's find a nice place and have a good meal," he says. "I hate those awful highway diners. Half a bottle of wine would do us no harm, right? After all, it's not every day we — er — elope, is it?"

"No, indeed." Impossible not to smile back at him as he pats my knee. And the wine he treats us to, a dry, cold hock, does enliven the not-very-interesting seafood that is Our Yo-Heave-Ho Special. Over dessert he makes me laugh with a ridiculous story about how Emma's husband, in hospital for removal of a mole, nearly got operated on for hernia by mistake. We linger over second cups of coffee. But as soon as we're back in the car, conversation dries up again: we seem to have nothing to say to each other.

"Would you like me to drive for a while, Willy?"

"Sure, if you'd like to."

We change places. He finds the gear-changes awkward at first, and he soon proves to be a fast but nervous driver with a tendency to change his mind in the middle of a decision; for example, when passing. My foot keeps pawing for an imaginary brake. My knuckles bleach as we sweep past a truck. Soon I try not to look at the road at all. Is it better to talk to him or not?

"I'm thinking of moving this spring, Bill. There's so much noise in my building it's getting me down. I don't know which is worse, those sex-acrobats next door, or the old battlers on the other side. I thought of looking for a little flat, maybe; or a coach-house, if I can find one. There's all kinds of furniture in storage in Toronto I could use. The extra space would be nice. And the privacy. I keep on running into our janitor, and he's — "

"Do you mind a lot, Willy? I find it a bit hard to concentrate when you're talking."

"I'll shut up," I promise quickly.

"Not nervous, are you?" he asks as I close my eyes.

"No, no — not at all." But despite a recent visit to the Ladies, I now feel a keen urge to do so again. Yet asking him to stop at a service station now (our tank is nearly full) would be so tactless that I feel I can't possibly do it. The next hour is highly uncomfortable for body and mind alike. Then, mercifully, he pulls up at a station and swings out of the car, saying cheerfully, "May I be excused?"

It seems to grow brighter as the long afternoon tediously melts into evening. The water-coloured sky is dappled with high, pale cloud. The roads shine with recent rain. After tea in a noisy roadside snack bar, we go on with me at the wheel. The car radio dispenses bland non-music. Bill leans back, yawning.

"Soon be near Washington," I remark.

"We might as well go on for a bit, don't you think? It won't be dark for ages yet. Lots of Vacancy signs."

"Of course," I agree, almost before he has finished. My cheeks are blazing. He yawns again.

When we stop at a small village restaurant for supper, a motherly waitress in bifocals, unabashed by the appalling leather eggs and cardboard pie she has served us, smiles warmly and says, "You-all come on back, now, you heah?"

"Don't hold your breath, you-all dear," mutters Bill. "Why don't you go back to the car, Willy; I've got a bit of shopping to do down the street. Won't be a minute." Soon he is back with a large paper bag, which he stows in the back seat. It clinks when I start the car. "Nightcaps," he says with a wink.

A little later, with darkness now total, we are moving along a four-lane highway out of Washington. It is nine o'clock.

"Do you think — " I begin, clearing my throat.

"What?"

"—nothing. Only we've covered nearly five hundred miles."

"Are you tired? Well, I suppose we'd better start looking for a motel."

"Yes, I suppose we'd better."

"That one's full."

"Look, that was a rather nice-looking one on the left. What do you think?"

"Nope; too near the road. The traffic noise would drive us nuts."

"Look, there's a list of recommended motels in the glove compartment—see it? Dozens of them listed. Can you find one near here?"

"Probably not, but I'll try."

"Wait, there was a place. It had a Vacancy sign."

"I don't think it had, Willy."

"Oh. Well, we'll just keep on."

"Here's one listed that sounds marvy. 'Colour TV in all air-conditioned units. Gourmet dining-room with view of lake.' Oh. It doesn't open till June."

"Well, we just passed a sign for the Shangri-La Motor Inn. Two miles west of here. Want to try it?"

"Oh, all right."

By now it is nearly ten o'clock. I am stiff with fatigue after so many hours at the wheel, and he must be weary too, for he keeps on yawning. At last we find the Shangri-La—Kumfy, Klean, Kosy — and there a hot-pink neon sign blinks the beautiful word Rooms. I switch off the engine with a sigh.

"You wait here, Willy. I'll see the office people."

He is gone long enough for me to wonder with a last-minute qualm whether by any crazy chance I've misunderstood him all along, and he intends us to have separate rooms—or whether at the last second he's lost interest and decided to arrange it that way.

"Right," he says, reappearing. "Number Seven."

And then, what seems too good to be true, we are setting down our luggage in a small room. Here not one but two double beds seem to loom in preternatural size. There is no TV, no view, and no air-conditioning—on the contrary, the stuffy air seems to have been there for years. But neither of us is in a mood to complain.

"It's all they had left," he says apologetically. "But it could be worse, I suppose. At least we're off the highway. Now you know what's going to happen next?"

"What?"

"Your Uncle Bill is going to make us a pair of lovely dry martinis. See, I got ice from the Boss Man's own fridge. Can you find us some glasses in the bathroom?"

"No gin for me, Bill—just give me a bit of the vermouth with an ice-cube."

"If you say so." He crushes ice in a handkerchief, pours with care from his bottles, stirs the mixture tenderly in one of the glasses. "You mustn't bruise the gin," he explains. Then he tastes. "Superb! Here, try yours, Will. Here's to us."

We clink glasses. A little colour has begun to creep into his cheeks by the time he pours the second drink. Perhaps it is only the white strip-lighting over the mirror that makes us both look so prematurely old.

"And next on the agenda, a gorgeous long, hot shower. Sound good? Would you like to — er — go first?"

"Yes, fine." I open my suitcase, then close it up again and manœuvre it with difficulty into the tiny bathroom with me. It's just too much, somehow, to take out my baby-dolls right there in front of him. Not to mention other, even more personal items. Then, just as I step out of the shower, the only light in the room fizzes and dies.

"Oy, Bill. The light's gone in here."

"Damn. There's only one bulb in this awful room. Want it?"

"Oh, never mind. It doesn't matter."

But it does. The all-important Familiplan must now be put into operation. Instructions are enclosed in the packet. Impossible to read them in the dark. Equally impossible to open the door a crack and—Oh God. Impossible even to emerge from this room clutching the damn box. There is certainly nowhere in the baby-dolls to hide it, and the only dressing gown I brought along is transparent. All I can do is put it back in the suitcase, control a fit of hysterical giggles, and edge myself and luggage back into the bedroom.

"Ah, there you are," he says brightly. A fresh martini tinkles in his glass. He is stretched out on the bed in his shirtsleeves, reading a paperback thriller. "My turn now?"

"Right. It's all yours."

He picks up his toilet case and a pair of pale blue pyjamas and disappears, martini still in hand. The door locks behind him. Something in the set of his back suggests that he may have need of a little privacy of his own.

Once I'm sure he isn't likely to come back for a few minutes, I unfold the Familiplan instructions. The thin paper crackles like a forest fire. I read the fine print hastily, holding it near the light. Then I read the whole thing again. I still don't understand exactly where ... or how ...

The shower-water stops. I freeze in panic. Then it starts again. Desperately I squat down between the beds and attempt to follow Familiplan's orders. It seems incredibly difficult. Either they have enclosed the wrong instructions, or I am constructed in some entirely original way. After a great deal of fumbling and increasing agitation, I manage to insert a small amount of the jelly. It immediately begins to sting fiercely, leaving the whole area in a condition of surprise. But the shower has stopped running. Hastily I hide the box in my suitcase and jump into one of the beds.

But it is a long time before he comes out. There is silence from the dark bathroom, except for a breathy sort of intermittent whistling from behind the door. It goes on and on, with occasional pauses. Once I think I hear him whisper "Shit."

I arrange myself as picturesquely as possible against the pillows. Soon my arms feel cold and I pull up the blankets. Bill's thriller lies open on the bed; I begin to read. Then my eyes begin to droop shut; sleep washes over me in wave after warm wave.

The unlocking door makes me jump. In he comes on a cloud of warm, moist air smelling of soap and gin. His blue pyjamas are crisp and his curly hair immaculate. But he looks very odd—his face is red and tight with some kind of distress or embarrassment. Or perhaps it's only the martinis.

"All right to turn out the light?" he asks in a constricted voice.

"Yes."

"Shall I — all right if I come in?"

"Of course."

The darkness is something to be grateful for, though it does seem a pity to waste the baby-dolls I've been counting on so much. He gets in under the bedclothes and puts his arm around me. His breath is heavy with toothpaste and martinis.

"Willy?"

"Yes."

"Um—I suppose we should have talked about this before, but
—are you on the Pill?"

"No, I'm not. But—"

"Oh. Well, in that case—"

"It's all right, though." (I hope.) "There are other—I mean—"
(No. I simply cannot go into details.) "But it's all right, really. Not
to worry."

"Because I — er — that is, I'd better use—"

"Yes, that would be a good idea."

"Yes." A brief pause. "But the perfectly maddening thing is
that I — I couldn't get it to stay *on* just now. Nerves, I guess."

"I know what you mean."

He gives an enormous yawn.

"The fact is, Willy, we're both terribly tired ... why don't we
just have a sleep first, and then ... "

"What a good idea. Let's do that."

"I'll take the other bed, then, just for now. Good night, Willy
dear."

"Good night, Bill."

One minute later he is snoring heavily. There is only time for
me to think sleepily, "It's all right, Mother. We didn't even bruise
the gin," before I am deeply asleep.

Virginia is blue and green, warm and beautiful. The dislike I
gradually acquire for its name is probably irrelevant. In the long
sunny days we enjoy the red-earth fields, and trees in rich leaf,
and the heavy Southern food. We chat and laugh as we explore
the handsome old districts of Richmond. We have long, leisurely
meals. One wet afternoon we go to the movies and sit in the back
row with our feet up like a couple of kids, eating popcorn.

It's only the nights that are awkward. As darkness falls we tend
to become spasmodically talkative, and to avoid each other's eyes.
On the second day of the trip, Bill eats something that disagrees
with him, and retires early to bed, groaning faintly. The night
after that is his regular weekly night to call his mother, and by the
time he gets back from phoning her, I am asleep. After that he
strains his back changing a tire. We are both always pleased when
day comes and we can take to the road and enjoy it without
complications. We send a great many postcards back to Canada.

Eventually, after one hot day's drive, we find a cabin for the night by the side of a small lake. It is a bare and primitive little shack, smelling faintly of kerosene, and the one bed is an elderly brass affair with a hollow in its middle. We avoid making any comment on this to each other. There is a small black stove, on which I cook us a delicious steak with mushrooms, and we share a bottle of good wine. Afterwards we sit outside on a little wooden jetty that runs out into the blue water. The sky is still bright, and the weather-whitened boards under us still feel warm. Bill brings out his martinis in a jug and we sit companionably close to watch the dusk come, with our tired feet dangling in the water. It is too early in the season for insects. An elegant little moon rises white in the east.

"This is nice, isn't it?" he says with a happy sigh. "You're such good company, Willy."

I lean against him. The muffled lub-dub of his heart is under my ear. Cautiously I relax. His arm and shoulder in a soft checked-flannel shirt feel warm and comfortable. As the martini jug empties and a few stars look out, he holds me closer. "Nice," he murmurs. Eventually he undoes a few of my blouse buttons. "Feeling sleepy?" he asks into my ear.

"Well, not exactly sleepy."

"Shall we go in?"

"Let's."

I whisk into my rose-coloured nightgown and hop into the bed, which receives me with a noisy jangle of aged springs. Soon he snaps out the light and joins me in the hollow. The moon looks in on us benignly.

Some time later he moves away. The springs give a loud, grinding clash.

"Sorry about that, Will."

"Not at all."

"Bit tired, I guess."

"That's all."

"You warm enough?"

"Yes, fine."

"Good night, then."

"Good night."

But now that I can define Bill's problem, the situation is actually easier. From then on we occupy separate beds without any comment or evasion, and feel a lot more at ease with each other. I sleep badly, but he is sympathetic and provides me with a bottle of tranquillizers.

And that is how we should have had the sense to leave it. But on the last night of the trip, after Bill has had one more martini than usual, my baby-doll pyjamas register a belated effect on him. Up to a point, that is. The same point. After which, with a parting kiss on the forehead, he returns to his own bed, and we say goodnight in small, polite voices.

The next day we are back in Montreal. It is a grey, chilly afternoon. The buds on the trees are barely open. Traces of snow still lie in patches of shade on the yellow grass of muddy lawns.

"It might be better if you just drop me off at a bus stop along Dorchester, Willy, and let me get home that way. You know what a bunch of gossips we've got at Cartier, and all our department lives so close to my place."

"Sure. This one do you?"

"Fine. Well, it's been really great, Willy. Terrific fun. Bless you." His brown eyes beam into mine. He smooths my cheek so tenderly my eyes prick with silly tears.

"See you around, pussycat," he says, and goes.

NINE

This Island's Mine

ELL, SO MUCH FOR THAT," I think as I pull away from the curb to merge the now-grimy Porsche with the flow of Sunday traffic. Last summer I grumbled because the truth wasn't enough like fiction. It's only fair now to admit that I don't like it much better when life unmistakably indicates the end of a chapter. The surprising thing is that I can accept this particularly emphatic end with so much equanimity. Perhaps I suspected all along that the relationship with Bill could never really develop. Anyhow, oddly enough, now he's gone, it hardly seems important, one way or another. The scent of the spicy lotion he uses on his hair lingers in the car and I wind down a window to let it out. Poor Bill. I wonder if, like me, he feels more light-hearted now our holiday is over than when it began. Does he wonder how that can be? Maybe he too is almost grateful to be left without expectations or hopes of any kind. For whatever reason, I am not—at the moment anyway—oppressed with any sense of failure. I don't dread going into my silent apartment. I'm not afraid of the painful thoughts and ludicrous memories that are certainly waiting for me there. Maybe, I think gratefully, I am actually getting tougher. Growing up. If so, what a good thing. Only wet-eyed sentimentalists think it's marvellous to be young.

On Dorchester I pass Archie's house sitting cubic, stubborn, and shabby in its desolate, empty lot. Two or three incorrigible crocuses have pushed up among the uncut bushes of his garden.

My foot lifts off the gas pedal. I have a sudden, irrational urge to stop here. Why don't I go up to his door and knock? I want to see him. But how ridiculous. I'm not *speaking* to Archie. Worse, he himself is being polite to me. Another end of a chapter. But why is this one so much harder to accept?

I find myself driving around the block to pass the house again. No one, not even Percy, appears at any of the windows. No smoke drifts from the chimney. Perhaps he's away. In Jamaica, perhaps? Or ill? Nonsense. He's at Molly's reading out of the dictionary, or watching Sesame Street with Emma's children, or at the library writing a Johnsonian letter to the Principal.

Once more I tour the block. Then I think, "No, the house is empty. But first thing tomorrow I'll go and see him in his office." Only then, as if released, can I pass the house and turn up the hill toward home. I stop along the way to pick up a newspaper and buy eggs, bacon, and cheese. I'll make a quiche for supper. Cookery is good for more than just the stomach. And I'll look at the Classified Ads, while I eat, for places to rent. One of these days I might even get myself a cat or a parrot. With a bit of company, there are worse places than an island.

Awkwardly juggling mail from my box with parcels and suitcase, I let myself into the apartment. The overheated darkness of the place is stifling. Too fine and private by far. I hurry to the window and open the curtains to let in the clear evening sky, on which a few delicate trails of silver cloud are floating. The light is pure and clear as water. I toss aside some bills and tear open a letter from Lou.

Dear Willy,

I must say I think it's selfish of you to rush off for no reason at all to the States instead of coming here to us. With all those long holidays teachers get, you surely could have gone there any time — but I've noticed that ever since you moved to Montreal your family doesn't matter as much to you. I suppose that's inevitable, really. Just the same, you might have thought of Dougie, if nobody else. He was terribly disappointed not to see you. I say nothing about myself, though it might also have occurred to you I could do with some companionship just now when I'm feeling so huge and rotten. And I could certainly use a hand with D., too — he's going through a horrible, whining stage these days and is a real drag. Of course Greg is out now more evenings a week than ever. He never thinks of anything but that damned law firm of his.

Well, single people never realize how lucky they are. It must be great to be footloose, with no ties or responsibilities at all. But I don't intend to criticize or complain. After all, I suppose you don't owe us anything. I hope you had a nice trip. Write soon.

Love, Lou.

Slowly but with some vehemence I tear up this message into very tiny pieces. I drop them into the wastebasket. After that I stand at the window looking out at the quiet air for some time. Then, suddenly, the buzzer sounds, making me start. Who on earth can that be?

"Hullo?"

"A word with you, miss." The rich voice growling out the speaker is unmistakable, but I can hardly believe my ears.

"Archie! Come on up."

While I wait for him to appear, I thrust the suitcase into the bedroom and dart into the bathroom to wash my face. My own eyes, large with astonishment, meet me in the mirror. The rasp of the buzzer still seems to tingle in the air.

"Come to apologize," he says, while still in the hall. He pulls up short in the doorway, a portly, aggressive figure, confronting me with truculence. He is wearing a handsome light-grey suit I've never seen before, the trousers sharply creased. A mulberry waistcoat with gold buttons adds a touch of splendour to the whole outfit. His blue eyes are diffident under a formidable scowl. He looks as defiant as an old boar at bay, except for those eyes. I pull him in, close the door, and without a word throw my arms around him. He returns a fierce hug redolent of cigars.

"I passed your house a few minutes ago and almost rang the bell."

"It's all right, then?"

"Of course it is."

"Shouldn't have said those things."

"Neither should I."

"Not fair to blame you for the Armstrong mess."

"No, but you were right. I handled it badly."

"Quite. But I had no right to speak like that. It was curmudgeonly."

"Damn right it was. Oh, I'm so glad to see you, Archie."

He beams at me. Each of my cheeks receives a smacking kiss. I blow my nose. He blows his.

"Come on in properly," I say, tugging at him. "Take off your coat. I was just about to make a bit of supper—have you eaten?"

"No, no. Sackcloth and abstinence. Haven't eaten a proper meal all week."

"Well, stay and have something now. I was going to make a quiche."

He follows me into the kitchen area and there at once begins to rummage in the grocery bag and inspect the contents of the little fridge with a critical eye. "*I* shall make *you* a quiche," he says. "Out with the pastry board, wench. Been away all week, have you? I have telephoned you several times." He throws me an eloquent look.

"Yes, I went down to Virginia."

"Enjoy it?"

"Not very much." I add no details, not because I am afraid or ashamed, but simply because the sight of him peering at me over the tops of his glasses as he breaks eggs makes me too absurdly happy. There is not a single detail about that week that I could not tell Archie, and because I know that, there is no hurry to do it. He will be perfectly furious, of course, when he hears the whole story. In fact, there will doubtless be another monumental quarrel. I'm actually looking forward to it. But it can wait.

"What's this about seeing your doctor?" I ask, girding an apron with some difficulty around the grey suit.

"More or less routine. He periodically links me up to an electrocardiogram machine that for some reason has his confidence. I had a heart attack some years ago. Healed up quite well. He's pleased I've lost some weight. The one compensation for giving up Scotch. You haven't even noticed that I'm wearing my last Savile Row suit, have you, miss? I can get into it again now, after ten years. Anyhow, the heart in this old fossil appears in fair shape for one of my temper and habits."

"Only fair?"

"Fair enough, one hopes, for ordinary purposes."

"Well, I hope they don't include retirement. I've heard hints you're thinking of resigning."

"From the Chair? Never."

The magnificence of this pledge is slightly marred when he adds, "Of course they are going to throw me out. But that is quite different."

"Quite," I agree, grinning. "But are they really ... ?"

"They are. Everybody's been informed but me, it seems. Adding insult to injury. They hope it will hurt. Instead it gives me a certain grim pleasure to find them so predictable."

"That's the spirit! How I love you, Archie."

Nevertheless, the row with Archie occurred punctually a day or two later when I told him about the Virginia trip. The scene wasn't quite the pleasure I expected, either, because instead of exploding with anger, he became (and remains) remote, sad, and cool. I find this so depressing that I accept Emma's invitation to a supper party the night before exams begin. She has pressed me to come, which is nice of her. After all, the world is not exactly spilling over with people who crave the pleasure of my company.

Early Sunday evening I zip up the blue mini-dress and apply some blue eyeliner, acquired in a light-hearted Washington moment. It gives me a highly bizarre look, which is perhaps not inappropriate in the circumstances.

For hours I have tried not to listen for the phone. Two weeks ago it would have been natural for Bill to ring and arrange to pick me up so we could go to the party together. Now, apparently, it is no longer natural. All week long I've only seen him for a moment or two at a time. The phone is silent as a toad. At eight-thirty I set out alone, with raincoat and umbrella, through mizzling rain. The street lights print swinging shadows of half-open leaves on the dark sidewalks. A lovely smell of earth and water breathes out over the city from the wooded mountain above and the broad river below. They enclose the vast city trivia of steel and glass and concrete with tolerance. It is spring. They can afford to be generous.

Reluctantly I turn up the path to the gaunt row of duplexes where Emma lives and furl my umbrella at her blue door. Well do I know I'd be far happier walking for a mile or two in the sweet, misty darkness, and then going peacefully home. But the penalty for being an optimist must be paid.

Emma swings the door wide. She looks even more immense than usual in a voluminous patterned robe like those fancied by the Queen of Tonga. Behind her in the hall and sitting-room I can see a swarm of people milling about with drinks; beyond, in the dining-room, others are thick around the buffet. Clasping my arm cosily Emma assures me, in the cheerful, lying way of hostesses, that I know everybody, but before abandoning me she hooks a passing male and introduces him as Rudolph Osmond, the new Registrar.

He is a cadaverous young man with a slight facial tic that at irregular but unnerving intervals arrests his mild expression in a look of violent alarm. He immediately fastens an intense and hopeful gaze on my bosom and forces a glass of clouded purple punch into my hand.

"Well, Miss Doyle, Emma says you're new at Cartier too. Where are you from?"

"Toronto." I look over his shoulder, while trying not to seem put off by the tic. I had thought Archie would surely be here, but there is no sign of him.

"Toronto the Good, eh? Ha ha ha." He actually accompanies this remark with an elbow-dig in my ribs. I edge aside. Off in a distant corner I can see Bill telling a story with animated gestures to Ruth Pinsky. She is laughing.

"Yes, sir, quite a contrast to Montreal the Bad, eh? Why the number of brothels in this town is higher than anywhere else in North America, did you know that? But what would a charming girl like you know about such things? Especially from Toronto the Good. Ha ha." In the middle of a tic he leers at me. A bubble of craziness rising in me almost makes me leer back. Wildly I look around for help. There is none. In a voice of appalling falseness, I say, "Lovely to have met you, but do please excuse me — there's someone over there I simply must see — " And I make for Bill, afraid to look back for fear Osmond is following. There is such a crush that for a moment I can make little or no progress.

"Of course they can do it," somebody says over my shoulder. Somebody else holds a cup of punch dangerously poised over my head as he tries to manœuvre sideways in the other direction. "The chairmanship is an annual appointment." Another voice says, "Somebody from Syracuse, I heard." I twist around, but both speakers seem to have disappeared. My party headache, I find, is already well established. Surely it was Archie they were gossiping about. But where is the man?

Bill is surrounded by a noisy group, including Molly and Harry, and at first he doesn't notice me. He is looking particularly well in the white sweater that sets off his new tan and the lustre of his dark eyes. Something in the timbre of his voice tells me he has had a little more of the purple punch than is altogether good for him.

"—my dear, insatiable!" he is saying. "They tell me it's the way with that age group, but *really*—" He catches sight of me then and calls gaily, "Hi there, Willy," but then turns aside to say something more to Ruthie that a burst of laughter behind me cuts off. I linger on the outskirts of the group for a minute or two, keeping a smile pinned firmly in place. Nobody else is near me that I know. I edge around a faded chintz armchair. Emma is a casual housekeeper. Under its pleated skirt a doll and a crust of toast have been imperfectly kicked out of sight. Cautiously I peer about. Osmond is mercifully invisible. After hiding my punch on a windowsill I help myself at the buffet to salad and spaghetti, carrying my plate into a deserted little breakfast bar to eat in blessed privacy. Not that I am hungry. In fact my throat closes after the first bite or two. No, it's neurotic to imagine that Bill was talking about me to those people. He couldn't possibly do such a thing. Nor would he. We are friends. There's no cruelty or treachery in Bill, I assure myself. But do I really believe this?

Someone is strumming "Georgia" on the piano in the other room. I take my plate out to the kitchen and scrape its contents into the garbage. As I do so I catch sight of someone sitting under the kitchen table. It is a girl of about three in a crumpled blue flannelette nightgown. She is eating Ritz biscuits out of a box with calm and silent absorption. Her bare feet are dirty and her banged fair hair hangs around a fat countenance full of complacent self-esteem.

"Hi," I say, squatting down.

"Hi."

"What's your name?"

"Jade."

"Jade! What a pretty name."

"I'm not in my damn bed," she says with satisfaction.

"No. Do you like parties?"

"They're silly. Why are your eyes so funny?"

"I don't know."

After a pause for thought she offers me a chipped Ritz. Her expression is severe as she judges how many are left in the box. She has nothing more to say, and no interest whatever in my boring presence. I look at her with admiration. Is she what I will be, with luck — or, poor little bitch, am I what she will become? But just then Emma's husband, a small and harassed-looking man, appears behind me, saying sharply, "Go to bed at once, Jane." Without the slightest loss of dignity or any empty farewells she scrambles out and disappears down the hall. When I turn, Osmond is there, tic and all. "Care to trip the light fantastic?" he asks. He takes my arm in a bony clutch. The player in the next room has moved on to "Jamaica Farewell", and there is some ragged singing. I pull my arm free and give Osmond a glittering smile to match his own.

"See you later, maybe," I tell him, and move off with decision to the bathroom. There I shoot the bolt and sit down on the one available seat, propping my feet on the tub. I light a cigarette. For some time I occupy myself with an old copy of *Punch*. Eventually, however, the knocks, rattles, and nudges at the door become more insistent and I get up reluctantly. The moment I unlock the door, an indignant redhead flounces in. I wonder whether she too is a refugee from Osmond.

After some search through a choked cupboard I find my coat and thank Emma's husband (now doing dishes) for the nice party. On the way out I glimpse Emma overflowing the piano bench, a sight that makes me think of Fats Waller's remark to himself before beginning a performance — "Is you all on?"

At the open door I meet Archie just arriving.

"Good evening," he says stiffly.

"Good evening, Archie."

"Off home already?"

"I'm early. But you're late."

"Spot of indigestion. Fell asleep over TV, if you want the truth."

"Oh."

We stand there looking at each other.

"Alone, are you?" he asks.

"Yes."

Another pause.

"I suppose you wouldn't like to walk me home."

He promptly buttons up his coat again. "Yes, I'll walk you home."

The rain has stopped and cleared room for a scatter of little stars. We walk along in easy and total silence. There is a faint chuckle of running water in the gutters. Down in the harbour a big ship hoots in its hoarse voice, and a police siren keens. Big-city music. He walks on the outside edge of the pavement to protect me from runaway horses. I find this soothing. Vaguely I think I'll not bother to go to any more Women's Lib meetings.

"Good party?" he asks finally.

"There are no good parties, really."

He grunts agreement.

As we approach my building we find ourselves walking more and more slowly.

"Once more round the block?" he asks.

"Yes, let's."

A few minutes later he takes my cold hand and puts it, folded in his large, warm one, inside his coat pocket. We walk more and more slowly till we hardly seem to be moving at all. I find myself smiling, smiling at nothing and for no reason at all. We go round the block once more, still in silence. At last he says brusquely,

"No, it would be ridiculous."

"What would?"

"Totally unfair to you. I'm sixty."

"I know that."

"And not even what the insurance people call a very good life. No, of course I could never ask you. I'm not even very well off."

"Archie, are you —"

"No. Don't say anything. Not yet. Please, not another word." The canopy of my apartment once more comes gradually into view. "I'll have to go back to Emma's now," he adds matter-of-factly. "Rude not to. But before I go —"

And before I can do anything to promote or discourage the manœuvre, he has engulfed me in a powerful arm and I am receiving a kiss of quite astonishing voltage. Afterwards it's hardly polite of me to look so amazed, I suppose; but I do, and he begins to laugh, in loud, explosive guffaws. I laugh too. A stout woman walking a pug of the same shape throws us a look of alarm. We clasp each other, feeling young, guilty, and happy. "There, be off with you," he says, giving me a little push. "And ponder the wisdom of Auden. His prayer was 'Make me chaste, Lord; but not yet.' Good night t'ye." And he adds, "My dear," in a voice so low I almost miss it. But not quite. Minutes later in the elevator, rising somewhat dizzily upward, I find myself still smiling, as it were, all over, in the most ridiculous way. Why didn't I say "Good night, love"? But perhaps there was no need.

Exam Week opens its jaws at nine the next morning and engulfs us all so totally there is no time for the minor metaphysics of the heart. At opposite ends of the gym, Archie and I pace up and down the aisles between long rows of desks where the candidates hunch over papers, desperately twisting their hair and munching Life Savers as they scribble. A brilliant sun plays heartlessly on the wall as these poor prisoners sit sighing through their ordeal, and the electric clock jerks away the rationed minutes. A rustling silence broods over us all. There is a feeling that the least life itself can do is remain suspended while this solemn academic ritual runs its course.

When not on invigilation duty I am crouched over a desk of my own, reading my way through volumes of handwritten exam books. This activity soon creates the kind of intellectual and physical fatigue that would result from trying to swim through jelly. Long class lists appear in our boxes; elaborate forms; stacks of computer cards. Deadlines for the submission of final grades are underlined in red with menacing politeness. I meet Bill briefly in the hall on his way to the coffee machine. His tan has faded to a wan yellow. He leans against the wall as if even light conversation might prove a dangerous drain.

"Ghastly, isn't it."

"Oh God."

"By the way, Bill"—here, uncomfortably, I lower my voice—"I found a silk tie of yours among my things; shall I — ?"

"Oh, just stick it in my box some time, Willy."

A brief, intensely constricted silence descends. I hasten into hectic conversation.

"I fell asleep over my Novel papers last night and woke up with my neck all crooked. Are you nearly finished?"

"Yes," he says heavily. "Well, I must be off." He then pushes himself away from the wall with the brisk air of a man who has just remembered important business, but a second later I see him turn into the door marked Men. Yet I feel no real resentment of poor Bill. He has been little more than a note on the margin for what seems like a long time.

At different intervals throughout the week I go to Archie's office to see him—though exactly why, or to say what, I really am not sure—but he is always busy. Once I find him patting a tearful girl who has apparently, in a panic, tried to answer all twenty questions on a paper requiring answers to only five. Another day he is on the phone shouting at some unfortunate soul on the other end. Late one afternoon I try again, thinking that at this hour he is surely likely to be alone. But this time I find him at his office door talking to a dark, short man in horn-rims and a striped suit. By the tension of their legs and the heartiness of their voices I can tell it is not a casual chat they are having.

"Miss Doyle, may I present the newly appointed Chairman of the Department: Dr. Mortimer Shift, from Syracuse."

"How do you do," I murmur, careful not to catch Archie's eye. "I just stopped by—it's not important—" and I make my escape without delay, having seized only a fleeting impression that Shift has large teeth, a dry hand, and the fixed eyes of a worrier. I am also aware that in a sardonic sort of way Archie is enjoying himself, which is a relief.

But he does not come to my office, or ring me at home. If I had the time for it, this would bother me. But as it is, I can accept that absurd episode outside my apartment last week as a momentary aberration, a touch of spring lunacy to be remembered only with a grin. It has no connection with anything. It has no importance whatever. It just makes me smile all over still, whenever I think of it.

On Saturday afternoon I finish checking my computer cards against long lists of marks, and am just leaving the building when I encounter Archie in the lobby. "I have been looking for you," he remarks crossly.

"Have you? Well, here I am." We walk out of the house together. Once out on the sidewalk, he stops short and stares at me with a challenging, almost bellicose, air.

"*Well?*" he demands.

"Well what?" I am tired and the brilliant sun makes my eyes ache.

"You've kept me waiting all week. Haven't said one word."

"One word about what, for pity's sake?"

"So I presume I am rejected."

"Archie, what on earth are you talking about?"

"You have rejected me," he repeats, offended.

I seize him by the arm and shake it. "I've done no such thing, you terrible man."

"Then don't stand nattering here. If you've accepted me, come along home and have some roast chicken. Fine thing when a woman can't make herself clear without all this fuss."

Not another word does he utter all the way down to his house. My thoughts are blowing all over the place like scraps of torn paper in the wind. For God's sake, does this mean I am engaged?

As soon as we get inside, he gives me another of his vehement and powerful kisses, terminated this time by a rousing slap on the behind. He now radiates such warm and masterful exuberance you could make toast on it.

"There!" he says. "That's settled, then."

"Is it?"

"Eh? Speak up."

"I said, yes it is."

"Good. About time, too. Now you see this bottle of champagne I'm about to put in the freezer. In half an hour we'll drink it all, to celebrate. Meanwhile, you can put that chicken in the oven — it's all stuffed and trussed; just shove it in." He throws himself into the old Windsor chair and thrusts out his legs wearily. "Exhausting, being in love; I'm really getting too old for it. Been a horrible week. Never been so bone-tired. My Convocation cold is three weeks early, and I ascribe that directly to you, miss. Disturbing the even tenor of my ways — and fancy keeping me waiting a whole week. Then of course there have been other things ... among them the ineffable Dr. Shift."

"I judge he tickles you very much. But he's not a fool, is he?" This subject is one I seize on because I feel suddenly, between gusts of joy and trepidation, terribly shy.

"No, not a fool. He's a villain. A climber. An operator. No scruples and no feelings. Admirable chap. He will doubtless run the department very efficiently — and I hope it chokes him. But when I think of next winter, when I don't have to prepare the budget *and he does*, I could dance."

The heat of the oven causes Percy to form a comma on the floor with his cream-coloured belly blissfully exposed. Outside, a gusty wind tears cloud into long, dark streamers that fly across the sunset. The kitchen windows rattle in their warped old frames.

The fridge hums as it cools the champagne. I busy myself tidying up the miscellaneous clutter at, in, under, and around the sink. The roasting chicken begins to scent the room deliciously. Archie watches me drowsily over the tops of his glasses.

"We won't tell anyone just yet," he says. "If that's all right."

"It is all right," I say quickly, thinking of Lou.

"I've got to go to Jamaica next week. My sister Jessie has a big Golden Wedding celebration coming up — months ago I promised to be there. But when I come back for Convocation ... "

"Yes. Plenty of time then."

There is a supremely comfortable silence.

"You won't want to live here," Archie says, casting me a rather shy look of his own.

"I don't care where we live."

"No—I've been thinking about it all week. Silly to hang on here, with that eighteen-storey monster about to go up. The only reason I—well, you understand. But I haven't heard her voice for a long time now. She's gone."

"Yes. Not that I'd mind staying here."

"Actually I phoned the developer on Thursday and told him I'd sell. He was livid. I've held out for over two years now, and his lawyer has got quite rich. But he still wants the land. Now I like this district, don't you? Still has character and charm. Or will until our city fathers finish turning the whole place into another New York. What I thought was, it's a buyer's market now — we could pick up a better house along the curve here — one of those with the stone balconies; ever noticed them? Two of 'em are up for sale, just west of here across the road. One of them is actually empty right now."

"The whole city is plastered with signs. It must be true that people are getting out of Quebec."

"All the better for you and me. While I'm away, you could be scouting around; go and look at those two across the road. See whether you like either of 'em."

"How long will you be gone?"

"Two weeks, worse luck. Loathe flying. And don't want to leave you."

"You do. You're already restless, admit it. Bored. And us engaged only half an hour."

After basting the chicken I go over and perch on his lap. He smells of eucalyptus and cigars and the lavender water sprinkled on the old-fashioned linen handkerchief he keeps inside his cuff. After eyeing us intently for a minute, Percy leaps up onto my lap, where there is no room for him. He balances there, purring and swaying perilously, eyes half-closed like some feline drunk.

"Archie, did you see that interview in the *Star* the other day with Harry Innis? He says he's going to move east of the Main and join the separatists."

"I did. But have you seen the reply? There was an editorial in *La Presse* the next day. Admirably short and to the point. I cut it out to show you." He begins to heave all of us about stormily as he tries to peer down beside the chair where he files clippings, cat-toys, and dirty dishes. Percy and I get off with as much dignity as we can muster while our lord and master stirs through a heap of objects, including gardening gloves and a monkey-wrench, till he fishes up a small newspaper-cutting in triumph.

"Here, I'll translate. 'We wish to register our polite but final rejection of the support of Mr. Harry Innis of Cartier College. The cause of Quebec independence has no need or wish to enlist Anglophone sympathizers of the kind represented by Mr. Innis.'"

"How devastating for him. Maybe that's why he and Molly—"

"Why they what?"

"Well, yesterday I stopped in for coffee at the Hideaway, that campus place, you know—and they were there with some other people in a booth at the back. They didn't see me. And . . . "

"Well?"

"I couldn't help hearing part of it. They were talking about me. Us, that is. Apparently they saw us when you arrived at Emma's and took me home before going in. They were . . . laughing. I couldn't tell what was so funny about it. Then somebody said 'Typical old maid. *Really* hungry.' Not very complimentary to either of us, was it?"

After a silence he says, "Remember how Crusoe longed to reach the mainland, until he stopped to think, 'I might fall into the hands of savages . . . far worse than lions and tigers.'"

"Yes," I agree, thinking of Bill. "Islands are not the highest-risk places. But let's forgive them."

"Sit down here again, miss. Much they know about it, eh? Much they know. Only you and me. Now that's enough, or I shall forget to respect your virtue. Which I intend to do, in my archaic fashion, until after the ceremony. After that, look out. Now get the champagne and we'll drink to our wonderful selves."

The night before Archie's departure we sit close together at one end of the long table, amid the faded Edwardian splendour of his dining-room. A large Tiffany lamp like an inverted tulip sheds warm light over our wineglasses, scrawled notepaper, ashtrays, dictionary, maps, and bottle of cough syrup. Swags of dusty gold brocade hang at the long windows, closing out a wet and windy night. A coal fire burns red in a small basket grate. Percy sits on the marble chimneypiece, pretending to be an ornament. He is well aware of Archie's suitcase in the hall and the catbasket stowed in readiness near my chair. A tall clock in the corner chimes eleven frail notes.

"It's getting late — I really should go." But I don't move to get up. Instead I study Archie's beaky profile bent in a scowl over the mass of papers he is studying. The last few days have been unromantically cumbered with legalities concerning the sale of his house. Lawyers' meetings, together with all the end-of-term paper work at Cartier, have kept him busy, tired, and extremely testy. I have been arbitrarily assigned a number of chores myself.

"Got your passport application off?" he demands.

"Yes. The picture makes me look like a criminal lunatic."

His only response to this is a grunt. I make a terrible face at him.

"What did your landlord say about your lease?"

"Well, you know it only has three months to run. But Louis-Philippe told me at first I couldn't sublet. Then he hinted that for fifty dollars he might just possibly be able to arrange something. And today it turns out he can find a new tenant for the place almost right away."

"Good." He yawns.

"Archie, you should go to bed."

"Eh? Have we finished the wine? No? Then pour me what's left. It helps the cough. And the travel twitches. If God had meant us to fly, He'd have given us all jet engines on our little fingers."

"What time shall I be here in the morning, Archie?"

"Time? What for?"

"To take you to the airport, of course."

"I don't want you there, miss."

"How rude you are. Why not?"

He shoots me a fierce look over the tops of his half-glasses. "Because I refuse to say good-bye to you in that seething brew of tourists. I refuse to say good-bye at all, in fact. Look for no sentimental farewells from me." He takes a large, noisy gulp of wine, and adds, "I wish to God I'd never promised Jessie to make this silly journey."

"There, there. Don't grind your jaws like that, love."

"Two weeks is a long time. You might come to your senses and change your mind."

"No such luck for you, Benedict. I promise."

He whacks me amiably across the arm with a rolled-up deed before tossing it onto the floor.

"You'll look after Percy. Don't let him bully you."

"I like that. Who let Percy sit on the table the other night and put his paw into the Charlotte Russe?"

"That was different. It was his birthday. What are you grinning at?"

"Oh dear, I hate this trip too. Being happy is so corrupting . . . makes you selfish and plaintive and full of crazy, creepy fears . . . But you will write to me, won't you?"

"I shall." He stares at me so comprehensively that I begin to blush. Then he says brusquely, "Go now, miss. At once."

I am glad of the effort necessary to corner Percy and stuff him into the catbasket. Captured, he deliberately makes himself heavy as a stone cat and fills the air with loud wails. I lug him out into the hall, then come back, buttoning my coat.

"Please take care of that cold while you're away."

"You may give me one dry kiss on the forehead before tiptoeing away with your cat. I will see you when these bloody two weeks are over."

"Bless you, in the meantime, Archie."

"Go," he repeats without looking up.

And I leave him among his papers. Just as I reach the door, his sonorous voice rises and reaches after me in a declamation threatened by laughter:

> "With a heart of furious fancies
> Whereof I am commander;
> With a burning spear

And a horse of air,
To the wilderness I wander."

He then adds "Dammit."

My letter comes from Jamaica on a brilliant May morning. The sky shimmers like tight blue silk. The trees flicker, yellow-green under a hot sun. All through the city a sort of euphoria sails on the warm air. People swing along the pavement gaily; the metal flashing on cars stabs the air with brightness. The glass towers downtown glitter like dreams. My letter is in my handbag, gripped to my side as I set out for Cartier. It is not a long letter, or even a particularly interesting one, to anyone but me. But certain phrases, hastily read in the glass apartment lobby, are already written into me permanently.

On the steps of the office building I catch sight of someone who looks vaguely familiar. A tall, thin lad with a slouch, the sun turning his long hair yellow. I hurry with a little skip to catch up with him.

"Mike, I haven't seen you for ages. How are you?"

He frowns down at me through a pair of huge dark glasses.

"I'm okay, thanks."

"I've been hoping I'd run into you. Have you got a few minutes—? Do tell me how things are with you. What are your plans?"

"Plans?" he says vaguely. "Well, that's not exactly my bag, plans. Might go off to the West Coast this summer with a couple of guys. Or might not. Like that. I've sort of got a deal on for this Honda ... just depends."

"That would be great—to go west, I mean. It's a whole different scene out there, they say. And who knows, maybe after a while you might even feel like finishing your degree out there."

He looks at me without expression.

"You sound exactly like my mother. *And* my father."

"Yes, I daresay." He edges a little away; he would like to go, not out of any unfriendliness, but simply out of boredom. I am no longer of any significance to him—if, indeed, I ever really was. Yet out of my own brimming happiness I would like to give Mike something of value to take away from here, even if it is only my loving concern.

"I've thought a lot about you this last month, Mike. Often

wondered how you were, and wished things . . . had been different. Blamed myself. Well, we over-thirties are talented worriers. How has your father . . . reacted?"

A faint smile touches his tender lips.

"I found him one night in the library looking at the old Mauser. Sitting there just looking."

"God, was he?"

"That was when we talked about me going west. And he mentioned I might go back to college out there some time. You see? You get it? He's got me now, for keeps. Wherever I go. Whatever I do."

He raises one hand in a lazy half-salute and without saying anything more, he lopes easily away. His short shadow bobs after him down the white pavement.

I watch him till he is out of sight. Then, gripping my bag, I jump up the entrance steps. It is deliciously cool and shaded inside the building. The lower floor is completely deserted, silent except for a lone telephone drowsily ringing somewhere behind a closed door. I climb the stairs swiftly, the oak banister smooth and cool under my hand.

Up on our floor, it is quiet too — so quiet that I am almost startled to find quite a large number of people about, many of them from other departments. They are just standing about in pairs, or silently going to and from offices. A little group is clustered around Sherri's desk. They are talking in low voices. Oh, surely not more secrets and conspiracies, I think lightly. Well, whatever it's all about, I must ask Sherri about renting Convocation regalia.

When Sherri lifts her eyes to me I see that they are red. She does not speak. A queer little buzz of shock goes through me.

"What's wrong, Sherri?"

"Haven't you heard? About Dr. Clarke? His sister sent the college a telegram a couple of hours ago. He had this heart attack yesterday. They took him to hospital, but he died early this morning."

The buzz escalates and then ebbs completely away.

"That's too bad," I say vaguely. "What a shame."

"Don't," someone says soothingly to Sherri.

I wander away down the corridor to my own office, and unlock it, and go in, and sit down in the armchair. Each action is a primly separate, deliberate, act of will. I am perfectly calm. I am proud of how perfectly calm I am. The most important thing in the world now — the only important thing — is the need to preserve this equilibrium. No cost would be too high to keep it intact around me always like a polished glass bell.

I sit there for a while thinking about Mike. He will be quite all right. In five years well-to-do, even successful. No need to be concerned for him. Then I do two or three minor items of paper work. After a while I go out into the hall again where Sherri's desk is, and ask her about renting a gown for Convocation. Bill is now among the people aimlessly lingering there.

"Isn't this the most miserable news?" he asks.

"Yes."

"To think he'd just go like that. Why, I saw him just the other day. He looked terrible, I thought. Just terrible. Poor old man. Well, I hope that bastard Fraser is satisfied."

"Yes."

"After all, Archie had nothing and nobody. His life here was *it*."

The talk drones on, joined now by others, a meaningless noise, made by empty, serious faces. Bill has disappeared, but I see Molly in a corner. Her mouth, her eyes, are dry and grim. She is saying nothing. I look away quickly.

"Will you ever forget the time he called the Principal a poltroon?"

"Bit of a problem with the bottle, wasn't there?"

"Actually, I saw him last Tuesday. He said the damn rain was making moss grow up his north side."

"Marvellous old guy, he was."

"There'll be a memorial service, I suppose — "

"No, no; Archie was an atheist."

"He wasn't. He was a Catholic."

I slip away. The glass bell is still intact. Through the blazing sun, the yellow-green and blue of painted scenery, the flash of silent traffic, I carry it carefully home. There, finally, the glass shatters. But I will never be able to describe how it is then with me. Grief has no vocabulary.

The one surprising thing about the next few days is that I sleep a great deal. For the first time in my life I sleep ten hours a night, and sometimes even drop off for a nap by daylight as well.

Unfortunately this does not last long. Sleep then deserts me completely, and I am left to drift through cycles of light and dark, stranded, dry, alert, endlessly awake. And this causes time to behave in a very curious way. Night and day cease to have any relation to each other or to me; so I keep the zebra curtains closed. I sometimes grill and eat lamb-chops at three in the morning. I may do a washing at ten, whether a.m. or p.m., or go to bed and doze at four in the afternoon.

I go out only when absolutely necessary to buy food. The streets frighten me. Something bad and dangerous is at large out there. I stay home behind the curtains.

Percy has settled down after those first suspicious hours long ago during which he growled at the furniture. He sits in the kitchen window bird-watching, or sleeps curled on my pillow. Occasionally, though, he pads restlessly through the apartment, yowling. This primitive noise gives me a deep satisfaction I don't trouble to analyse. I never discourage his yells. I like to hear them.

Louis-Philippe comes to the door.

"Yes?"

"Can I talk to you a moment, mees?"

"All right." But I keep the chain on.

"You been sick, I don' see you around?"

"No."

"Well, I'm sorry, but we have a few complaint. Tenants in Six and Two, they say, 'I hear a child cry at four every morning'— well, I know you got no kids, but your cat she's disturb people just the same. . . . " His Indian eyes rest on me curiously. It is the first time he has looked at me without a trace of lechery. Instead he looks wary, as if something in my appearance, while creating no pity or even interest, may mean trouble for him.

"Mr. Mackenzie. We're moving out at the end of May."

"Yes, I know, but—"

"Then tell Six and Two that." And I close the door.

This is the first occasion for some time when I have talked to anyone. The encounter leaves me restless. I walk up and down. With vague surprise I notice a sort of track in the carpet. I must have been doing this quite a bit lately. But it's good to pace up and down, up and down. This time, though, the restlessness mounts, builds, swells, like a dangerous supercharge, until I'm afraid of it.

I take a couple of aspirins. They are no help. Then I remember the little bottle of tranquillizers Bill gave me years ago in

Richmond. I take one. Return to walking up and down. The drug must have lost its potency. I take two more. Nothing whatever happens. I can't remember now just how many I've had, but swallow one more. Then, without any plans or motives whatsoever, I put on a light coat and leave the curtained apartment. The elevator slides down noiselessly and delivers me into the lobby. I see through the heavy glass doors that it is night.

Outside, the darkness is quite warm and still. A faint sweetness of lilac hangs in the air. The streets are quiet, and my shoes make a loud, hollow tap on the pavement. I turn uphill, toward the dark height of the mountain. It would be nice to walk on the earth. Nice to be up there alone in the silent, velvet dark.

I find steps and climb them. A broad pathway winds upward. But it is not the familiar scuffed, almost rural picnic-path I know. City lamps follow its curve; the trees keep a respectful distance. Still I climb on mechanically. I have forgotten why. A mounted policeman rides slowly past, giving me one careless glance as he jogs by.

Abruptly I come upon a sort of clearing before a small chalet-style building set among trees. Spotlights in these trees shed a green glare that bathes a large crowd of people standing about on the grass. Many of them are in evening dress. They are all chatting and laughing. Some couples stroll a little away from the rest, their arms or hands linked. I stare at this scene for some time in wonder. Why are all these elaborately dressed people here on the mountain at night? Then I remember. The chalet is a new little summer theatre. This must be intermission-time. Slowly I move closer and mingle with the crowd. A pleasant theatre-smell of cigarettes, new fabric, perfume, and fresh programs floats on the night. No one so much as glances at me. "Why, Bottom, thou art translated," I think vaguely. Of course no one can see me under this freckled ass's head. No one ever has—but one. Who was that? It doesn't matter. He's gone. I can't remember his face.

Suddenly I recognize one of the women, in a long green gown of some delicate material that lifts in the warm air. It is Molly, with Harry. They stand shoulder to shoulder but turned a little aside from each other. They are not talking; in fact Harry is reading a newspaper, frowning intently over it. He has become stouter. A soft little chin doubles itself under his beard. Neither of them notices me.

As I turn away I see someone else I know. Her dress is short, of brown crêpe with a yoke of lace. I know that dress. I know the old-fashioned worn gold rings set with diamonds on her thin hand. It is my mother. But when I move toward her she frowns coldly and turns away to disappear in the crowd.

There is Bill Trueblood. He would like to avoid me, but it is too late. He frowns too, impatient but polite. "Enjoying the play, Willy?" He looks very elegant in a blue velvet jacket. "Have a cigarette?" But I see a spider in the case he holds out and jerk away, almost losing my balance. "No? Good setting for Chekov, isn't it? Didn't see you at Convocation. Or at the service for Archie. Out of town, were you? I must say you don't look too well; get yourself a good vacation. I'm going in for a sinus operation next week; then it's off to Halifax to recuperate. Take care. See you around."

A buzzer is sounding from inside the theatre, and people begin to drift inside. I see George MacKay—or is it Emma's husband?— something seems to be wrong with my eyes. His arm is around a very young girl in yellow with waist-long dark hair. She gives a great yawn as they pass me, showing all the coral interior of her mouth as candidly as Percy does. Whoever he is, he nods pleasantly to me as they go by, and says, "Hi there, Milly."

Music sounds from inside. Everybody is gone now except a small man who sits on the steps and tilts a flask to his mouth. It might be Gerald Wellesley Doyle.

"You left me all alone," I say to him.

"What's that, baby?"

I look at him steadily, thinking 'You left me all alone with her. Remember once you told me she was a cold, selfish woman? I didn't believe you, of course. I gave her my whole life. And she didn't even really want it. Maybe it was you that really needed me. Shall we be two horses laughing?'

"Baby, you worry me," mutters the little man, putting away his flask.

"You are making a mistake," I tell him coldly. "I don't know you."

"Sorry. I do apologize." With a somewhat blurred bow, the little man, now on nimble feet, turns and goes inside. I realize then that my father and mother will never come back: I have seen them truly and for the last time. The spotlights glare on the deserted green-yellow of the scene. All the actors are gone, but me. Who will dismiss Caliban? If that is my part.

I move off up a narrow path and continue my climb. Energy hums through me, though my feet feel heavy. I am only vaguely aware of twigs and brambles that tear at my legs and coat. It is darker as I move up higher. The path is hard to see. Once I stumble and fall, rising with earthy knees and stinging palms. After some time I go back to that place and pick up my shoulder-bag.

On and on, the ground rising as if it breathed. The distant, muttered roar of the island city floats around me like a memory. When I look down at the tide of light, it sways and drifts; it is an illusion. Yes, I understand it all now. There is no more to know.

I took the tranquillizers not to die; only to quiet a raging pain, and to achieve this distance. They have done their job at last. I can go back now.

But I stumble again on the way down. This time I feel very dizzy. It is hard to get up. Too hard. Instead I drag myself a few feet off the path onto a grassy area thickly overhung with bushes. They form a sort of shelter. The earth under me feels soft. The air is warm. I sleep.

"You're crazy. She ain't dead."

"Aw shit."

I sit up, not without difficulty. Every moving part is stiff and sore. The dirty faces of two squatting little boys confront me at close range. Their gaze is full of pleasurable curiosity untainted by compassion. I fumble to extract twigs and curls of dry leaf from my hair.

"You got mud on your face, lady."

"So have you."

My head feels very large and my limbs thick, as if I had swollen in the night. But I know where I am, and who. Yesterday, today, and tomorrow are in their proper places, not deplorably in each other's beds as they have been lately. Best of all, perhaps, I have things to do and the intention of doing them. The clumsy thickness of my body makes me impatient, that is all. Getting to my feet is an enterprise that has to be achieved in instalments, and with effort. The boys watch, interested. At last I am upright, breathing heavily and hanging onto a low branch for support.

"Do you know what time it is?" I ask them. It is the first time for a long while I have wanted to know the time.

"Quarter to nine."

The air is soft with coming rain. The sky is silver-grey.

"Will you hand me that bag there, please?"

One of them seizes the long strap and drags the bag up toward my hand. I clean my palms and face with a tissue soaked in cologne, and tie a headscarf over my chaotic hair. Then, balancing with one or two unsteady crises that greatly amuse the boys, I turn my grubby coat inside out so the reverse side of Black Watch tartan is outermost. As soon as I have put this on and slung the bag over one shoulder, my entertainment value disappears, and so do the boys. Like Crusoe rescued, I now look too much like the dull rest of human creation to be of the slightest interest. No one but himself knows how separate, how uniquely different, the island-dweller will always be. This makes me smile, using stiff muscles.

Slowly I make my way down to Westmount Boulevard, where I find a taxi to take me home.

Percy meets me at the door, yelling indignantly for his breakfast.

I drink a lot of coffee. Then I pick up the phone and ring the number of a real-estate company.

A week later I am sprinting wildly across the dirty marble concourse of Central Station. Several fellow-travellers with whom I collide in varying degrees of violence glare at me irritably. Of course the club car is the very last carriage of the Turbo to Toronto, so I have to run the whole length of the platform, suitcase battering my legs without mercy. The conductor, a silver-haired man of episcopal dignity, is intoning "En Voi — ture", as if I needed any urging. Hastily I scramble aboard, thinking, "What a ridiculous effort just to get back where I started from a year ago." The doors hiss shut like an answer.

I sink, breathless, into the nearest empty seat. The bald man beside me in the window seat looks up from his *Gazette* to say cheerfully, "Just made it, eh?" There seems no polite answer to this, so I make none. I wonder whether Percy is safely aboard the baggage car. And that is the one and only philosophical speculation I intend to have on this trip. Travelling light this time. No intentions. No projects.

An old woman in black across the aisle frowns with disapproval when I sway against her in the effort to heave my suitcase onto the overhead rack. She is knitting something white in small, dark hands knotted with age. One wonders what kind of bereavement it can possibly be that has plunged her into such intense mourning. She wears laced-up black shoes, black stockings, black dress; even a black hat, skewered with jet pins to her meek white hair.

The train skims past the flats, factories, shops of west-end suburbia caught in the cheerful act of rape on areas still innocently and endearingly green. We cross the bridge over sparkling water. Picking up speed, the Turbo aims us at Toronto with a formidable air of purpose and significance, just as if this journey were not, like most, circular. It feels like a long, long time since I advanced upon Montreal at the same speed and with the same illusion of progress. And since then, absolutely nothing has happened to me, unless you count a comic sequence of deceptions and self-deceptions, some sad, some just ridiculous. Then the meaningless, violent blow of loss.

All this would be depressing if one allowed it to be. But I am determined not to brood over those absurd plans, hopes, fears, all anished now, totally and forever. I look at the old widow across he aisle with her black stockings, dowager's hump, and air of sour endurance, and instruct myself to be grateful that at least I don't look like that. There's no visible difference in me at all after this year in Villette. A developed sense of irony doesn't show.

"Cigarette?" the bald man asks. "Hot for May, isn't it? Off to Toronto for a visit, are you?"

"My sister had a baby boy this morning. I'm going to look after my young nephew while she's in hospital."

I take out my magazine and open it purposefully. The memory of George MacKay is still alive and kicking among the dead remains of The Project. This nice man with his pink skull and Masonic ring is safe from me. Unfortunately, the article I'm now assiduously studying for his benefit is headlined "Achieving the Female Orgasm". I close the magazine, trying not to laugh.

"What did you think of the election results?" I ask.

"Oh, just what I expected, really. Bourassa's all right. At least he'll keep Quebec in Confederation."

"Well, I was a bit surprised *he* was what Quebec wanted after all . . . a true-blue accountant. Bit of an anticlimax. The fact is I'm a bit of a . . . separatist myself."

"So am I, same way as I'm a romantic about the Acadians and

the Doukhobors. That's what this country is all about. Differ
ences. But there's nothing like owning a few shares or a few acres
of land to turn a romantic into a realist, right?"

"I suppose so. My notary is a kid fresh out of Laval; you'd
expect him to be with the revolutionaries, but he told me he voted
for Bourassa. Come to that, I voted for him myself. It must be
becoming a property-owner that did it."

"Yeah?"

"I've just bought a big stone house with three fireplaces and a
garden. Big, high rooms, ceilings with garlands of flowers
moulded into the plaster, that kind of thing. And it cost me about
a third of what a house like that in Toronto would fetch."

"Big family, eh?" asks the Mason absently.

"No, just one." I think of Percy, who is doubtless making life
hell for the baggage-car attendant.

The bald man drifts amiably back to his newspaper and I sit
back and close my eyes. I think of my new house, of the broad
floors with their borders of inlay, the wide, high windows looking
out at the city and the dark hill at its centre. It will be good to live
there alone. It's good now to sit back and say nothing, wrapped in
my own privacy. Restful to be ignored. Peaceful to be all but
invisible. The old woman's needles click steadily on. Curious that
at her age she should find it worth while to make a jacket for some
baby to be sick on. But perhaps that's her way of not letting God
down. Mine was to buy that house, all twelve rooms of it, braving
all Lou's squawks and hisses of protest.

A boy drifts down the aisle, holding a transistor like a poultice
to his ear. The speaker is belching out that song about poor Mrs.
Robinson, and his listening face is blank with pleasure. 'Much you
know about Mrs. Robinson, my lad,' I think. But when I consider
the case of acne the poor kid has, I'm willing to admit he may have
some idea after all. One seat up from me sits an exquisitely
dressed woman of perhaps fifty, with jewels flashing in her
pierced ears and on her delicate hands. She has a repetitive sniff.
I time it: once every two minutes. A pregnant girl manœuvres her
bulk toward the washroom, carrying her new identity in front of
her wearily. She sighs, as she goes by me, with so much self-
pitying importance that I could get up and hug her. No, this trip is
not, after all, exactly like the last one. It's completely different, in
fact. More interesting. Who knows, perhaps I am too. I intend to

believe this, anyway, because otherwise knowing Archie and loving him would all be stupidly wasted. I won't have that. Nor am I going to brood over his memory like a fetish. No black stockings for me.

Yes, I am alone, I think, as train and landscape scoot past each other, making their own statement about Canadian isolation. I am alone. So are countless thousands of other people — a fact which doesn't help one damned bit. Solitudes rarely touch, much less merge. Mine will not change. I know that now. I will remain alone and what I am—what my parents made me—till the end. Is there any point in resenting that?

I will always be alone. Single. Celibate. And I will make no more ridiculous efforts to be otherwise. I belong to no sisterhood, unless it is of aunts. I am a schoolteacher. A bachelor. A cat-owner. Soon I will be a solitary householder, surrounded by the furniture of my parents' lives. I will take up gardening. One day at a time is how I will live. Perhaps I'll become a bird-watcher or go to yoga classes. Doubtless I will lie awake at night, and sometimes ache and sometimes weep. But by day two tough cords in my neck will develop from keeping my head up and my jaw shut. I intend to ask for nothing and clutch at nobody, not even Dougie.

I shall look in no mirrors, except for laughs. If I feel like it, I will get fat, or adopt Christian Science, or rent a dog.

Loneliness is just a condition, like arthritis or claustrophobia. Incurable. And far from enviable. But it's my condition, and I'm at last prepared to face it; even accept it. Eventually, in spite of my talent for being absurd, it may be possible to salvage a kind of dignity out of it. There is a modest satisfaction, even a sort of art, in island-dwelling. Lucy Snowe found it, and so will I, in time.

The train cuts through the afternoon, carrying its freight of separate identities. I look through the running shadow of the windowpane, and the face there flashes me a small, grim smile of recognition.